SMALL TOWN LAWYER

Defending Innocence

Influencing Justice

Interpreting Guilt

Peter Kirkland is a pen name created by Relay Publishing for co-authored Legal Thriller projects. Relay Publishing works with incredible teams of writers and editors to collaboratively create the very best stories for our readers.

www.relaypub.com

SMALL TOWN LAWYER - BOOK TWO

INFLUENCING JUSTICE

PETER KIRKLAND

BLURB

A small-town murder hides a dark secret.

When social media influencer Simone Baker asks Leland Munroe to defend her on charges stemming from another influencer's death, the former prosecutor initially says no. He wants a quiet life practicing business law and continuing to rebuild his relationship with his son, Noah. But with bills to pay and no other clients coming through his door, Leland takes the case.

At first, he figures the prosecution's weak evidence should make for a simple defense. But Simone's situation isn't as straightforward as it seems, and she weaves a tale of evidence tampering by local police, missing young women, and online manipulation.

As Leland and his PI friend Terri Washington investigate, they realize the case goes far beyond a single murder. Innocent women may be entangled in a criminal organization Leland hoped was gone from Basking Rock for good. And as the jury's verdict looms closer, it's not just Simone's freedom that hangs in the balance...

Leland's and Noah's lives are on the line as well.

CONTENTS

PROLOGUE

EASTER SUNDAY, APRIL 12, 2020

I'd come up to Charleston alone, to the graveyard, to talk to my wife. I parked around the corner, grabbed the little box I'd brought off the passenger seat, and walked to the entrance on the old side of the cemetery, because it had always been her favorite part. The trees were draped with Spanish moss, and the gravestones tilted at weird angles, with moss and lichen growing over the names and dates. Weeds grew between the broken flagstones I walked along. Even in the bright sunlight of Easter morning, the place was spooky, but Elise thought it was romantic. We never thought she'd end up here so soon.

It took a few minutes to get to her spot, in the new part. The stones here were upright and shiny. Pink granite, white marble. But there was nothing on her grave yet besides grass—a little overgrown—and a flat plaque with her name. They'd advised me to wait six months or a year for the earth to settle before placing a stone. Fifteen months had come and gone, and I still couldn't afford what she deserved.

Nobody was around. It was time for folks to be in church. I looked down at the ground she was under and tried to say, "Happy Easter." The words stuck in my throat, so I tried again.

A breeze made the grass flutter.

"Brought you a piece of king cake," I said, opening the box. Elise was born in New Orleans, and her traditions had become mine and Noah's. I hadn't made it up to Charleston for the Feast of the Epiphany, so this cake was the Easter version, frosted pink. I took it out and set it on the grass.

"I hope you're watching," I said. "I hope you can, because you'd see Noah's doing better." I smiled and shook my head. "Those binoculars you gave him when he was, what, seven years old? That he used to spy on the old man across the street? I think you were on to something. If you were here, you'd see—he actually *wants* to go to school now, because it has a purpose. Says he wants to be a detective, and I think he means it."

She'd understand why I was spending what little I had on his physical therapy and his community college tuition. She'd say that's exactly what I should do, not put that money into some hunk of stone for a woman who wasn't here anymore. But the fact I couldn't do both made me feel lower than dirt.

"Not detective," I said, correcting myself. "He says 'private eye' instead. I guess it's more romantic. He got that from you."

No breeze came. The grass didn't flutter.

I dropped my head. I didn't know why part of me still expected a response.

———

1

TUESDAY, APRIL 21, 2020

On the way to work, I stopped at Basking Rock's only bakery to get donuts. I'd gotten in the habit of bringing half a dozen to the law firm once a week—enough for me, Roy, his secretary, and whichever clients or FedEx guys happened by—but world events had cut down my regular purchase considerably. Over the past few weeks, the governor had issued some executive orders, trying to keep the pandemic that had clobbered Italy and New York from hitting us too hard. It looked like Roy and I would be mostly working from home for the next little while. His secretary, Laura, was still coming into the office every day to take calls, check the mail, and drive the checks that came in down to the bank. I'd been dropping by every few days to get my mail and bring her favorite donut for her troubles.

The owner, Hank, came out from the back, wiping his hands on his apron, and said, "Morning, Leland. Just two today?"

I nodded and said, "Wish I needed more. But I'm glad you're still open."

"Yeah, food's an essential business. Even donuts, I guess. How's that little dog of yours doing? He stuck at home too?"

He meant my ancient Yorkshire terrier, Squatter. I chuckled. "Well, governor's orders are governor's orders. I've set up the dog's office on the couch." I pulled out my wallet. I'd been back in town for a year, since losing just about everything and leaving Charleston. Friendly chitchat and being a regular with an order that the guy always remembered wasn't half bad. I was starting to think I might finally fit in here.

Hank handed over my donuts and said, "That king cake meet expectations?"

"Yes indeed." I'd found a recipe online and brought it in for a custom order. I'd never seen a proper New Orleans king cake in South Carolina, except the ones Elise used to make.

"Yeah, it was damn good," he said. "I made two so I could see for myself what you liked about it. My boy ate half of it in about ten minutes."

I laughed and said, "Mine too. I think that's what teenage boys are for."

We wished each other a good day, and the bell jangled as I headed out the door. It was another sunny morning. Small-town life had a lot to recommend it.

As I got back to my car, the downside of small towns came into view. The old guy who ran the antique store I'd parked near was sweeping his porch—his shop was in a little Victorian house—but when he saw me, he scowled and went inside.

In the murder case I'd won a few months earlier, some of the evidence I'd unearthed to help get my client off had also ended up bringing the feds down hard on two local businesses. The larger one, Blue Seas Yacht Charter, had been seized by the feds and auctioned off. That did a number on the tourist trade—no charters meant fewer rich folks ready to drop a grand on a fancy chair or an old mirror—and the governor's orders hadn't improved the situation. I guessed the antiques guy blamed me, for the first part anyway.

And maybe he was right to. I wasn't sure there was a way to practice criminal law that didn't upset somebody, and understandably so. Whether committing it, prosecuting it, or defending someone charged with it, crime wasn't anyone's happy place. It sure as hell wasn't mine.

———

Roy's office was a genteel gray bungalow near the causeway. Palm trees edged the parking lot, and after I slammed my car door and headed up the walk, I heard a seagull squawking not far off. When I got inside, Laura smiled—not so much at me as at the donut bag.

"I swear, Leland," she said, "you are trying to weaken my resolve."

She was an older lady, the kind who gets leaner with age instead of rounder. I thought she could probably eat six donuts a day and still be as skinny as a blade of grass, but she liked to chide me for bringing them.

"Just making people happy," I said.

"Well, maybe this'll make *you* happy: I just took a call from a young lady who's in need of criminal defense counsel. She asked for you by name."

"That so?" I kept my smile where it was, but it was no longer sincere. I was tired of reading autopsy reports, and beyond tired of fearing that criminals might come after me or my son. I wanted to reinvent myself as a business lawyer, helping local enterprises do what they do and getting paid twice as much as I'd ever earned for dealing with the worst that humanity had to offer.

"It's not often a caller asks for you instead of Roy." Laura tore the top page off her pink message pad and held it out.

I traded her donut for the message. It was just a phone number and a name I didn't recognize. "She say what the charges were?"

With a smile, she said, "Manslaughter!"

I chuckled. "You're pretty cheerful for someone talking about homicide."

"Well, it's your bread and butter," she said. "Isn't it?"

"I'm a little tired of bread and butter."

"Oh, she also mentioned drug charges. Heroin? Could that be it?"

"I expect it could be. That's a drug people go to jail for, if that's what you mean."

"Leland," she said, sounding excited, "I am going to have to learn a whole new vocabulary if you'd like me to help you with your clients! My favorite TV show is *Murder, She Wrote*, but they never talk about drugs on that."

"Or we could just stick with the kind of business Roy's used to," I said, thinking of all the local suits he wined and dined. "Although I'd have to learn to play golf. You know I only took that murder case because the kid was my friend's son."

"Oh, and the whole town was sure he did it. I heard stories like you would not believe down at the hair salon. Wasn't it something, though, to get him off? Do you truly not want to keep helping folks like that? This young lady sounded very nice."

"The killers who sound nice," I said, "are usually psychopaths." I shook my head. "And, see, that's the prosecutor in me talking. I'm not cut out to be a criminal defense guy. Which is why I signed up for that business law CLE. It's online, but I'm stuck in it all day tomorrow and the day after too—so if anyone needs to reach me, it'll have to be on the lunch break."

"Well, if anybody else calls, I'll let them know."

We exchanged looks. We both knew clients didn't call for me. What money I made was from Roy asking me to do the work he didn't like. Research, writing—the quiet side of being a lawyer. Roy was the glad-hander, backslapper, and expert golfer. I was none of those things.

As I walked back to my car, I couldn't help but think of the advice Roy had given me when I told him about my upcoming CLE. His white hair and fatherly manner added gravitas to whatever advice he gave, so it was a gut punch to hear him say, "You know, Leland, it's a whole lot easier to build on a reputation you already have than to make a new one from scratch. Seventeen years as a prosecutor, plus defending a murder case that everybody and his cat were talking about, counts for a lot more than a two-day CLE."

On top of that, Roy didn't have as much work for me as he used to, since I'd inadvertently helped the feds destroy the yacht-charter company, one of his biggest clients. I was lucky he still let me have an office in his firm.

Still, I knew what I wanted and what I didn't. When I got in the car, I crumpled up the message Laura had given me and tossed it in the shopping bag I used for trash.

———

2

THURSDAY, APRIL 23, 2020

It was dinnertime, and since I'd been in my CLE for two days straight, Noah had brought home some take-out shrimp with rice and fried okra. We were eating it with the TV news on, though we were talking instead of paying attention to happenings in the world.

"So right when I start learning about criminal justice, you're going to bail on me?" It seemed Noah, like everyone else in my life, was less than impressed with my desire to focus on business law.

I took a bite of shrimp and said, "I still got eighteen years of it under my belt. That's not going anywhere. You got a question, you just ask."

"Naw, but I mean, it's weird, changing gears like that. Is it even interesting? I don't get how, like, real estate could be more interesting than fraud and murder and… y'know, right and wrong."

On TV, a worried-looking blonde newscaster was talking about how the pandemic was hitting retailers. Would they survive? Was the economy going into free fall?

I gestured to her with my fork. "See what she's talking about? All of that falls apart without the law. The whole economy. I mean, say you want to go into business as a private eye after school. You need an office, right? Would you give a landlord a grand or whatever in rent every month and spend more getting your office equipped how you want if you thought he was going to change the locks one day and take your computer for himself?"

"Course not."

"Right. And the reason you know he's not going to do that is, you got a contract. You got a lease, and there's rules about that, and if he breaks them, you can take him to court and win."

"Well… but most people wouldn't do that anyway, so…" He shrugged.

I looked at him. I sometimes forgot how clean the world could look to people who hadn't spent nearly two decades working in criminal law. I wondered, not for the first time, if I'd sheltered him too much.

"There's no shortage of people who'd do that," I said. "But most of them aren't in the office-landlord business *because* they know the law makes it hard to get away with. If that's how they want to operate, any normal business is not a good proposition. And at the same time, the law's set up to make it a pretty good proposition for people who want to run their business more or less the right way. I mean, you know that when you go to the bank, the money you had in there yesterday is still going to be there, right? Nobody ran off with it. Or if they did, the bank's insured, and you'll get it back."

"Yeah. Oh." He was starting to get my point.

I nodded. "The law makes things predictable and… I'm not going to say fair, but *more* fair. You can make plans, invest in your business, and so forth, because you can mostly count on banks and landlords to run pretty much how they should. Nobody ever thinks about the law until things go wrong and somebody gets arrested or sued, but it's there all along. It's the reason things mostly work."

"Huh," he said. "I guess I never thought of it that way because—I don't know. Most of the people I've ever met were pretty much okay. But then, I guess—" He laughed. "I guess there's a lot of circles I don't run in."

I looked out the window at the sunset. "Yeah, well," I said, "I'm glad of that."

Even with the carefully chosen circles Elise and I had put him in back in Charleston—the private school, full of lawyers' and doctors' kids— he'd still gotten so far into illicit prescription drugs that we almost lost him. Maybe I hadn't sheltered him enough. Or maybe it was a fool's errand to think I could protect anyone from the world, or from themselves.

We munched on in silence for a minute. Then I heard a familiar name from the TV. I glanced over and saw a split screen with the blonde newscaster listening to Travis Girardeau, Charleston criminal defense lawyer extraordinaire. He was sitting at his desk talking earnestly about some case. It was the kind of rousing speech lawyers usually prefer to give on the courthouse steps, with the wind in their hair and a dramatic architectural backdrop, but all the courts in the state were closed; the pandemic had forced him onto Zoom. His office looked nice. On the wall behind him was a framed photo of himself shaking hands with the governor.

"Wait for it," I told Noah. "He's going to say it's un-American to prosecute his client."

"You know him?"

"Had a few cases against him, back in the day."

"And as every one of your viewers knows, Maureen," Girardeau said, "this country was *founded* on the principle that every man is innocent until proven guilty. And in this case, the solicitor has just torn up that basic principle and thrown it in the trash."

Noah laughed, picked up his glass of Coke, and held it out across the coffee table. I raised my glass and let him clink it in congratulations.

"He's a pretty good lawyer," I said. "Knows how to grab a jury's attention. But he's about four hundred times flashier than I could ever be."

"That's still not very flashy," Noah said with a grin. "I mean, four hundred times zero is still zero."

"Dammit," I said, laughing. "Show some respect."

"Oh, hey," he said. A box had appeared onscreen with the name and photo of Girardeau's client, a pretty, young Black woman. "She's, like, famous! I mean, famous for someone from Basking Rock. I tried to get into that party, but she had security."

"What party?"

"The one where that other lady died. The one she's charged with killing."

"Here in town? How did I not hear about this?"

"It was right around when you took Jackson's case," he said. The defendant in my big murder case from the year before was his best friend. "And you know how you get when you're on a case. Like, nothing else exists."

That was hard to hear. I'd missed a lot by burying myself in work. Most of Noah's childhood, and all of Elise's warning signs.

On TV, Girardeau was complaining that the solicitor was convening a grand jury to consider a murder charge when, according to him, even the manslaughter charge "hangs by the very thinnest of threads." The victim, he said, "was—and I'm sorry to say this, but telling hard truths is part of my job—she was a drug user. A heroin user. And down that path lies tragedy. But that is not my client's fault."

I thought about the crumpled pink message slip in my car. I wished it was at hand so I could check the name on it—Girardeau's client was apparently Simone Baker—because manslaughter and heroin sounded familiar.

I asked Noah, "What's this Baker woman famous for?"

"She's an influencer."

I waited for him to finish his sentence, but apparently that *was* the sentence. "What the hell is that?"

"It's…" He thought about it a second. Then he said, "It's hard to explain," and chomped his shrimp.

"Well, what's she famous for?"

"She, like… I don't know, I think she might have a clothing line? She's disabled or has some health issue or something, and she inspires people. I don't know. I don't follow her. She's just sort of famous, and I thought it'd be cool to get into her party."

"Well, I'm glad you didn't, since somebody died there. What was it? Overdose?"

"I don't know. That's what folks thought, but a while later she got arrested."

Girardeau had disappeared from the screen. It was time for the heart-warming human-interest part of the news, and after that we'd get the weather.

I said, "Don't know if they got to this yet in your criminal justice class, but if a person overdoses, whoever gave them the drugs can be liable for manslaughter."

"Huh," Noah said. He wasn't really paying attention. He was probably sick of me reminding him of the countless ways that being involved in drugs could get a person in trouble.

I figured the drug-delivery scenario was most likely the reason Girardeau's client was facing charges. He liked to make every case he touched seem uniquely and dramatically compelling, but manslaughter charges for supplying drugs weren't uncommon, and the basic concept seemed pretty reasonable to me. I also didn't subscribe to his view that there was something unjust about, as he put it, "using the tragedy of a global pandemic as an excuse to add charges that we were about to go to trial without." Apparently, the trial would've begun this very week if it hadn't been for the court closures, and Girardeau found it unfair to use the delay to bring additional charges.

To start up the conversation again, I went for the most boring question a parent can ask: "How you liking your online classes? What all are you studying now?"

"It's fine. We're mostly studying the justice system. Like, how the courts and the police work."

"How they work? Or how they're supposed to?"

"I guess how they're supposed to," he said, "because it doesn't sound much like how you and Terri talk about it."

Terri Washington was a friend of mine, an ex-cop turned private investigator who'd worked on my murder case. She deserved a hell of a lot of the credit for digging up the info that helped get Jackson off. What I valued even more, though, was how she'd inspired my son to start caring about life again. After the accident that had killed my wife and broken half the bones in his body, he'd lost his baseball scholarship and watched all his friends head off to college while he was stuck doing months of physical therapy just to try to get back to 70 or 80 percent of baseline. Watching her work on Jackson's case had gotten Noah interested in what she did for a living, and now he had something to aim for again.

My boring question had led to another lull in the conversation. The TV blathered. The weather, to no one's surprise, was supposed to continue being sunny and seventy-five. It was South Carolina in the springtime, after all.

Noah said, "Terri thinks there's something weird about that girl's case."

"Does she?"

"Yeah, she said something about the cop who arrested her. I don't know. You'd have to ask her. Although maybe you're more interested in real estate and business now—maybe it's just going to be Terri and me who'll keep fighting the good fight."

He was teasing, but it stung a little. I said, "We're all fighting the good fight."

He leaned back on the couch, elbows out, hands behind his head, and said, "I mean… I guess."

———

3

TUESDAY, APRIL 28, 2020

I was heading up the walkway to Roy's office on my weekly mail run, enjoying the shade from the palm trees, when my phone dinged. It wasn't a text. It was a sound I hadn't heard in a good long while: an appointment reminder. My career had recently been in a lull, to put it nicely, so I was surprised. As I jogged up the front steps, I checked the screen and saw I had a Zoom meeting in half an hour with none other than Simone Baker.

When I handed Laura her donut and asked about it, she said, "Well, she called back this morning, and she just sounded so professional and so nice. I knew you'd be here soon to get your mail, and since Roy's been saying we need some more income streams coming in…"

She was speaking diplomatically. Roy would've said that I, not we, needed more income. I'd been handling his castoffs and representing the occasional friend of a client on DUI or drug possession charges. It was mind-numbing work, and it barely kept me and Noah afloat.

I said, smiling so she'd take it as a joke, "He just does not want any competition on the business law end of things, does he."

She chuckled. "Well, now, to be fair, this kind of case can bring a lot of attention to the firm. It could really liven things up around here. Anyway, I took some notes when I spoke to her just now, so I'll email them."

I started heading to my office, then stopped to ask, "She say why she wants to switch lawyers? Her trial's going to start up again as soon as the courthouses reopen. Seems like a real strange time to ditch your lawyer and bring in a new one."

Laura, on her way to the coffee maker, said, "I didn't feel it was my place to ask, but she said something along the lines of she didn't feel her lawyer was on her side."

"Travis Girardeau, the criminal defense guy up in Charleston? He'd be on the side of a potted plant if it paid him enough."

She laughed again.

I used the time before the meeting to read up on Simone's case. The news articles described her as an Instagram health and wellness influencer, which to me still sounded more like a string of random words than an actual job. If I did take her on as a client, I'd have to ask Terri or Noah to walk me through Instagram so I could get a sense of what the heck she did.

The facts of her case seemed pretty straightforward, although the timeline was weird. In May of last year, she'd thrown a party for another influencer woman she knew from Charleston. The party had caterers and security, like Noah had mentioned—evidently Basking Rock now had glitterati, and she was it. Her guest of honor slept over that night and was found dead of an overdose the next morning.

I kept searching to see where the manslaughter came in. I soon learned she'd been pulled over six weeks later and booked for drug possession because a syringe with trace amounts of heroin was found on the floor of her car. Any amount of heroin was a guaranteed possession charge, and more than four grains—or nine one-thousandths of an ounce—was felony possession with intent to distribute. I wasn't sure how heroin dealing fit with her health and wellness thing. But there were plenty of hypocrites in the world, and I'd seen a lot of crimes whose perpetrators were not who you'd expect.

The next detail raised my eyebrows a little. According to the solicitor, this syringe had the victim's fingerprints on it. That seemed miraculous, as evidence found in traffic stops went. I wondered what their theory was. That Ms. Baker had taken it from the crime scene before the police got there, then driven it around in her car for six weeks? In my experience, when people purposely removed evidence from crime scenes, either they were calculating enough to wear gloves and wipe it down to erase any prints, or they were too upset to think straight and got their own prints all over it. One way or the other, that usually made any earlier fingerprints unusable.

Carrying incriminating evidence around in your car for a month and a half also seemed like a pretty stupid thing to do, especially when that evidence was small enough to easily get rid of. But that said, I was well aware that stupidity is abundant in the human race.

A box on my computer screen alerted me that my meeting would start in five minutes. I put on the suit jacket and tie that hung in my office —they were intended for unexpected meetings and court appearances, but I guessed now they were for Zoom. I clicked into the meeting early and cringed at the image of myself on the screen. My face seemed misshapen from every angle. And why did I have a wall of legal books I never touched behind me? It looked pretentious. On top of that, although my suit jacket and tie were both dark blue, on the screen they looked black. This woman was going to think she'd called an undertaker.

When Simone Baker appeared, I thought perhaps a Hollywood celebrity had joined me. She was a pretty girl, immaculately put together, with a low white bookshelf behind her. Above it was what the home-improvement shows called an accent wall, painted a deep turquoise. Her bookshelf held four or five little sculptures and a single long-stemmed purple flower draping gracefully out of a glass vase. I understood from the news articles that she was all of twenty-three years old. How a girl that young from Basking Rock had achieved this level of sophistication, I did not know.

We introduced ourselves, and after a few pleasantries, I got to my first order of business. "Now, Ms. Baker, just so I know, is Mr. Girardeau the only attorney who's represented you in this matter?"

I was trying to figure out whose fault it was that she was ditching Girardeau: hers or his. If she'd been lawyer-hopping already, that'd be a red flag.

"Yes, he is. I spoke with him the Monday after Veronica died."

"Oh? So you contacted him, what, about six weeks before you were even arrested?"

My tone was too sharp, and she took it the wrong way. "Mr. Munroe," she said, "a woman died in my house of unnatural causes, I assumed, since she was only twenty-two. I wasn't about to talk to the police without a lawyer by my side."

"Of course not," I said. "You were absolutely right to handle it that way." I wondered if any of the cops or the prosecutors had seen her decision to do that in a bad light, though. Some folks thought lawyering up was evidence of guilt.

"Thank you." She sounded brisk and businesslike, and she wasn't smiling.

"All right," I said. "It's my understanding your trial would've started last week, but it got postponed at the end of March when the courts closed down." She nodded to confirm that. "And as yet we don't know when it's actually going to take place?"

"Mr. Girardeau told me it'd be as soon as the courts reopen, but he wasn't clear on when that might happen."

"Okay, so as I'm sure you appreciate, it's pretty unusual for a defendant to change their trial counsel this late in the game. It can create difficulties since the new attorney has very little time to prepare. So, to make sure this is the right choice, could you just explain what's led you to want to move away from Mr. Girardeau?"

What I didn't mention was that in addition to being unusual, it was a huge red flag. I suspected Girardeau had told her she had no good defense and ought to take a plea, but she didn't want to face facts. Or he might be firing *her*, either because she was impossible to work with or because she didn't pay. If any of those things were true, I was not going to take her on as a client.

She dropped her chin like she was about to school me. "Mr. Munroe, I am aware of the pros and cons. I've spoken to other attorneys, and they've explained why they think changing attorneys is a bad idea. To be honest, they've been a little patronizing. If our meetings had been in person instead of on Zoom, I think one or two of them might've patted me on the head. I would hate to get the same impression from you."

I said, "No, ma'am. Of course not." Then I realized that was probably the first time in my life I'd ever called a woman her age "ma'am." She had a weird kind of charisma, something commanding, and I wondered how it'd play to a jury. It could backfire.

She was still staring at me, so I continued. "Okay, then, could you tell me why you're certain this is the right decision?"

"He doesn't believe me," she said. "I mean, not that he's said so, but I can tell."

"Believe you on what? The death, or the heroin? Or both?"

"He does not even believe— Look, I have relapsing-remitting MS. I'm okay most of the time, but I drive a wheelchair van so that even during relapses, I'll be able to get to my doctor's appointments and so forth. My health is everything to me. But Mr. Girardeau seems to have no trouble believing that I drive around with syringes of heroin."

"I'm sorry to hear that," I said. I couldn't help but notice she hadn't said anything about the woman's death.

"And he doesn't understand my business. So he's pushing me to do things that might make his job easier right now but don't work for me long term. Do you know what it is I do?"

"Broadly speaking," I said. "Health and wellness influencer?"

She nodded. "I'm a health and wellness influencer who's been charged with heroin possession and manslaughter. And maybe murder, God forbid, if the grand jury says so."

"Yeah, it doesn't sound good."

"And it's all over the web. Mr. Girardeau wanted me to plead to first-offense misdemeanor heroin possession, if he could get them to offer that. Which could be two years in jail. And I cannot maintain my health in jail. The diet I follow, the sleep schedule, the physical therapy—what I need, to hold off disability as long as I can, is just not possible there. So how could I accept that?"

Girardeau's idea surprised me. I didn't know what prosecutor would let a killing go completely unpunished, but I let her continue.

"And when I said no to that, he laid out a trial strategy where he'd try to get the heroin evidence thrown out because it was an illegal search."

"So, when you got pulled over, you didn't consent to them searching the van?"

"Mr. Munroe, excuse me for putting it this way, but I am a Black woman in the twenty-first century. I am not about to let a police officer search anything of mine. I'm not saying they're all bad. Just that you don't know until it's too late which kind you've got in front of you."

I nodded. "I can't fault your logic there. But in criminal defense, you want to get the court to throw out all the evidence you can. And it seems to me that syringe of heroin is the linchpin here, since it sounds like it's what ties you to that young lady's death. Depending on what other evidence there is, getting it thrown out could mean not a single one of the charges would stick. That's a strategy I'd have to agree with."

She sighed in a discouraged way, like she was tired of people failing to understand. Then she looked up for a second, like somewhere above her she might find a way to get through to me. After a second, she said, "Okay, so right now, I'm a health and wellness influencer who's been charged with these terrible crimes. I'm losing followers and sponsors, and I've gotten messages like you would not believe. Just hateful, hateful things. So if Mr. Girardeau follows that strategy you like, and he wins, I don't go to jail. But for the rest of my life, I'm a druggie and a killer who got off on a technicality. How do you think that will work out for me?"

If she was innocent, the fact that our system was making her choose between ruining her reputation and going to jail was yet another example of why I wanted to get out of criminal law. "You do have a point."

"I'm glad you can see that," she said. "None of the other lawyers could."

"I mean, I can't tell you what to prioritize. That's your call."

"Well, I might not have explained my priorities." She paused and looked up again like she was searching for the right words, then said, "My relationship with God is number one. Are you a man of faith, Mr. Munroe?"

Every crime I'd ever tried flashed through my head, and then the image of my wife in the morgue where I'd had to identify her. Faith was not part of the picture. I wasn't about to get into that, so I said, "I like to think we each have our own relationship."

She waited, but I didn't say more, so she went on. "I actually don't even need to mention that, since none of these problems interfere with that relationship at all. So, besides that, my health and my mother are what I care about the most. And that means my business and my brand are essential. I need sponsors and followers. They're how I can afford to maintain my health and support my mother. If I lose my business, what do I do? Go on Medicaid and just die? And watch my mother suffer? How is that better than going to jail?"

"Honestly," I said, "that all makes sense. But to make sure I truly understand, are you saying you'd rather take the risk of a jury trial, which could put you in jail for many years—or even life, if they come back with a murder charge? You'd prefer that over pleading to anything or getting the evidence tossed?"

"Yes. I would."

"That's a hell of a gamble."

"I've got no other choice. No good choices, anyway."

"Okay, I— This isn't my bailiwick at all, but I'm asking so I can understand for myself what your choices are. Or, I mean, what exactly you're willing to roll the dice on. So, for instance, do you have any qualifications? Other ways of making a living?"

"I went to school for nursing, like my mom, and I got my associate's, but then I got diagnosed. And that profession is *so* hard on your body. I can't do that and stay healthy."

She also couldn't get a nursing license with a manslaughter conviction, but mentioning that, or using it to argue that she ought to let me get the evidence thrown out, seemed pointless if she physically couldn't do the job.

"Okay," I said, thinking things through. "What you're talking about is something I don't think any attorney would ever recommend, but I do hear what you're saying. That said, though, it's not just up to me. I would have to check with the ethics folks and my insurance to see if I'm even allowed to purposely not try to throw out such critical evidence. That might be malpractice even if you okay it."

"Well, I appreciate that you're at least considering it. It's more than Mr. Girardeau was willing to do."

I shrugged. "You've got what strikes me as a good reason for it. And it's your life. But I still would have to check."

"Okay. Looking at the time, I have to go now, but you should know that if I find a lawyer who believes me and who's willing to fight for what matters to me, I am prepared to offer a $100,000 retainer."

I forced myself not to blink. I'd never earned more than $63,000 a year in my life.

I said, "That seems very reasonable."

"Let me know about the ethics and the insurance as soon as you can."

"I will."

4

TUESDAY, APRIL 28, 2020

In my car, headed to the causeway so I could get home and walk Squatter, my mind was racing. I could not fathom that amount of money suddenly dropping into my account—or, I reminded myself, Roy's client trust account, where retainers were held and then disbursed to the attorney as they did the work. Damn, Roy would be blown away if I brought that kind of money in. He might even stop making snarky remarks about my lack of business skills.

I put the window down to feel the breeze—it was, as usual, a beautiful day—and tried to get the money out of my head, since after all, I still didn't know if it was even possible for me to help Simone.

It probably was, if I papered it right—meaning if I sent her a letter laying out exactly why leaving that evidence in and going to trial was about as high-stakes a bad bet as it was possible to make, and she answered in writing that she understood and wanted to do it anyway. After all, every client had the absolute right to take a plea or to refuse and go to trial. Spurning the opportunity to throw out damning evidence was a weird way to insist on going to trial, but the law probably did see that decision as hers to make.

As the palm trees on either side of the causeway whizzed past, the western ones casting shadow stripes on the hood of my car, I thought of another problem. Even if it was lawful to do what she wanted, was it right? I'd be paid a hell of a lot more to go to trial than I would to get the evidence thrown out and the trial canceled as a result. Would that be taking advantage of her desperation? All she was likely to get out of this was a few more weeks or months where she could still feel hope. Still think, in other words, that her life might get back to normal. But it wasn't going to. I could picture a Basking Rock jury looking at a successful young Black woman the wrong way and being only too glad to seize on that syringe evidence to render a guilty verdict.

Maybe the other lawyers she'd consulted were right to decline. A woman that young, with no knowledge of the law or of how trials really worked—could she truly comprehend the risk she was asking to take?

At the stoplight at the end of the causeway, I picked up my phone and called Terri. She had the smarts and good sense I needed to think this through.

"Hey, Leland," she said. I heard barking in the background. "Wait a second, I just got home." I heard her sweet-talking her hound, whose collar was jangling, and dropping something on the floor. "What's going on?"

I turned and cruised up the next long street. "I've got a new case, maybe. Although taking it might make me feel about on par with Mephistopheles, morally speaking. I don't think the client can possibly understand what she's getting into."

"Sounds interesting!" Her dog woofed in the background. "Buster needs a walk. Want to meet up somewhere and walk Squatter with us?"

"Yeah, maybe the beach? I just drove down the causeway, and there was nobody there. We and the dogs might have the sand to ourselves."

———

In the time it took to get home, feed Squatter, and put him in the car, another train of thought got going. How, I wondered, did Simone have that much money? Were her sources legitimate—or, to put it bluntly, legal? Given my ignorance about social influence people, or whatever they were called, and my lack of any clue as to how they made money, I knew my suspicions might be off base. But as I sat at a light looking at the ocean, a ship in the distance reminded me that the last time I'd helped a rich person deal with their legal troubles, he'd turned out to be up to his neck in corruption. Henry Carrell, who I'd thought of as a friend, or getting there, had his yachting company seized by the feds. And he himself had disappeared, along with his family—into witness protection, I assumed.

As I turned back onto the causeway, I wished I'd brought a towel and some shades. Every new thought made this potential case seem like quicksand to me. I just wanted to lie on the beach and think about nothing.

———

I parked and waved to Terri, who was down by the water watching her rottweiler, Buster, attack the waves. I let Squatter out of his carrier, and after skittering around sniffing our front tire and the curb stop we'd parked behind, he noticed Buster and ran toward him across the sand. I hadn't realized my elderly Yorkie was capable of moving that fast. But he hadn't seen his friend in a while, and I knew how he felt. It must have been five or six weeks since we'd hung out with Terri and her dog.

"Hey there!" she called out when I was still fifteen or twenty feet away. "How's the shutdown treating you?"

"It's been killing Squatter's social life. You know how he is."

She laughed. "Places to go, places to pee…"

I laughed. Then it hit me why she looked different: "Oh, your hair!"

"Yeah, I got tired of that wavy Oprah do. It's high maintenance, and I realized, you know, life is short. Plus I read some bad stuff about the chemicals."

"Well, it looks good. I'm probably going to need to buy some clippers myself, if the hair places don't open back up soon."

"It's a good thing I got locs when I did. Right before the shutdown! And they're supposed to last up to six months."

"Wish I could only hit the barber every six months without looking like a damn hippie."

We started walking up the beach. Our dogs were racing back and forth at the water's edge.

"Don't tell Buster," I said, "but Squatter doesn't have any other friends." I stopped to take my shoes and socks off. Leather shoes such as I'd worn to drop by the office didn't work too well in the sand. Apparently, I'd been too distracted by the case to think of that before leaving the house.

"Oh my God! No! Give me that!" Terri blocked her dog in mid-run, squatted down to pry his mouth open, pulled out a starfish, and threw it back in the water.

"Thank you," I said. "That thing could've grabbed Squatter and drowned him."

"Aw, not without a fight."

"Maybe not."

We watched the dogs playing for a minute. Then she said, "So, what's this new case?"

I told her. Two sentences in, without me mentioning any names, she asked, "What's up? Is Girardeau asking you to be co-counsel?"

"Oh—no. Haven't spoken to him at all." I hadn't mentioned his name either; she was following the case.

"Did she seek you out herself?" There was no one around to listen in, but even so, she avoided saying Simone's name. I nodded. "Good. I wasn't sure how a flashy Charleston lawyer would play down here. Those guys who look like they'd represent the Mafia, you know—maybe it's the cop in me, but I always think whoever they're repre-senting must be guilty."

I laughed. "Well, however he comes across, he's a pretty good lawyer."

"But were his clients guilty?"

"The ones I saw in court? Yeah, I sure thought so."

A hundred yards out on the water, a white motorboat was buzzing over the waves.

She said, "I've actually been keeping an eye on her case since—well, since before there was a case. When it just looked like an overdose at a party."

"How come?"

"I don't know," she said. "I just… pay attention."

I knew already that she had a mental library of the lives and secrets of what seemed like everyone in Basking Rock. Terri paid attention, and she remembered what she learned—better than probably anybody else I'd ever met.

She said, "I don't know if you remember, but her mom was in high school with us. Two years ahead, I think. There was always something weird about her."

"How so?"

She watched the motorboat for a second, thinking, and finally said, "She was just… damaged."

"You know why?"

She shrugged. "I got an idea."

Buster brought a shell over and dropped it at her feet. She stooped to praise him. I doubted she was going to share what more she knew about Simone's mom unless it turned out to be relevant to the case. Terri didn't just remember secrets, she respected them.

I was reminded of my own responsibilities in that regard: I couldn't tell her what Simone had told me because even prospective clients were covered by confidentiality rules. I wondered how to unravel, solo, my conflicting thoughts about taking her case.

A wave hit Squatter and dragged him two or three feet out to sea. "It's okay, boy," I called, jogging over to fish him out. He was whining, and Terri pulled a hand towel out of her bag and passed it over. As I dried him off, I thought about the unfortunate fact that the only person I was allowed to talk to about anything Simone had said was Roy, since I was of counsel to his firm. And Roy was a smart man, but business-smart: savvy, good at getting people on his side. He wasn't someone with insight and common sense I felt I could rely on.

Buster bumped my hip to check on my dog's well-being. I set Squatter back down, and they ran off again.

There was one thing I could ask Terri about without breaching confidentiality. "You know," I said, "I know nothing about these social influencers, and I don't understand how they make money. I'm probably being a little paranoid here, and she didn't say one word to make me suspect this, but the last thing I want to do is get mixed up with someone who's got God knows what illegal sources of income."

"You worried she's selling drugs?"

"I mean, you know how it is. They did allegedly find heroin in her van, although what they found is so miraculous for their case it seems like it almost *has* to have been planted."

"Mm-hmm." Terri had a very emphatic way of saying that.

"But even so, I've got no way of knowing at this stage if she's innocent, and I might never be sure."

"I'd be truly surprised if she's dealing. I haven't heard anything like that about her, or about her mother, for that matter."

"Well, that's good."

"And they—influencers—they can be rich, and they can get that way fast. I mean, I follow Tabitha Brown, and three years ago she was nothing, just some woman talking about vegan sandwiches to the camera on the dashboard of her car. Now she lives in some gated community in Los Angeles."

"But how? What on earth do they do that folks pay them for?"

"They entertain people," she said. "Or teach them something. You watch them kind of like you'd watch a TV talk show. And Tabitha Brown's got, let's see, spices with her name on them in the grocery store, some other deal with Whole Foods—that sort of thing. Sponsorships. You know how TV stars used to advertise, I don't know, like, exercise equipment? It's that sort of thing. They're influencers because they influence people to—well, to buy stuff, among other things."

"Huh." The way she put it, it did kind of make sense.

"So if she can pay," Terri said, "and you think she might be innocent, what's stopping you from taking the case?"

I sighed and watched the dogs for a second. Buster was standing in a few inches of water, looking back at Squatter. A wave came and he jumped it, then looked at Squatter again. I thought he might be trying to teach my dog some basic water safety: *Here's how we avoid getting swept away.* Though that worked differently when you weren't much bigger than a squirrel, I supposed.

"Mostly it's things I can't talk about," I said. "Except in the abstract. So, let's say there's a strategy she's dead set on, and I can see why, but it's about the highest-risk thing a defendant could do. There's an easy way to win—it's not guaranteed, obviously, since nothing is, but trying it is easy and low risk, not to mention quicker and cheaper than a full trial. Any attorney would tell her that's what you got to do. I understand why she wants to go the other way—I mean, she explained her priorities, and it makes some sense. But chances are, she'd lose. And she's only, what, twenty-three? She's never seen even one trial in her life. I'm just not sure she has any real way of understanding what she's up against or how completely this might ruin her life."

"So you don't want to take her money and go to trial? Because you're worried you'd get rich off destroying her life?"

"I mean, I'd do my damnedest to stop it from being destroyed," I said. "Because, my God, she's barely older than Noah. She ought to have her whole life in front of her. But yeah, that's the concern."

"That's the father in you," she said. "It sounds like you already care more about her best interests than Girardeau ever could."

I looked at her in surprise. That was a take that had not occurred to me.

"Damn," I said. "Yeah, dammit, I think you're right."

She was smiling. I got the sense she had another thought, but instead of saying it, she was going to let me get there myself.

"I can't leave her with that clown. He doesn't even know Basking Rock juries. He's a city guy."

She nodded.

"All he cares about is a client's money. She needs a lawyer who actually cares about what's right for her."

"Mm-hmm."

I looked back at the ocean. The sky was getting a darker blue.

Without looking at her, I said, "I'm going to need a private investigator. You available?"

———

5

MONDAY, MAY 4, 2020

By the time I heard back from ethics and Roy's insurance company that I could move ahead with Simone's high-risk strategy, the South Carolina Supreme Court had issued an order allowing grand juries to convene remotely because of the pandemic, and I heard from the solicitor that they'd be convening to consider adding murder charges to Simone's case on Monday, May 11.

That was a blow. As the saying goes, grand juries would indict a ham sandwich if the solicitor asked them to. The chances of Simone not getting indicted were slim, and what followed that was the nightmare she'd already told me she was willing to risk everything to avoid. An indictment meant an arrest and a bail hearing—and accused murderers were hardly ever granted bail. If she had to sit in jail for months awaiting trial, I didn't know what that might do to her health, and I assumed it would destroy her business.

I gave her a call to share the bad news. She sucked in her breath, and I thought she might cry. But when she spoke, her tone was measured.

"Okay," she said as if she were psyching herself up. "Okay. Um, so, I understood from Mr. Girardeau that what normally happens after somebody's indicted is the police come out and arrest them. Is that—I mean, would you say that's correct?"

"I would. And then the bail hearing's within twenty-four hours after that, although with the court closures it'd be virtual, so you'd attend the hearing from jail—"

"I'm not going to be in jail." I heard a little background noise, like she was moving around the room. "I'm on my way to Charleston right now."

"Oh. So— Wait, are you planning on staying there into next week?"

"I'm being admitted to a skilled nursing facility. It's to get physical therapy for my illness. I hope the judge will understand that as the reason I'm not in the county anymore."

I debated whether to tell her that wasn't going to buy her much time. I could tell the judge she was in a medical facility, and that might get him to forgo having her hauled off to jail immediately, but it wouldn't stop her bail hearing from happening. As an accused murderer, her months of being free on bail while awaiting trial were almost certain to come to an end.

To get a sense of whether she was trying to line up some way to flee, I asked, "Did you have this planned? I mean, with the grand jury thing coming up?"

She hesitated, then said, "I have a concierge doctor. She's very responsive to my needs."

"A concierge doctor?"

"She trained at Johns Hopkins. Her practice doesn't take insurance. Instead, patients pay a monthly fee for— Well, it's sort of like the retainer I'm paying you, Mr. Munroe. It means I can call her any time, day or night, and she'll address whatever's wrong."

I'd given her Benton & Hearst's bank details the previous day. I scribbled a reminder to myself to check whether her $100,000 had arrived.

"Okay," I said. "Well, I would just ask that you make sure I can get in touch with you." If it came down to it, I needed to be able to represent to the court that she wasn't fleeing from justice.

"Of course. I'll have my phone."

"If you could let me know what facility you're going to be at, that'd be good. Meanwhile, I'll need to get Girardeau's files. If he's available, I'll head up there today."

"I think that's a good idea," she said. "I'll send you his cell number."

I heard a zipper, like the sound of a suitcase opening, and a couple of things being tossed into it. I wondered if she had a passport. I decided not to ask. I wasn't a prosecutor anymore, and I needed to get in the habit of putting my client's interests before the interests of the state. If I somehow got the judge to consider granting her bail, he could ask her that question himself.

"Mr. Munroe," she said, still packing from the sound of it, "I try to face things squarely. I know from Mr. Girardeau what it means for the grand jury to convene. But I am *not* going to jail. I will answer any call or text you send me to help you get ready for the bail hearing, if it comes to that. And so will my doctor."

"That's good to know."

My phone dinged, and a text from her appeared on the screen: *Girardeau*, it said, followed by a Charleston number. The clock at the top of the screen said it was already past one.

"Thanks," I said. "I'll let you go now. Got to give him a call."

I hung up, and the phone dinged again. This text had the name and address of what I took to be the nursing facility up in Charleston.

Before calling Girardeau, I dialed Roy's number.

"Leland!" he boomed, so loud I had to hold the phone away from my ear. "I checked the balance on the client trust account this morning. There's an extra hundred grand in there! I thought we'd been hacked!" He laughed loudly at his own joke, and I chuckled too. I had to admit it was pretty funny.

"Strange thing for a hacker to do," I said, "putting money in somebody else's bank account."

"Oh, you know, money laundering, that sort of thing. Just about anything seemed more likely than you landing a big client." He burst out laughing again. "Hoo boy," he said, quieting down. "Seriously, I got to hand it to you. Nice work. Even nicer if you can win it, of course."

"Well, I like to think my courtroom skills are even better than my business skills."

"That's one way of putting it. Setting the bar a little low, but okay."

———

Girardeau's office was in Charleston's business district, a couple of blocks north of the courthouse. The city was quieter than I'd ever seen it on a Friday afternoon—or, I realized, at any other time in the two decades I'd lived there. The pandemic had shut everything down. I parked right across from his building, which at five stories of brick and stone was one of the taller ones in town. He was meeting me there because, he said, even his receptionist was working from home; nobody would be around to hand over Simone's case files.

As I was paying the parking meter, I heard a low hum and looked up. A metallic blue Lamborghini was gliding up the street. From inside, Girardeau waved. He parked, checked for traffic—there was none—

and opened his door with a sound like the seal breaking between two modules of a spacecraft in a sci-fi movie.

I'd only ever seen him suited up for court, never dressed down for a day off. He had gold-framed sunglasses on top of his head and was wearing a bright pink polo shirt with a tight pair of dark jeans so perfectly distressed I knew they'd come that way from the factory. I crossed the street, shook his hand, and walked with him to the glass doors of his building. While he ran his key card through the slot, I noticed that his black-and-red shoes had the bumpy look of alligator leather.

The lobby was deserted. Calling the elevator with his key card, he said, "I guess we can forget the elevator rule, since there's not a soul around to overhear us. So, this case. It is a *dog*."

"You think?"

The rule he'd mentioned, which was drummed into every student in law school, was a reminder not to discuss your cases in elevators or any other public place, since you never knew who might overhear.

He hit the button for the top floor. "My God, yes," he said. "You are welcome to it. Ms. Baker has not listened to one word of my advice since I took the case. And I don't foresee that changing, even though as of Monday she's probably looking at a possible life sentence."

I shook my head. "You never want to see a grand jury considering murder charges. Not if you're on the defense side, anyway."

"Yeah," he said. "By the way, what brought you over to the defense bar? I figured you thought we were all on the dark side."

"Well, things change." I wasn't going to tell him exactly what had changed for me, although with the Charleston legal community being as small as it was, he might've heard rumors.

"You develop a sudden love for the United States Constitution?" He laughed. "Everyone presumed innocent until the government can damn well prove its case? Here, this is my floor." He held the door for me to get off.

On the wall facing the elevator were two large flags: one the Stars and Stripes, the other South Carolina's blue and white. Beside them, painted in gold letters a foot high, were the words "Travis Girardeau, Attorney at Law." He swiped us in through another set of glass doors and led me down the hall.

I recognized his office from his appearance on the TV news. His desk —mahogany, I assumed—was about eight feet wide. The two corners that I could see were carved into stylized eagles, their talons gripping brass balls that sat on the red carpet. I silently revised the equation I'd given Noah: Mr. Girardeau was well over one thousand times as flashy as me.

He gestured to three file boxes and a couple of Redwelds sitting on the floor. "I'll help you carry those down," he said. "Inside you'll find everything we've got to try to change Ms. Baker's fate—if she'll let you. Two of the boxes are discovery, and the rest is from her or from my own investigations."

"Thanks."

Discovery meant the evidence that the solicitor's office had turned over to the defense. Two boxes seemed like a lot more information than Simone had given me. This weekend, I hoped, I'd come to understand how the other side could look at this case and see a homicide.

"Damn," Girardeau said, "I forgot how much I'd been missing this place." He went around his desk, sat down, and kicked his alligator shoes up to rest a few feet from his mouse pad.

"Yeah, this pandemic's turned things upside down."

"Have a seat," he said, gesturing. "It's been interesting, having hearings on my computer instead of in person. I sure as hell hope they don't start doing trials that way. I think, to connect with a jury, you got to be in the same room."

"I'm with you on that. What'd you have in mind for Ms. Baker's case? How were you thinking you'd tell them her story?"

"Oh, I never thought we'd have to get there. That syringe has got to get kicked out. The whole thing comes down like a house of cards once it does."

"That was my thought, too."

"It's criminal defense 101. But I could not get that through to her. She start talking to you about her conspiracy theories yet?"

I laughed. "Not as yet. I haven't had the pleasure."

"Hoo boy," he said, shaking his head. "You look at this case, first glance, it looks like a garden-variety overdose. Right? Girl went to a party, partied too much, and ended up dead. Happens all the time, unfortunately, and the state's got a hill to climb to convince a jury it was anything else."

"Yeah," I said. "Maybe I'll feel different after looking through those boxes of yours, but back when I first heard about the case, I assumed it was one of those things where they know she's the one who gave the victim the drugs."

"Right. And that's the prosecution's theory, based on a couple of witness statements that maybe pointed that way, but there were holes in those that I could drive a truck through. The syringe is what ties it all together. As it stood when we were supposed to start trial, the case goes up in a puff of smoke if you get that tossed. But that's not the way she wanted to go. If that indictment comes down tomorrow, I dearly hope she'll change her tune."

"You got any idea how they think they can get from manslaughter to murder? That's quite a leap when the manslaughter was just giving somebody drugs."

"You're the former prosecutor," he said. "If you've got an autopsy report from nine months ago, a dead woman who's been buried since last June, and a private residential crime scene that the cops haven't set foot on in close to a year, how do you convene a grand jury to add charges?"

"A witness. Or some kind of digital evidence they somehow didn't have before now... although for a death in someone's home, that'd most likely come off somebody's phone, so—"

"Right, so it still means a new witness. Somebody whose phone they didn't already have. And I have no solid ideas as to who, since according to her, she's kind and fair to one and all, has no enemies, and doesn't let drugs into her life."

"You think that's less than true?"

"I have no illusions," he said, "about *any* member of the human race. And she may be kind and fair, but when you look in those boxes, you'll see some text messages between her and the dead girl that I assume they're going to use if they do add a murder charge, to try to show motive. Professional rivalry type of stuff, pretty nasty. Although nothing I couldn't have handled, if she'd let me do my job."

Professional rivalry struck me as a flimsy motive. Among gang members or in organized crime, maybe, but that was not this case. "Unless they've unearthed something big," I said, "it's a little hard for me to see the prosecutor actually *believing* that this was murder."

"Yeah, and more importantly, getting a jury to believe it. In most cases that have a gray area, I assume they throw murder on just to get the defendant to take a plea. And I told her that, of course, because you and I both know what she's looking at if she doesn't take one."

"Mm-hmm."

"That went nowhere. She even asked me if she could testify before the grand jury."

We both laughed and shook our heads. Grand juries could hear testimony from the accused, and on rare occasions that was a good idea, but usually it was like dropping a cat into a cage with a pit bull. The only lawyer allowed in the room was the prosecutor, and there was no judge to keep things fair.

"So, yeah," Girardeau said. "Her problem, it seems to me, is she doesn't see how bad things could be. I mean *at all*. Even though she had personal problems with the victim, she can't even *imagine* that woman might've been a heroin user. So she comes up with some outlandish murder plot—" He sighed, almost in disbelief. "That's what I meant by conspiracy theories. When I've asked her what might've happened, she comes up with something straight out of the movies, and then she wants to, you know, work doggedly to help uncover the *truth*. But we are not on TV. This is real life."

I tried not to seem too surprised. I didn't want him to know I hadn't heard anything like that; so far she'd seemed very grounded. "Yeah? Who's her suspect? Or does that change from day to day?"

"That's the thing! Is it the dead girl's boyfriend? That's an easy story to tell, right? And if I can tell the jury a plausible alternative story— emphasis on the *plausible*—I've practically won already. Any juror that's ever watched the news knows it's usually the boyfriend or the husband."

"Absolutely. Have you talked to him?"

"No—he's gone! He split town! How's that for raising a juror's doubts? But no. It can't be an overdose or the boyfriend. For her, it's got to be complicated." He looked at his watch, which was chunky gold and, if I had to guess, probably weighed close to a pound. "God,

I'm sorry. I wish I could talk more, but I've got to run. Work was not on my agenda this evening."

"Oh, I'm sorry to keep you." He stood up, so I did too. "Listen, do you mind if I stay in touch? I might have some questions about what I find in those boxes."

"No problem. You got my cell now, give me a call if you want. Now, let me just grab a cart from the library. Be right back."

He went out and down the hall. I looked at the file boxes and Redwelds, wondering what land mines I might find in there and how long my list of questions to ask Simone would be by the time I was done going through them.

Girardeau returned, wheeling a cart. I helped him load the boxes, and we headed back down the elevator.

As I was loading the files into the trunk of my car, Girardeau, holding the cart steady, looked around and gave a low whistle. "Never thought I'd see Charleston looking like a ghost town."

I saw what he meant. "Kind of suits it, though, doesn't it?" I said. "As cities go, this one's always been a little spooky."

He laughed. When I stood up, all done loading, he nodded to the boxes. "Thanks for taking that girl's ghost off my desk, at least." Then, with a smile and a wink, he added, "Welcome to the dark side."

———

6

MONDAY, MAY 11, 2020

Terri and I were enjoying the spring sunshine at my backyard picnic table, looking through Girardeau's boxes while our dogs sniffed various parts of the grass and the fence. When it had started getting breezy, I brought jam jars and cans of soup out to use as paperweights. It was a nice way to work.

But the grand jury was convening at that very moment on new evidence I didn't yet have. And given how grand juries worked— eighteen regular citizens listening to a prosecutor telling them why they ought to indict somebody, and looking through the evidence he presented—there was a good chance they'd come back the wrong way.

"So, this boyfriend," Terri said, snapping photos of each page of his witness statement. "From what's in there," she said, gesturing to the file box next to her, "it looks like the cops focused on him at first. Which you'd expect in a case like this."

"Right, and why did finding the syringe in Simone's van change that? He was there the night Veronica died, and Simone told me she parks right outside. He could've planted the syringe that night, or seen the van later and planted it then."

She put his statement back in its manila folder. "Yeah, unless there's a smoking gun in that last box there, I don't know."

"There's not." I'd spent the weekend going through everything.

"Well, then I would think the investigating officer probably got pressure from above."

I nodded. Police higher-ups did that sometimes. For good reasons, usually, but not always.

"Okay," she said, writing the boyfriend's name in her notebook: *Austin McKrall*. "I'll pull his criminal record, if there is one. And whatever else I can find."

She'd already given me Simone's record, which was no record at all. She'd never even been pulled over until the stop last summer that had gotten her arrested in this case. The victim, with her handful of speeding tickets and, two years earlier, a suspended thirty-day sentence for misdemeanor weed possession, looked like a hardened criminal by comparison.

"Right. And I'll get in touch with the caterer," I said, typing his name into my laptop. "Luke Delacourt. With restaurants closed for coronavirus, he's probably back in Charleston, unless he's down here supervising the renovations."

"Yeah. At least some of his workers would probably have stayed at the party pretty late, for cleanup, and maybe he did too. I'm surprised the cops didn't get statements from any of them."

"You hear anything about why he took over the Broke Spoke?" Our local truck stop and strip club had been the second-largest business in town until my big case the previous year had ended up landing the owner in federal prison. That was by far the most interesting thing that had ever happened in Basking Rock, so every development since then, including the hiring of a new restaurant manager, was a major topic of local gossip.

"It was a moneymaker," she said, shrugging. "Even before the notoriety. What *I* was curious about was why the feds let it keep running. Why'd they put Blue Seas in forfeiture, but not that place?"

"You know Cardozo's not allowed to share that kind of thing." I pulled a sheaf of papers out of the last box and handed it to her. "But I can guess." Cardozo, my law school buddy who was now a federal prosecutor in Charleston, was in charge of the case that had brought both Blue Seas and the Broke Spoke down.

"And what'd you guess?"

"It was probably mortgaged to the hilt," I said, "and maybe underwater. You don't normally bother with forfeiture proceedings unless there's some equity."

"Huh. So I wonder where the money for renovations is coming from."

"Maybe that was part of this, uh…" I glanced at my laptop. "This Mr. Delacourt's deal."

"Yeah." She was drumming her fingers on the autopsy report. "You know, it might be a coincidence, but I keep coming back to the fact that the investigators got this report back barely a week before Simone's traffic stop."

"So, did that shift their focus to her? I've read it three times, and I don't see why it would. Wish I could decipher Girardeau's chicken scratches." He'd made a fair amount of mostly illegible handwritten notes in the margins. Something about it had given him ideas or gotten him excited, but I was going to have to call him again to find out what.

46

"I don't know either. I mean, they already had Veronica's medical records, so the diazepam shouldn't have been a surprise."

Veronica Lopez had died from combining two drugs: heroin and diazepam, otherwise known as Valium. The report said she had enough diazepam in her system to knock her out. Her medical records showed she had a long-standing prescription for it.

"Yeah. If she'd overdosed at her own house, or even if the needle had still been there when the cops arrived, it would've been pretty open and shut."

Noah leaned out the back door and yelled, "You feed Squatter yet? He was scratching at the door."

"Oh! No—I got distracted, I guess."

He laughed and shook his head. "Well, at least it's for a good cause. Okay, I'll feed him."

He let Squatter in. When the door shut behind him, Terri smiled. "I think he's proud of you. For taking this case, I mean."

"Well. I don't know." I pulled the police reports out of a Redweld. "I guess he didn't like my business law plan. This is more up his alley."

"Yup. I can tell."

"Here." I tossed her the file on the traffic stop. "When I saw the photos from when they impounded her van, I thought she must've bought the thing that *day*. It's pristine. My car looks like a dumpster compared to hers."

She laughed and paged through. "Yeah, and a light gray interior? How could there be a syringe rolling around in there for six weeks without anybody noticing?"

I skimmed through the initial police report again. It said that upon their arrival, at 7:04 a.m. after a 9-1-1 call twelve minutes earlier, the victim was deceased and they found no signs of trauma, no syringe, or anything else that might indicate her cause of death.

So someone had moved it, obviously, but Simone and the dead girl's boyfriend had both claimed ignorance, and nobody else was there. The two of them had been asleep, they said, and after the boyfriend woke to find Veronica dead, his shouting had alerted Simone.

When more cops showed up forty minutes later with a search warrant, they didn't find the syringe in the victim's bag or the trash or anywhere else. Photos showed each room and a couple of different angles of the yard. No drug paraphernalia was found, no drugs, nothing incriminating at all. The names of party guests were obtained, and the investigation proceeded as I would've expected after that, with the boyfriend as the person of interest, until Simone's traffic stop in July.

"This guest list," I said, tossing it across the table to Terri. "I don't get it."

"What is this, like, fifty people? And they only interviewed... apart from Simone and Austin, *two* of them? Really?" She gave me a look.

"I know." Although the boyfriend was the obvious suspect, it was appalling how little effort they'd put into investigating beyond him and Simone. They had short statements from the victim's cousin, Sofia Lopez—who Terri described as a wannabe influencer—and two other party guests, but nothing else. The statements talked about an argument Simone and Veronica had gotten into at the party. It sounded bad, but while I'd handled cases where an argument spiraled into manslaughter because some fool grabbed a knife or a gun, I'd never seen one that went from heated argument to friendly sleepover to fatal overdose. For me, that story didn't hold together.

"If it were me," Terri said, looking over the guest list, "I mean, if I were still a cop, I'd want to talk to her stalker, even though he's not on the list."

Simone had told us some basement-dweller named Shawn Gifford had been Veronica's most obsessive fan, and he'd shown up at a couple of her public events. There were four or five sentences about him in the police investigation files Girardeau had provided, including the notation that he had not attended her funeral. They hadn't interviewed him.

To lighten the mood, as anyone working in homicide had to do sometimes, I told Terri, "Remind me to hire that caterer if I ever need one. It looks like they cleaned up better than most folks do after a party—I don't even see any empty liquor bottles in these photos."

With a smile, she said, "Your house looks worse than that right now."

I laughed. "I'm a widowed father trying a homicide case," I said. "I'm lucky the house is habitable at all." With a sigh, I picked up the autopsy report again. It was time to get back to business. "The only difference I can see this thing making is that the sheer amount of diazepam and heroin in her system made it absolutely clear Veronica couldn't have gotten rid of the syringe herself. She must've dropped like a brick as soon as the heroin kicked in."

"Yeah, but you assume that anyway, as a cop. You don't need to wait for the autopsy report. Even if it takes five or ten minutes for the overdose to really hit, you're high as a kite that whole time. I never saw an OD where the victim had, like, tidied up before dying."

My phone rang. It was Aaron Ruiz, who I'd come to think of as a friend, but he was also a prosecutor with the local solicitor's office. I picked up. "Afternoon, Ruiz. Or evening, I guess." It was just about six o'clock.

"Evening, Leland. Hope you're well. So, uh, cutting to the chase, I'm calling to let you know the grand jury's come back with a true bill for murder."

That meant an indictment. Simone's life was about to get a whole lot worse.

"Okay." I gave Terri a look and a head shake to let her know the news was bad. "Well, I'll look forward to the discovery. How are we handling the bond hearing? Virtually?"

"Yeah, every one I've been at for the past four or five weeks has been that way. They set up a room at the jail with a video camera for it. You'll see your client on a screen up by the bench."

"Oh, I should mention, my client's in a medical facility right now. Doctor's orders. I don't know if you're aware, but she's got MS."

"Multiple sclerosis?" I heard him scribbling something down. "Yeah, I knew it was something like that. Okay, what's the facility? Is this a hospital?"

"Skilled nursing. Not here in town—she's got complex medical needs; she gets her care up in Charleston. What I'd like to do is see if we can put an officer outside her door at the facility and proceed to the bail hearing that way rather than putting her in jail first. I'll get you a letter from her doctor."

"That's what I was going to ask for next. Can you give me the doctor's name? And the name of this facility?"

I scrolled through the last few texts I'd gotten from Simone and read out her doctor's name, but I hesitated to let him know where she was. "As for the facility," I said, "do I need to bring a motion, or do I have your word you won't send any boys up there to drag her out in cuffs?"

"Of course you do. I save that kind of maneuver for the Charles Manson types. Or I would, if we ever had that type down here."

"What about Ludlow? Would he send them?" Ludlow was his boss. Neither of us thought highly of him.

After a second, Ruiz said, "I'm going to leave that facility name off the file for now."

"I appreciate that."

"But that said, I need it so I can order an officer up there tonight. If I wait until tomorrow morning, Ludlow will be back on the clock, and he might suggest, uh… handling it differently."

I knew what he meant—it was why I'd asked about Ludlow in the first place. Since moving back to Basking Rock a little over a year ago, I'd noticed a lot of perp-walk photos in the local news. Ludlow was the kind of guy who wanted everyone to see that he was hard on crime.

"Okay," I said. "Let me know when you've got a pen."

"Oh, I got one. I'm looking for a Post-it so I can tell Ludlow that, unfortunately, the facility name and address fell off the file by accident." I heard him rummaging. "Okay, what is it?"

I told him. When he was done writing, I asked, "So that would make the bond hearing, what, tomorrow afternoon?"

"Yep. I'll call the clerk now and let you know what time they set. The clerk will send a link. And I can overnight you the discovery or drop it off, either way."

"Whichever's fastest. Thanks again."

Terri was digging for something in the giant blue handbag she used as a briefcase. As I got off the phone, she found a folder and tossed it across the table.

"What's this?"

"Something you're going to need, it sounds like. For the bail hearing, whenever that's going to be."

"Dammit." I shook my head. It was almost impossible to get bail for a murder suspect. Magistrates weren't even allowed to consider granting bail for murder, and the General Sessions judges who could almost never granted it.

Inside Terri's folder was a document entitled "Land Contract."

"Oh, she owns property? Or almost?" That was a bit of good news. For bail purposes, it would make her seem like less of a flight risk. I flipped through to the last page. The contract was dated four years earlier.

"The payoff date is two years from now," Terri said. "With how her business has been going, she could've paid it off early, although if she did, it's not up on the county property site yet. But they only update that quarterly, and with the pandemic they may not have even done that."

On my laptop, I added that topic to the list of things I needed to ask Simone. As I typed, I said, "What kind of person signs a land contract when they're, what was she, eighteen or nineteen? Seems like she's got more sense in her and more ambition than most people twice her age."

"Money counts for a lot," Terri said. "And she knows it."

———

7

TUESDAY, MAY 12, 2020

I drove up to the skilled nursing facility after lunch, having phoned the night before to let Simone know what was going on. For her bail hearing, I needed to know a lot more about her. I still hadn't asked her anything about the night Veronica died.

The facility she was in, just south of Charleston, looked a lot nicer than my mental pictures of nursing homes. It was set on about an acre of land overlooking the island where rich folks liked to go golfing. Flowers grew alongside the parking lot and on bushes running down the side of the white building. I parked and went inside, where the woman at reception pointed me to boxes of masks and gloves. I put them on, signed in, and headed down the hallway she'd pointed me to.

The cop outside the door was the big, silent type. He scrutinized my ID and bar card, called home base on his cell to get permission, and finally stepped aside to let me get near the door.

I knocked, Simone called me in, and I swung the door open to see a spectacular ocean view through her plate-glass windows. She was sitting up in bed wearing what I thought might be silk pajamas. She smiled and put on a surgical mask. To my surprise, she was tiny.

She'd seemed bigger on my laptop screen than she did in real life, and without makeup she looked even younger than she was.

"Pleasure to meet you, Ms. Baker."

"Likewise." She gestured me to a chair.

"I see you're not handcuffed to the railing," I said, sitting down. "Glad the letter worked."

"Yes. Thank you for that. My doctor had the bed switched right after you called."

I noticed that her bed, unlike every other hospital bed I'd ever seen, didn't have any railings. When I'd spoken to her doctor the previous night about the letter I needed for Ruiz, I'd told her that patients under arrest normally got one hand cuffed to a bed rail. The letter she'd sent back detailing why Simone needed inpatient treatment mentioned that due to potential neurological damage, the doctor strongly recommended "against any type of restraints" on her wrists. Apparently, she'd felt the need to go one better and make cuffing her to the bed impossible.

"Your doctor must have some sway around here," I said. "Good thing. I've had family in facilities like this, and getting a different kind of bed for them was more like a week-long ordeal."

"Well, my doctor's a partner in this facility."

"Oh. Okay." I was silent for a second, processing this—not the fact about her doctor, but the bigger thing: how differently Simone lived from nearly all the criminal defendants I'd ever seen in court, and what kind of resources we were going to be able to bring to bear in her case.

She leaned over to her side table and pulled out a little silver laptop. "I hope you don't mind if I type while we talk," she said. "This has all been, um, a lot to deal with, and taking notes helps me feel like I can… I don't know, manage it, I guess." She laughed at herself. "And I need to update my followers about what's going on."

"Actually… would you mind running posts by me first? Just the ones about your case."

"Oh! Oh my goodness. You mean, so I don't say anything I shouldn't?"

"Exactly. I know when I was a prosecutor, combing through a defendant's social media came in very handy sometimes." I didn't want to put it this way to her, but I'd won several trials in part due to stupid things that defendants had posted.

"So if I'm creating a post about that, you'll vet it for me first?"

"Yes. I think that's a good way to proceed. Now, since we've got limited time here, I'd like to get right into things. At four o'clock today, we're having your bond hearing. Virtually, of course. My recommendation would be for me to be physically here, not just logged in from my house, because it makes it easier to confer with you if I need to."

"That makes sense." She exhaled hard, like she was trying to calm herself down. "Okay, so, what do we need to do? I've been through one bail hearing already, for the original charges. Is this basically the same? Do they just want a higher amount?"

I leaned forward. "Well, the thing is, this is a murder indictment." It felt too blunt to deliver the bad news right away, so I explained, "First off, it's not at the magistrate's court. Magistrates aren't even allowed to consider granting bail on murder charges."

"Oh. So is it the main judge? I mean, the one who's going to do the trial?"

"Probably not. It'll be one of the judges who *could* preside over your trial—the ones up in General Sessions Court who hear cases like this

—but since bail hearings have to be held within twenty-four hours of arrest, it's just whichever one of them is available."

"Okay. Do you have a sense of how much bail would be?"

"Uh, well… it'd be a good deal more than it was already, and we should discuss that, but, Ms. Baker, I've got to be clear with you that the amount is not likely to be the problem. The issue here is that South Carolina judges almost never grant bail on a murder charge."

She stared at me for a second, speechless, and then looked away at the ocean. After a few seconds, she said, "I've been to jail once. Overnight, when they booked me for the drugs and the manslaughter. I don't ever want to see the inside of that place again."

"I understand. So, our best shot at avoiding that—"

She turned back from the window. "Didn't you say they almost never grant bail?"

"Almost. Yeah." I'd never seen it happen myself, but I'd heard of a couple of cases. "But almost is all we've got. And I plan to fight like hell."

She looked at me for a long moment. I had the impression she was checking whether I meant it. "Okay," she said. "Tell me what you need."

We worked through preliminaries. First, everything I could think of to show that she wasn't a flight risk. She had her land contract—it wasn't paid off, but it was better than renting. She'd been raised in Basking County, although she was born out of state and had family there; I hoped the judge wouldn't ask about that. The fact she could work from anywhere weighed against bail, since she could skip town without losing her income. But her illness weighed in favor. All her doctors—I got every name and specialty—were in Charleston.

In case we got one of the more religious judges, I asked the name of her church and how frequently she went. And I asked her height and weight, explaining that it might be relevant to an argument that she was no danger to the community. Five foot one, she said, and a hundred and three pounds; I wrote that down.

"Okay," I said. "Now, since we've got some time before the hearing, could you walk me through what happened on the night Veronica died?"

She sighed and shook her head—not to say no, but to say it was a lot and it was hard. "I don't really know where to start. I mean, it's complicated."

"Well, let's start with how you knew Veronica."

"Um, I'd known her a long time—we went to the same high school— but our relationship was mostly professional. She'd reached out to me about, I don't know, eight or ten months before… um, the events. So I put her in touch with my management company, up in Charleston— Apex Image Management—and they took her on."

"Okay. And how'd you come to be throwing a party for her at your house? Or am I misunderstanding what that was?"

"No, that was the management company again. A publicity thing, their idea. We livestreamed part of it for our subscribers."

"Uh-huh." I wrote that down. "You still have that footage?"

"I think it's backed up somewhere. Didn't Mr. Girardeau talk to you about that?"

I hadn't seen anything about that in his boxes. "Not as such," I said. "I'll ask him about it." I hoped the new evidence the grand jury had seen wasn't some damning video evidence from the livestream. I'd find out soon enough when Ruiz gave it to me.

"So," I said, "how well did you know Veronica?"

She shook her head again. I got the sense this was not something she wanted to talk about.

I tried another approach. "Did you hang out together, or mostly stay in touch electronically, or…"

I was trying to get a read on whether there was anything more to, as she'd put it, their professional relationship. What had she felt when the young woman was alive, and what was left now? Animosity? Regret? Part of me truly wanted to know whether she was innocent. That was the part that wasn't cut out for criminal defense work, since you had to fight just as hard for the guilty clients, and I didn't think I could.

"Mr. Munroe," she finally said, "I didn't like Veronica." I felt the truth in her tone. "We weren't friends, and we were never going to be. But I respected what she'd accomplished since her accident and what she was doing for other women like her."

I knew from the news articles that Veronica had been paralyzed from the waist down in a car crash a few years earlier and that her niche as an influencer was connected to that. "I hear what you're saying, and I appreciate the honesty."

"She copied some of my ideas," she said. "Videos I made, or wanted to make. Themes I was talking about. That kind of thing."

"Yeah, I saw some of the messages between you two in Girardeau's files."

"Oh. Yes. But, I mean, some of that was blown out of proportion. And some wasn't even real—management had us pretending to accuse each other of plagiarism."

"What'd they do that for?"

"They'd seen how it made her followers come to my page and vice versa, trying to compare our posts. So they'd suggest some theme for us to both work on and then tell us to basically fight in public. Whatever drove traffic."

"Okay," I said, jotting down a note. "Shouldn't be too hard to explain that to the jury, if it comes to that. But let's get back to what happened. If you two weren't friends, why'd she spend the night?"

"Her boyfriend got drunk. He was the designated driver, but that went out the window. And they'd come in her van, which she could drive, but she was having some spasms in her legs."

"Oh? How come?"

"It's just a thing that happens. I get them too, in a flare, but with paraplegia it's worse. That's why she used diazepam."

"That helps?"

"You inject it into the muscle," she said. "I use it too. And with the spasms and the diazepam, she didn't feel safe driving. And my home's accessible—she could get to the guest room and the bathroom —so, you know, it worked."

"Uh-huh," I said, writing that down too. "So was she mad at her boyfriend for getting drunk?"

"I think so, but it's not like they had a public fight."

"Do you recall who was there when you-all decided she was going to stay?"

"Well, the guests were gone. But there were still several people—a couple of production people taking down the lighting, and catering cleaning up. Then they left, and we all went to bed."

"You sleep well? All night?"

"Yeah, until Austin started shouting." She shuddered. "That was maybe 6:30 or 7 a.m."

"And what'd you do?"

"I ran out. In my pajamas. He was coming out the guest room door, and he was—" Her eyes were wide, looking off into the distance like she was reliving it. "Mr. Munroe, I'd never seen anybody act like that. I didn't realize until then how much he cared about her. He was so overwhelmed and so in shock. He was not even coherent. I remember when a policeman was asking basic stuff, like his name, he still couldn't talk. He just pulled his wallet out and showed him his ID."

That kind of reaction, I thought, was as consistent with shock at having killed someone as it was with shock at finding a loved one dead. "Did you actually see Veronica? That is, did you go into the guest room?"

She nodded, looking haunted. "She was just... I could see she was gone. Her eyes were open, and she was— I mean, I already believed in the *soul*, you know? But to see a person when it's gone out of them..." She shook her head slowly. "You can tell it's gone. It's... horrible."

"Did you have any idea at the time what might've killed her?"

"Not at all." She was talking louder and faster. "At first it didn't even occur to me drugs could be involved because the one thing we did have in common was health, you know, taking really good care of our health. I mean, she was vegan!"

"Uh-huh."

"So I thought maybe it was a heart thing. You know, sometimes you see on the news some high school kid dies suddenly, and it turns out there was something wrong with his heart that no one knew about until then?"

"Right, I've seen stories like that."

"But I heard the police talking, I mean, the second set of police, the ones who came with a warrant. They were looking for a syringe. That's when I realized drugs were involved, and I thought maybe it was the diazepam. Maybe she took too much by accident."

I wondered if the boyfriend could've given her an extra dose of that, in addition to the heroin.

"Ms. Baker, did Veronica ever talk to you about her boyfriend? Any problems with him?"

"Oh, no. She talked to me a lot—it kind of always went one way; she thought I was her mentor or something. But not about him. What she'd been talking about the most those last few weeks was some of her subscribers who had disappeared. Girls she'd been in touch with, video chatted with—friends, basically. And they disappeared all around the same time. She was obsessed with it. She thought there was a connection, and she was going to prove it."

"Huh." I was afraid we were about to go down the rabbit hole of what Girardeau had called her conspiracy theories.

"Mr. Munroe, you're looking kind of skeptical."

"Well, no. I just want to make sure we don't get too off track, since we've got the bail hearing in about ten minutes and I'm still stuck on one thing." I was actually stuck on two, counting the issues about the boyfriend, but I didn't want to get into that, especially since Simone had just said Veronica didn't talk to her about him. Terri was digging for more information on him, and there was no point speculating until she told me what she found.

"What are you stuck on?"

"Well, in a word: motive."

Her expression didn't change. She nodded for me to go on.

"Because manslaughter can happen by accident. Or, as the theory was in your case, it can happen when you give somebody recreational drugs that end up killing them."

"I didn't do that."

"Right, I hear you. I'm just explaining how this case might look to the prosecution. They didn't need a motive for manslaughter, but they need one now. Juries know people don't generally kill somebody for no reason at all. Prosecutors know that to convince a jury, you need a motive. So, are you aware of anything that could've made the prosecutor here think you wanted Veronica dead?"

She looked at me. She blinked.

My phone beeped to remind me to log on to the bail hearing.

"No, Mr. Munroe," she said. "I'm not aware of anything like that."

She was lying.

8

TUESDAY, MAY 12, 2020

In the five minutes we had left before the hearing, Simone put a light pink blazer on over her pajama top, moved her rolling bedside table a few feet over so she could have the only artwork in the room behind her, and clipped a ring-shaped light about six inches across to the back of her laptop. She got another light out of a cabinet and set it up for me.

The clerk waited until all parties were signed in, then went to get the judge. In her square on my screen, Simone looked as polished as a newscaster. Another square popped up, this one containing a serious-looking man in his forties wearing black-framed glasses. The clerk announced his name: "Judge Lucius Davenport, presiding." I'd never appeared before him or heard anything about him, good or bad. I checked the screen to make sure my hands were out of sight and texted his name to Terri. If she knew anything useful about him, she'd let me know.

"Good afternoon," Davenport said. "I understand this is State of South Carolina versus Simone Baker, case number 2020-A1012-4143, and with respect to this proceeding, Ms. Baker is facing one count of murder."

"Yes, Your Honor," Ruiz said.

The judge hadn't glanced down at the paper in front of him before speaking. He'd memorized her name, case number, and charges. He was sharp.

He said, "On my screen I see, apart from my clerk, the court reporter, and myself, three more people. Could you all please introduce yourselves and state your roles so my clerk can confirm that everyone's present who's supposed to be." His request came out like an order.

After we introduced ourselves, he stated for the record how the proceeding was unfolding: virtually for us, but in person for court personnel, who were sitting "in a socially distanced manner," as he put it, in a courtroom downtown. Davenport didn't seem to be a casual, chitchatty judge at all. I was paying close attention to his style, since it was all I had to go on unless Terri sent me something. I'd learned a long time ago that you had to present your arguments the way the judge wanted to hear them. For that reason, I always made it a priority to research the judge, but with a bond hearing, there often wasn't time to do that.

"Today's hearing," he said, "as I'm sure you all appreciate, is limited to one issue. And that's whether the defendant is entitled to a bond on this charge. If she is, I will also determine the appropriate amount. With that, anything further, counsel?"

"Yes, Your Honor," I said. "For the record, although I trust we're all aware of this, Ms. Baker is not being charged for any new crime committed since she was released on bond on the earlier charges. Her behavior since that point has been exemplary."

My phone, sitting next to my laptop, lit up with a text. Terri's message: *Duke JD. 5th Cir clerk.*

Smart guy, in other words. Intellectual arguments welcome. Emotional arguments, probably not.

"Mr. Ruiz," Judge Davenport said, "is that correct?"

"To the extent Mr. Munroe stated she hasn't been charged with a crime committed after the facts underlying this charge, that's correct."

"Is there any way in which it's incorrect?"

"Well," Ruiz said, "I was just trying to indicate I wouldn't characterize it as 'exemplary.'"

"Understood. Mr. Munroe, I'd appreciate it if counsel kept color commentary to a minimum. The facts and the law should be sufficient for me to make a determination."

"Certainly, Your Honor. And again, to make this clear for the record, Ms. Baker had never been charged with any crime or infraction prior to the events of May 31, 2019, nor has she been charged with anything else since. I mention that both to make clear that this isn't a situation where a defendant was arrested for a new crime while out on bond and also due to its relevance to several subsections of Section 17-15-30."

That was the section setting forth what facts the judge should consider in a bond hearing. Judge Davenport nodded. "Understood. Let's proceed. Mr. Ruiz?"

"Yes, Your Honor." He shuffled some papers in front of him. "It's the state's position that given the seriousness of this offense and the lengthy sentence Ms. Baker faces here, bond should be denied. We are talking about the taking of a human life. There is no greater crime. And as I'm sure Your Honor is aware, it's the practice of courts throughout the state that bond is essentially never available on a murder charge. This is not a situation, as in *State v. McLaren*, where the defendant had preschool-aged children to care for and was a domestic violence victim who claimed self-defense—"

"Does Ms. Baker have any children? Or other family members she's caring for?"

"No, Your Honor, not to the state's knowledge."

"Mr. Munroe?"

"No, Your Honor, although as I'm sure Your Honor is aware, *McLaren* does not present the only scenario in which South Carolina courts may grant bail."

Judge Davenport gave me a few seconds to go on. When I didn't, he said, "Mr. Munroe, do you have a case that's on all fours with this one, where bail was granted to a murder defendant?"

I didn't. I'd spent a good part of the weekend looking for one, with no luck. "Your Honor, I do not. But if I may, I would suggest that what we have here is an unusual case and an unusual defendant, so the lack of similar fact patterns in prior cases really shouldn't come as a surprise. First of all, and I think this goes to Ms. Baker's lack of danger to the community, she has walked the straight and narrow her entire life. She graduated from high school, went from there to nursing school, supported herself, and until this whole ordeal, she'd never set foot in a courthouse at all. She had not one blemish on her record, not even a speeding ticket."

Davenport said, "A speeding ticket is not inherently trivial, Mr. Munroe."

"That wasn't my implication, Your Honor." I wondered if he'd lost somebody in a traffic accident. It was hard to tread carefully when I knew so little about him. "I was merely pointing out her history of complying with the law, which is pertinent to Section 17-15-30 sub (B)(1). And more broadly, Your Honor, I think it's fair to say that in

66

all these respects, Ms. Baker is quite different from the average person appearing before this court."

"Granted. That said, not to state the obvious, but your client has been charged with murder. To my knowledge, there is no legal system on this earth, and no religion, that sees that as anything but the most heinous of crimes."

"We acknowledge that, Your Honor. And Ms. Baker and I fully recognize the value of the life that was lost. But she is presumed innocent, and at this point the state is very far from proving otherwise."

"Mr. Ruiz, anything to say on that?"

"Yes, Your Honor. As counsel for the defense just acknowledged, they're not aware of any authority holding that on these facts, a murder defendant should be granted bail. And the state would posit, Your Honor, that on the facts we have, it appears that Ms. Baker may have used what little nursing training she got—because, just so it's clear for the record, she never did complete her nursing degree—but what training she got, she misused. It's the state's position, based upon the new evidence we've received, that Ms. Baker drugged the victim into unconsciousness and then injected her with the heroin that killed her."

Simone gasped. "Your Honor! Your Honor, I did *not!*"

"Ms. Baker," Davenport said, "you'll have your turn to speak. Please wait until then. Mr. Munroe, what's your response to that?"

"Your Honor, the state has yet to provide any such evidence to the defense. At this point I have not even been informed of the nature of that alleged evidence, but I have read the autopsy report, and it didn't suggest anything like what Mr. Ruiz is alleging now."

"Mr. Ruiz," the judge said, "what's the nature of this evidence, and if Mr. Munroe is correct that you haven't yet provided it to him, what's your timeline for that?"

"I'll be sending over a DVD of the interview as soon as our vendor provides it. It's testimony from the only other person present at the murder scene."

If we'd been in the courtroom together, I would've whipped my head around to look at Ruiz like he'd lost his mind. "The victim's boyfriend? You mean the original suspect himself, who fled the jurisdiction however many months ago?"

"Mr. Austin McKrall," Ruiz said, "who was at the scene, yes."

"Your Honor—"

Davenport held up a hand for silence. "Counsel, we're not going to debate this evidence here. I've got a line about a mile long of folks with hearings that got rescheduled from last month due to this coronavirus thing, on top of the hearings that were already scheduled for this week, and we've only covered one of the two issues I have to consider in a bail hearing. Let's get to the second one, then maybe hear from the defendant if she still wants to speak, and call it a day. Mr. Ruiz, what does the state have to say about Ms. Baker as a flight risk?"

"Your Honor, the state has serious concerns in that regard." As Ruiz flipped through the papers in front of him, my phone vibrated: another text from Terri. This one said, *Religious.*

Ruiz found his notes and said, "As we were just informed by counsel for the defense, Ms. Baker is an unusual defendant in some ways. One of those ways renders her absolutely a flight risk. Ms. Baker is a person of some means, Your Honor, and her earnings come from posting videos and so forth on the internet, which is something she could do from anywhere. Unlike defendants who earn their living from a local employer or who depend on benefits from the state, Ms. Baker could simply pick up her laptop, cross state lines or even leave the country, and continue making a very comfortable living from wherever she might care to go. In addition, as we've also already heard, she has no dependents here relying on her. She has literally nothing to lose if she were to leave the jurisdiction, and everything to gain, in that here in South Carolina she's facing a potential sentence of thirty years to life."

Davenport had a look of distaste on his face as he said, "Can I ask the nature of those videos?"

I jumped in to say, "Health education videos, Your Honor. What they call health and wellness. Ms. Baker suffers from relapsing-remitting multiple sclerosis, and she shares what she's learned about maintaining her health with others who suffer from similar conditions."

"Oh," he said. His expression shifted to one of sympathy. "That's just a terrible disease."

"It is, Your Honor. And I didn't mean to interrupt, so I'll ask Mr. Ruiz if he was finished before I continue, if that's okay."

Ruiz said, "That's fine with me, Your Honor."

"Thank you." Of course I had meant to interrupt. The judge's reaction had made me suspect he was imagining "videos on the internet" meant Simone was some sort of online porn star, so I wanted to correct that impression ASAP by describing what she did in the most wholesome way possible.

"So, Your Honor," I said, "if I may give a little background on Ms. Baker's condition. Right now she's confined in the Alston Gardens skilled nursing facility up here in Charleston to receive medical treatment. Her medical team is right here at the Medical University of South Carolina, and with their help she's been able to maintain her mobility and so forth since her diagnosis. It's taken several years of very careful and attentive care to get her where she is now, and given the lifelong nature of her illness, that's a very strong motivator for her to remain here. Also, and especially given her health condition, I think we should heed the recent order from the state supreme court advising that due to the pandemic, courts in bond hearings should consider home detention and other ways of reducing the jail population. That's from their April 22 order at sub (h)(1)."

Judge Davenport was paying close attention, but I sensed I hadn't yet stirred him.

"In addition," I said, "Ms. Baker was raised in Basking Rock, and so was her mother. Both graduated from Basking Rock High School. And shortly after graduating, despite her young age, Ms. Baker entered into a land contract to purchase a home, which she has since renovated for handicap accessibility. Ms. Baker's church home is here as well. She was raised in Grace Baptist Church, and she is still an active member there today. Her family life, her religious community, and her health are all very strong ties to this area. She's never lived anywhere else, and as I'm sure Your Honor can appreciate, given her medical needs and the need for an accessible home, she is not the type of defendant who could just get in their car and go find a new life someplace else."

Judge Davenport said, "Do you have any response to Mr. Ruiz's point that her income and the nature of her work would enable her to easily flee?"

"I do, Your Honor. Ms. Baker is a fairly well-known online personality. She appears in all of her videos. So, unlike the vast majority of defendants, she's not an anonymous person who could just, for lack of a better word, skip town and disappear into the woodwork. She'd most likely be recognized, and from what I understand about how the internet works, the location that she's posting from is something that authorities would be able to determine."

"If I may, Your Honor," Ruiz said, "our concern with any defendant who has what you might call portable income is that they can flee to a jurisdiction we don't have an extradition treaty with, so the fact that she might be recognized or her location might be traceable wouldn't be any bar to her fleeing. And while I'm happy to concede it might be difficult initially to get set up with doctors and so forth, I think Mr. Munroe also has to concede that when the alternative is spending thirty years to life in state prison, that initial difficulty is not going to dissuade most defendants. It's the consequences of *not* fleeing the jurisdiction, in addition to the severity of the crime, that's led courts to generally deny bail for murder suspects."

"Okay," Davenport said. "I think we've covered what we need to."

In her box on my screen, Simone raised her hand.

"Oh, Mrs. Forstater," the judge said, looking at his clerk, "would you swear the defendant in so we can hear what she's got to say and then get this wrapped up?"

The clerk did so. Simone didn't just answer "I do" in response to the clerk's questions. She echoed back the words, "So help me God," with what seemed like absolute sincerity.

"Ms. Baker," the judge said, "is there anything you'd like to make of record before we close these proceedings?"

"Yes, Your Honor. And I'm sorry if I say anything wrong because I'm not familiar with Your Honor's rules or what a person is supposed to do in court. But as God is my witness, I am innocent of these crimes, all of them, and that's why I refused the plea bargain they offered me last year. I am not taking any plea bargain, and I am not leaving the state, because I am determined to clear my name."

"Okay, thank you. Mr. Ruiz, was there a plea offered? And the defendant refused?"

"Yes, I believe last summer we offered that the heroin possession would be dropped in exchange for a plea on involuntary manslaughter. Her counsel at that time declined it."

That checked out. Girardeau's files included a printout of the email thread where he'd "strongly advised" her to accept the plea, and she'd just as strongly refused.

"Okay," said Judge Davenport. "And Ms. Baker, do you have a passport?"

"I don't, Your Honor. I've never been anywhere but South Carolina and Georgia. And once to Jacksonville when I was little."

Judge Davenport shifted in his seat, slapped a hand on his desk, and said, "I'm going to take all this under consideration. But I have three more hearings today, and my understanding is that Ms. Baker is currently under arrest in some form, but not in jail?"

Ruiz said, "Yes, Your Honor. She's at the healthcare facility Mr. Munroe mentioned, which I can get the address of to your clerk, and we have a guard outside her door 24-7."

"Okay. If she's not actually in jail, my decision can wait. The next three folks coming before me do not have that luxury. My clerk will be in touch to let you know a time tomorrow when I'll deliver my ruling in this matter. Afternoon, counsel."

His video went off, and the clerk formally ended the proceedings.

I exited the Zoom meeting and looked over my laptop at Simone.

Her eyes were closed, and she had one hand on her chest. She was taking slow, purposeful breaths, trying to stay calm, I supposed.

I didn't blame her. If this went the wrong way, the cop outside her door would come handcuff her and take her to jail, and she'd stay there until trial, pandemic or not.

————

9

WEDNESDAY, MAY 13, 2020

At nine in the morning, Judge Davenport's clerk called to say the judge and Ruiz were available for a nine thirty Zoom hearing, and would that work for me? The only right answer was yes. The timing meant I wouldn't be able to get to the nursing facility and be there in person with Simone when she heard her fate, but I couldn't risk annoying the judge.

I called Simone and gave her what reassurance I could.

A few minutes before it started, as I was settling down at my laptop with my coffee, Noah wandered past my office door in his T-shirt and boxers. I called out, "Hey, you want some real-world experience? See the criminal justice system in action? Come sit where nobody can see you, and you can find out with me if Ms. Baker's going to get bail."

"For real? Wait, is that allowed?"

"Bail hearings are public," I said. "If the courts were open, you could walk right in and sit with the spectators. Not dressed like that, obviously."

I turned my camera on, and we made sure he was out of sight but could see my mute button.

The clerk came on, let us all into the meeting, and did her little speech. I said good morning and muted myself again.

"She looks nervous," Noah said. He meant Simone, who looked polished as usual, but her face was tight with fear.

"Mm-hmm."

"Man, she must be just terrified. I'm glad Jackson's not here, or this would give him PTSD."

His friend Jackson, who I'd represented the previous year, had spent six months in jail awaiting his murder trial.

I shushed him and unmuted myself just long enough to say, "Good morning, Your Honor. Leland Munroe, counsel for Ms. Baker."

"All right," Judge Davenport said. "I've obviously taken into consideration the two factors with regard to the danger posed and the risk of flight, as well as the factor related to the pandemic that counsel mentioned. All that has been thoughtfully considered. I note also that apart from the letter from Ms. Baker's doctor describing her condition and her medical needs, we do not have any of the letters on the record that you sometimes see at bail hearings, along the lines of character references from teachers and the like."

I clenched my jaw. I wanted to remind him that the hearing had been held only twenty-four hours after the grand jury came back, so there wasn't time to get such letters, but you don't interrupt a judge.

"In the final analysis," Davenport said, "given the nature of the crime alleged here, the law of the state of South Carolina points toward a denial of bail."

Noah gasped, and Simone blinked hard, like she was fighting tears.

"The law also," he said, "points farther than that. When each of us is judged from on high, as we all will be at our appointed time, we will witness a justice greater than human justice, and also, I believe, a mercy greater than human mercy. I bear that in mind as I propose that in this case, Ms. Baker be permitted, if she is able to post a bond that I will set at an appropriate amount for so heinous a crime, to be released to home detention pending trial, as the state supreme court has exceptionally allowed due to the pandemic. This would be upon her release from the medical facility she's currently in, and subject to the following conditions." He looked down at some papers in front of him. "First, an ankle monitor. Second, to remain at all times in her home or on its grounds, with exceptions only for medical reasons, to travel to her attorney's office if needed, and to attend church, if services are not available remotely."

"Whoa," Noah said. "Like basically house arrest?"

On the screen, Simone looked like she was shocked but trying to stay composed. We'd discussed the possibilities of jail or being freed on bond, but this outcome—avoiding jail but being in every other way confined—had not been part of the conversation. I took it as Judge Davenport's way of deferring to the state's coronavirus rules while still expressing his strong belief that she ought to be behind bars.

"Third," Judge Davenport said, "given the narcotics charges in this case, total abstinence from alcohol and any other intoxicating substances, apart from any medications she may be prescribed. Fourth, of course, no contact or communication with any witness or potential witness in this case, or with the victim's family. Fifth, no use of her computer or phone, except strictly for the purposes of her business or to communicate with her medical or legal team, her family, or any friends she may have who have no connection to the victim or her family, nor to the events of May 31, 2019. And to be clear, because I am basing this decision primarily on the state supreme court's emergency order regarding the pandemic, if that order is changed or rescinded, at that time I will consider revoking this order and remanding Ms. Baker to the custody of the county jail. Of course, any violation of the conditions I've just set out would result in her immediate arrest and incarceration until trial."

He looked up, adjusted his glasses, and asked, "Mr. Munroe, are these conditions acceptable?"

Simone gave a little nod.

"Yes, Your Honor," I said. "Uh, and what is the bond you're setting?"

"One million dollars."

"Your Honor, I'll confer with my client. Thank you."

Ruiz mumbled, "Thank you, Your Honor."

"Okay. I believe that concludes this proceeding."

After that, I had Noah leave my office so I could call Simone to walk her through what was required. She didn't have a million dollars lying around, so I helped her find a bail bondsman and broke the news that she was going to have to pay at least $100,000 in cash and put her house up as collateral. Then Ruiz and I talked about logistics: when she was going to be ready for release from the nursing facility, and who he was going to send up there to fit her ankle monitor.

When all that was done, I had to ask him about the witness statement he'd sent over.

"So, I got that discovery last night. Thanks."

"No problem."

"The thing is... Don't take this the wrong way, but as a lawyer, and as a human being, do you believe it? I mean, the self-interested statement of the guy who was suspect number one until Simone got pulled over with the syringe?"

He was quiet for a second. "Well, you know, Leland, we didn't offer him a deal, just so that's clear."

He meant the kid wasn't offering testimony in exchange for having some charge or other against him thrown out. "Okay," I said, "but he's the boyfriend. You and I both know who's usually to blame if a young woman gets killed. And it's not like he has an alibi—he was right there."

He heaved a sigh and said, "I'll grant you this is no slam dunk. But I have to at least consider what an alleged eyewitness says. Whether to believe him isn't my call, it's the jury's."

I could tell there was something else he wanted to say, but he wasn't going to. I said it for him: "Is this another Ludlow thing?"

"Well, you know where the buck stops."

Ruiz was a deputy solicitor. The buck stopped with his boss.

By the time we hung up, it was nearly lunchtime. I called Terri to see if we could get together. I needed to know what she'd found on the boyfriend. And also what ideas she might have about why Simone wasn't being completely honest with me—or, more importantly, what she might be hiding.

———

We met at the beach with our respective dogs. It was pretty deserted for a springtime afternoon. The stay-at-home order was still in place, but walking dogs was among the exceptions, and working on the beach was preferable to an office anyway. The hot dog stand was open again after a brief shutdown, with only one person working inside and neon-orange stakes stuck in the sand at six-foot intervals to show where patrons should line up. I got enough food for all of us, dogs included, and we sat on two adjacent benches to watch them chase each other along the waterline.

"So I tracked him down," Terri said, "in Florida. Gainesville. And while I was gathering information on what all he was up to down there, he came back to Charleston."

"Any idea why?"

She shook her head. "He got busted for weed in Florida and skipped town before his hearing, but I'm still figuring out why he came back here. It doesn't seem like what you'd do if you were guilty of murder."

"I've seen cases where that happened. Seemed almost like a compulsion. The killer had to return to the scene of the crime."

She shuddered and said, "I sure hope Dupree and Porter, or whatever his real name is, don't feel that way. You ever get around to doing that security system upgrade?"

She was talking about the two ringleaders from our murder case the previous year. Their local lackeys were all in prison, thanks to us and my friend Cardozo, but the two of them were still on the run.

"Yeah, I did," I said. "Called the guys you recommended and got alarms on every window and door. I set them like clockwork, right before I brush my teeth. And then there's my guard dog."

She laughed. I bit off the end of my hot dog and held it down for Squatter. "Maybe this boyfriend came back to the scene of his crime and then gave this supposed witness statement to make sure somebody other than him goes down for it. He have any history of violence?"

"There was a domestic with a previous girlfriend. No severe injuries, but she filed for an order of protection. She didn't show for the hearing, so he got off. She's fine now, apparently," she added, anticipating my question. "He got together with Veronica pretty soon after that."

"Any DV history with her?"

"Not that I could find."

"That's a good thing," I said, looking out at the waves. "If I heard about some punk abusing a girl who's in a goddamn wheelchair, I'd probably kill him myself."

She laughed. Buster ran up with a wet branch he'd found stuck in the sand, and she took it from him, stood up, and hurled it into the water. "I followed his last girlfriend on Instagram," she said. "Commented on a few of her posts."

"What, as yourself?"

"My God, of course not. I create at least one new profile for every case." She sat back down. "This time I'm a twenty-year-old White girl called Kayleigh."

"Oh, yeah." I chuckled. "Forgot you could do that. There's at least two ethics rules I know of that say lawyers can't use fake profiles to investigate folks."

She smiled. "And that's why you need me."

"Among many other reasons."

It occurred to me that I wasn't 100 percent sure what the ethics rules were on lawyers having PIs use fake profiles. I made a mental note to check.

Buster was still running after waves, but Squatter was walking back up the beach toward me. I could tell he was out of energy.

"I want to talk to the girlfriend," she said, finishing the last bite of her hot dog, "but in the meantime, it might be a good idea to drop by the

Broke Spoke. That caterer's been spending time there—I saw his silver Audi in the lot."

With faint sarcasm, I said, "There's no way that counts as working from home." Squatter flopped down beside me in the sand. I gave him a dog biscuit.

"I think construction's still allowed," she said, "if the workers are distanced enough. Right before lunch he was there with a couple of guys in dust masks, carrying in drywall."

"Today? Why don't we head over right now?"

"I suggest you go talk to him alone. Some folks know what we did on Jackson's case. If we show up together, it won't look like a social call."

I nodded. "Makes sense. I'd like to know what he remembers—and who else he had working that party."

"I've already got the names of three of his staff." She sucked the last of her soda up through the straw. "One of the girls who was there tagged the cutest catering guy in a couple of her Instagram posts, and through him I found the other two."

I laughed. "I'm guessing Kayleigh must be pretty cute herself."

"Oh, she's about the cutest stock photo I could find, and then I put some even cuter filters on her. You *know* honey attracts more flies than vinegar."

I thought for a second, then looked around to confirm the beach was still as deserted behind us as it was in front. "I wonder," I said quietly, "what honey I could come up with to get Simone to be straight with me."

"Oh, is she not?" She put her fingers in her mouth and whistled for Buster.

I shook my head. "I mean, nothing I can confirm." I parsed my words, making sure not to betray confidences. "I sometimes get the impression that she's, like… *managing* me. And I don't think I'm anywhere close to having a good understanding of her relationship with Veronica."

"Well, the cop gossip is that there was a grudge. Your client had been nursing it since high school, I heard, and finally let it rip."

"What about?"

"Depends which cop you ask." Buster ran up, shivering with excitement, and let her put his leash back on. "It was jealousy over a boy, or some mean-girl stuff, or racism, one guy said. Or bullying straight out of Stephen King's *Carrie*. And I'm sure there'll be another story next week."

"I wonder what the hell is true."

"Don't we all." She stood and picked her bag up off the bench. "We also need to figure out which one the prosecution thinks is true, because that's going to be their motive. That whole professional rivalry thing's not convincing enough on its own."

"I wonder if Noah knows anything. He's only a couple of years younger, and it's a small town."

"You ask him," she said. "But you know what, I want to talk to her mother."

"Simone's mother?"

"Yeah," she said. "The nurse."

———

10

TUESDAY, MAY 19, 2020

Simone was being released from the nursing facility Tuesday morning, so I drove up to be there when the sheriff's deputy came to put on her ankle monitor. The roads were still more deserted than usual—that was about the only good side effect of the pandemic —so I left my windows down to catch the salt smell of the ocean as I drove. I'd asked Terri to meet me there, partly to introduce her to Simone and partly so she'd have a chance to meet Simone's mother, who was coming up for moral support.

Terri and I met up in the parking lot, walked in, and went through the usual rigmarole to get past the cop guarding Simone's door. Inside, a woman I took to be her mother was standing by the window. Simone was in the armchair beside her bed, dressed like I would've told her to dress if we ever went to court: nice gray pantsuit, light pink blouse. As we said our hellos and I got introduced to her mom, I noticed Simone even had on a string of pearls. I took her outfit to be an effort to reclaim her dignity from whichever sheriff's deputy was about to show up and treat her like a criminal.

"So, Simone, and Ms. Baker, ma'am, this is Terri Washington, who I've engaged as the private investigator on this case. She was also the investigator on that murder case I had last year, and she's a large part of the reason that young man got off."

Simone's pensive expression relaxed. "Oh, it's nice to meet you, Ms. Washington. Thank you so much for helping me out."

"Happy to," Terri said. "I've actually had my eye on your case since last summer. The charges against you never sat right with me, and I'm glad to have a chance to do something about it."

Simone, I could tell, was instantly won over. Her mother was not. She was dressed like a church lady on a day off—tasteful skirt suit, but no hat—and along with her regal bearing, she had a look of skeptical reserve. I got the impression she'd seen about every kind of misbehavior and wrongness that there was, had scolded those responsible and righted their sinking ships about four hundred thousand times, and had long ago lost any belief that things would ever improve.

"So, Ms. Baker," I said, "I understand you're a nurse?"

"Yes, I am," she said. "Twenty-three years now."

Simone mentioned the nursing home outside Basking Rock where her mother worked.

Terri said, "That's a real good thing, having a nurse in the family, when you've got health problems. Ma'am, I'm sure you've done a lot to make sure your daughter gets the care she needs."

"I do what I can."

A knock came at the door, and the sheriff's deputy let himself in. I was not pleased to see it was a guy I'd known in high school as a casually racist good old boy. The mustache was new, and he was heavier, but his name was on his badge and I remembered his red hair. Time had not improved his arrogant demeanor.

"Okay," he said, looking a little annoyed as he glanced from Terri to Simone to her mom. "Which one of you's the murder defendant?"

"Afternoon, officer," I said. "I'm Leland Munroe, Ms. Baker's attorney. These three ladies are Ms. Washington; Ms. Simone Baker, my client; and her mother, who's also Ms. Baker."

"Uh-huh. Well, I'm up from the Basking County Sheriff's Department, and I got an ankle monitor your client has got to wear 24-7, pending trial." He held up a blue plastic case. "Now, I did see her name on the door and I know law enforcement is outside, but since we got three different African American females in here, I'm going to need to see some ID from her, and then I got to explain how to keep it charged and so forth."

"Okay, well, let's get that taken care of double-quick." I stepped closer to Simone and stood more or less between the deputy and everybody else, hoping—probably pointlessly—that I could shield them from his obnoxiousness.

While Terri got to talking with Simone's mom and Simone reached for her purse, the deputy set the case on the bedside table and snapped it open to reveal what looked like a big black plastic wristwatch. The strap was about three inches wide, and the box with the GPS in it was the size of a pack of cigarettes.

He looked at her ID and nodded. "Okay, now put your foot up where I can reach it."

"Let me get a chair," I said, and brought one over for her to rest her foot on. As he put the monitor in position to check the length of the strap, she looked away in disgust. I wished they'd at least sent a female deputy, since there was no way to do this without touching her bare leg. Although, as I thought about it, I wasn't sure our sheriff's office even had any female deputies.

He removed the monitor to cut the strap down to the right length. She was too tiny for any of the standard sizes.

He set it back on her leg and announced, "Yessiree, that's just what you need."

She looked away again while he attached it. I did not know how this young woman was able to have so much dignity at her age at all, much less in such a demeaning situation. His rudeness was irritating, but it was just a proxy. This whole case, and what it was doing to her life, offended me to my core.

The deputy went into his spiel about how the ankle monitor worked and what Simone could and could not do. Shock registered on her face as he explained that she'd have to sleep in it, shower in it, and essentially plug herself into the wall for an hour or so daily to keep it charged.

Behind us, I heard her mom clear her throat. "Excuse me," she said. "Excuse me."

She was looking at the deputy. I noticed she wasn't doing him the courtesy of calling him officer or sir, and I couldn't blame her.

When he looked her way, she said, "What is the procedure if she needs some sort of a medical scan? I'm referring to an MRI or a CT scan, that kind of thing."

"For that, she'll need advance permission. It ain't compatible, if that's what you mean, but she cannot take this off herself. And from what I've seen, she don't even want to try." He shook his head, but he had a little smile on his face. I got the sense he enjoyed witnessing the consequences—the cops swooping in, the humiliation—when people did try to take these things off.

After he'd relieved us of his presence, Terri and I helped carry Simone's things to her van. We waved as she and her mother drove off.

As I walked Terri to her car, I asked, "You get anything good?"

"From her mom, you mean? No, this was just step one. Make her acquaintance, help her get familiar with me." She got behind the wheel, leaving the door open so the heat could escape, and said, "She's the kind of person where it's going to take a while."

"Yeah, I don't know." I shook my head. "Getting information out of someone like her—I think it'd take about as long as trying to pick the locks on Fort Knox with a bobby pin."

She put her seat belt on, stuck her key in the ignition, and smiled up at me. "I got a lot more tools at my disposal than bobby pins."

———

As I drove back toward Basking Rock, I decided to head past the Broke Spoke to see if the Audi that Terri had mentioned was there. I wanted to talk to the catering guy; I'd left him a voicemail a few days earlier.

Coming off the exit toward the rest stop that the Broke Spoke sat behind, I spied a lone traveler filling up at one of the pumps. The restaurant was still closed due to coronavirus, but I could see through the windows the remodeling that had been done. The same was not true of the strip club behind it; that run-down building had just a couple of tiny windows, and the blinds, as always, were down. A silver Audi was parked in the restaurant's lot, a few spaces away from a white van. I pulled in, got out, and took a little walk around.

A minute later the door banged open, and Luke Delacourt came out. I recognized him from a news article Terri had sent me about his last restaurant up in Charleston: tanned, slim, brown hair on the longish and fluffy side.

"Afternoon," he said, as pleasantly as the maître d' I knew he'd once been. "Anything I can help you with?"

"Afternoon. Luke Delacourt?" He nodded, and I stepped forward to shake his hand. "Leland Munroe. I left you a voicemail, but I can see you've got a lot on your plate. Were you in charge of the renovation here?" I gestured to the restaurant.

"Yeah, that's been my main project." He smiled and shook his head regretfully. "We're a little behind on the launch date. As you can imagine, I did not foresee the coronavirus in my business plan."

"Well, it looks damn good. I don't know what kind of magic your architect worked, but the thing is, it looks about twenty times better than it did before, but it still doesn't look too expensive. You know what I mean? It's not going to scare anyone away."

"Well, thank you," he said. "Yeah, they got restaurant design down to a science now."

"Seems that way." I reached in my chest pocket for a business card. "So, listen," I said, handing it to him. "You know that party you catered last May, where the next day that poor girl ended up dead?"

He shuddered. "Oh, yeah. My goodness, that's not something you forget. I remember hearing they arrested someone?" He looked at me like he couldn't quite believe it.

"Yeah, they did. My client, unfortunately."

He shook his head and looked back at the restaurant. "As I recall, at the time I thought it was just an overdose. That's what people were saying."

"And did that make sense to you? In terms of what you'd seen there?"

"Well, you know. Rich kids, the young and the beautiful, a party… The fact is, it happens."

"It sure does. Did you happen to see anything like that? I mean, kids getting high?" He had a look on his face like he wanted me to think he just could not recall, so I added, "I know, in your profession, you got to be discreet. Hell, even in restaurants you probably see affairs happening, fights, who knows what else. And as a caterer, going into people's homes? Watching people get drunk? I cannot imagine."

He chuckled. "I'll grant you, I don't always see people at their best. But we all have things we'd like to be forgiven for."

"Yep." I left a bit of silence for him to elaborate. When he didn't, I said, "If you prefer to see people at their best, it's a damn good thing you decided not to keep running this as a strip club."

He gave me a sort of man-to-man smile. "Well, it *is* still going to be a bar. With a dance floor. Just not *that* kind of dancing."

I heard the door start to open again, but then it stopped. A guy in a dust mask leaned out, and Delacourt told him to hang on a minute.

"Oh, I don't want to get in your way," I said. "I'll let you get back to work. But would you mind if I gave you a call? Or dropped by again sometime?"

"Not at all."

"Great. And tell you what, if you could get me a list of who you had working the party, I've just got to do my due diligence on that." Terri had already tracked three of them down, but I wanted to cover all the bases. "My number's on the card, of course, if you or they want to reach out."

"Sure enough." He looked at my card and then tucked it into his pocket.

As I was pulling out of the parking lot, I paused to let a car go by and glanced in the rearview mirror. Delacourt was holding the door open for two guys, both in dust masks, carrying a rolled-up carpet. They flung it into the van.

I shook my head at the thought of what the hell might be on a strip club's worn-out old carpet. I'd need a hazmat suit, not just a dust mask, before I'd carry that thing around.

———

11

SATURDAY, MAY 23, 2020

I'd just gotten off the phone with Simone, advising her on another video she was planning to post, when Noah knocked on the open door of my home office.

"Dad, I found something. About Simone and the girl who died. Thought you might want to see it."

"Yeah?"

"Yeah. Just a sec, I'll get my laptop." He padded off down the hall to his room. I still noticed his limp, probably always would, but it was good to see he was moving a lot more easily than he had been even six months ago.

I was going through what I'd gotten from Girardeau and Ruiz, making piles: a stack of documents that related to Veronica's death, a stack about her relationship with Simone, a stack about the party and its guests. Arranging and rearranging all this paper into different categories was my way of figuring out what elements of the prosecution's case or our defense were weak, and which puzzle pieces I still needed to fill in.

Noah came back and sat down at the folding table that served as my overflow desk.

"So, maybe this is weird," he said, "but I've gone through both their social media, just trying to figure out… I don't know, who they were? In case that helped figure out what happened, you know?"

"Yeah. I've done the same thing. More than once."

"And there was this whole feud, supposedly, right?"

"Right." Simone had told me their management company had all but manufactured it, for publicity reasons, but I couldn't tell Noah that. Everything a client told me was confidential.

"And there's those posts flying back and forth arguing about how Veronica copied those SpokeTruth things Simone was selling?"

I nodded. Simone had designed a line of decorative tubes you could attach to the spokes of a wheelchair that looked jazzy even when you weren't moving. When the wheels turned fast enough, they threw off some kind of hologram thing that spelled out an empowering message, or in a couple of models a whimsical picture: little iridescent birds flying around your wheels, stuff like that.

"And she copied her themes of the month and whatever else. So Simone went off on her about plagiarism and cultural appropriation, and—"

"Do you buy that? As a motive for murder?" I didn't, but then I didn't exactly have my finger on the pulse of American youth. Things that would've been a huge insult when I was a kid didn't matter to his generation, and vice versa.

"I mean, it's not like it only happened one time," he said. "It's not like it was an accident. And it seemed like Simone kept losing the argument, somehow. So losing, like, millions of subscribers."

"Millions? Really?" I wondered how much money that meant.

"Oh yeah. I saw the stats." He looked at me like it was weird that this was something he had to explain. "But that's just background, okay? Because what I found is, like, a lot more about their fights. They had this whole secret chat thing going on Explode—"

"What's that, one of those disappearing-messages things?"

"Yeah. Anything you post there disappears sixty seconds after it's read, and you can't screenshot it. I guess that's where they had their real fights." He tapped at his keyboard and brought up a pixelated photo of what looked like two chat bubbles. The first one, from BlkGrrlTruth—Simone, I assumed?—said, *Ur a user, manipulator, thief. Nothing's changed. This is how you say thx?!*

The response, from VLoGlo, was, *Chip on your shoulder much, bitch?*

"Huh," I said. "If they disappear, how'd you get this?"

"Some new account is posting them. I don't know who it is. And what these look like to me is photos someone took of her phone. Somebody was there snapping photos as the messages went back and forth."

"Could you expand that a little?" I peered at it. "Okay, so this must be Veronica's phone we're looking at?" The numbers and whatnot at the top of the screen looked like mine. I had an Android. Simone had the latest iPhone.

He zoomed out enough to show the phone case and a fingertip holding it. The nail was long and not just painted, but intricately decorated; airbrushed, maybe.

"I thought maybe that nail job would be a way to identify her," Noah said. "I assume it's Veronica's finger, but with that we could confirm it."

"Uh-huh. Good thinking."

"I don't know if the police have these yet, but it seemed like you'd want to see them."

I nodded. He flipped through several more photos. BlkGrrlTruth said, *I made u. I brought u into this world, I can take u out.* That did not look great.

Noah's words replayed in my head. I looked at him. "I do need these. But how'd you know I hadn't seen them yet?"

I saw a flash of guilt on his face before he turned away.

"Noah, did you come in here, into my private office, and look through my case files?"

He stared at the floor for a long moment before saying, "I just wanted to help. I wanted to do something real."

"Noah, I *understand* that. But Goddammit, almost none of this is public yet, okay? This is not stuff that anyone outside the case is supposed to know!"

"Shit. I'm sorry. I didn't think of that. You're not going to get in trouble, are you?"

"I… You know what, dammit, I don't even know how I'm supposed to handle this. They didn't write the ethics rules for lawyers who worked from home."

"I won't tell anyone," he said. "I won't talk about the case at all. If anyone asks me about it, I'll just… I'll shrug and say I don't pay much attention to my dad's work, that it's boring to me. That way I won't get in a conversation and accidentally say something I wasn't supposed to know."

I gave him a little nod, since that was a good idea. "You got some sense," I said. "That'll serve you well if you do become a PI. Acting bored works a heck of a lot better than clamming up if you're trying to make someone think you don't know about something."

"Not enough sense to know not to look in legal files in the first place, though." He shook his head. I could tell he felt like a heel.

"Well, I didn't have the sense to think about keeping them safe here. Roy's office has locking file drawers. We don't. That's going to have to change if I keep working from home."

"I could look for those," he said. "File cabinets, I mean. Like, on Craigslist."

"That'd be really helpful."

"And I could go pick them up in the crappy car."

"Sure. Uh, you sound way more excited than you'd normally be about shopping for office furniture."

He exhaled sharply and tossed himself back in the chair. Something was bothering him. Shaking his head, he said, "I just, I sit here on my laptop watching some professor drone on about how the police department is organized, and... I don't know, I'm sick of sitting around the house. I want to *do* something."

On the one hand, I felt for him. On the other, having abundant free time on someone else's dime—mine, in his case—was something I was pretty sure I wouldn't complain about.

I noticed he was wearing a gray shirt with what looked like multicolored zombies sitting on top of the word FLEABAG.

"What's that," I said, "one of your bands?"

"Oh, yeah. British guy. Real cool stuff." He held his arm out so I could read the word YUNGBLUD written down the sleeve. He cracked a smile and added, "You wouldn't like him—he doesn't sound anything like Tom Petty."

I laughed. It was good to see him shift back to a joking mood. "He's sure got a different aesthetic," I said, looking at the zombies. "Man, you are *going* places in that shirt. You know what they say: dress for the job you want."

He gave a laugh, then leaned his head back against the chair. "You know what," he said, talking to the ceiling with his eyes closed, "I'm not sure I *want* to go places, whatever that means. Seems like a lot of the places there are to go mostly suck."

I thought about how to answer that. "You mean as in, the things there are to do in the world? The things adults do?"

"Yeah..." He screwed up his face like it was hard to explain. "I don't know, like, how is Ruiz getting paid to try to put Simone in jail?" He looked at me. "And... that used to be your job. If you were on the other side of this case, would you believe—I mean, without even thinking about what she's like or what she's got to live for, would you really believe that little-bitty girl, who's even freaking *handicapped*, or kind of, somehow snuck in and pulled some ninja shit and, like, in the middle of the night managed to inject a fatal dose of heroin into someone else's vein? *Really?*"

So he had read a whole lot of what was in my files. Possibly everything.

"I wish you could be on her jury," I said, trying to lighten the mood.

———

Around sunset, Ruiz called me with an update on discovery, namely the video of the police interview with Veronica's boyfriend, Austin McKrall.

"I had it put on a DVD," he said, "since obviously the file's way too big to email. And we outsource that, but with the shutdowns and then apparently a few folks out with COVID, everything's backlogged, so it's taking even longer than usual."

"You guys don't use Dropbox or anything like that?"

"No. Ludlow's firmly stuck in the stone age."

"Understood. So, for the DVD, they give you an ETA?"

"They gave me one that already went past, earlier this week. Whenever it does come in, I can bring it by or drop it at the post office to get it overnighted to you."

"Thanks. We'll figure that out when it comes. But by the way, since when do you do work calls on a Saturday? And at"—I looked at my phone—"quarter past eight at night? I mean, I'm glad to hear from you, but I'm just wondering."

"Is it that late? Oh, hell, I don't even know what day it is anymore. All the trials and half the hearings got canceled, the kids are home all day, Marisol's losing her mind trying to homeschool them or whatever, and I'm working in the garage. I'm literally looking at a can of motor oil right now. It's on the windowsill. I do not have the brain cells left to pay attention to the clock or the calendar."

I laughed. "You and me both."

I heard him take a gulp of something. "I probably shouldn't be having another cup of coffee if it's this late. Oh well."

"I had one maybe an hour ago."

"I guess we're on the insomnia express."

"Yeah." After a second, I said, "Listen, can I ask you something?" I was thinking about what Noah had said. How Simone's case looked to him.

"Sure."

"So… I'll see the video when it comes, but I've obviously already read the boyfriend's written statement, and I just have to ask: Do you *believe* that?"

He paused. "Believe what?"

"That Simone did this. For his story to make sense, you've got to believe she knocked them both out with Valium and then—what—snuck into their room in the middle of the night and injected his girl-friend with a fatal dose of heroin? I mean, to me, that's not even something you'd see on *CSI* or wherever because it's so implausible. From any witness, but especially from the former number one suspect!"

"I actually did see a murder committed that way on… Oh, I don't know what show it was. It might've been a movie. It doesn't matter." I heard him take another gulp of his coffee.

I sighed. "You know what, go ahead and forget I asked. I know Ludlow'd rip you a new one for even listening to defense counsel, much less responding."

"Yeah, but this is my personal cell phone, and as I'm pretty sure you know, Ludlow has nearly succeeded in crushing the last shreds of integrity and optimism out of the last few deputy solicitors who had any to start with. So if he did fire me, it'd come as a relief. For about five minutes, anyway, until I remembered I've got four kids to feed."

"Leadership skills are not his forte, are they?"

"You don't want to know what I think is his forte. But look, I hear you on the boyfriend's story. It's weird. And we both know how often this kind of death turns out to be the boyfriend or the husband. But I can tell you this: I've watched that video a few times now, and one thing I think anyone watching it would agree is, he absolutely did love that girl. And I don't mean, like, in a crazy way or a psycho ex way. I mean, he just, transparently, really did care about her."

"Huh," I said.

What I meant, though I wasn't about to say it to the prosecutor, was, "Shit."

If the boyfriend came across that way on the stand, it would complicate my ability to create reasonable doubt by convincing the jury that the cops should've gone after him instead.

It could do more than complicate it. I wouldn't know until I'd seen the video, but my alternate theory of Veronica's death—my best shot at keeping Simone out of prison—might not fly at all.

———

12

SATURDAY, MAY 30, 2020

S imone's kitchen, where Terri and I were sitting with her, looked like something off a cooking show: sleek white cabinets with crystal knobs, stainless-steel appliances, and yellow walls brightened further by the morning sun. We were perched on barstools at the marble-topped island, which had nothing on it but our laptops, the glasses of sweet tea she'd served us, and, in the middle, a green glass bowl full of oranges and bananas so perfect I wondered if they were real. I made a mental note that even if I did somehow find a way to get Simone out from under the charges she was facing, I should never invite her to my house. My countertop was Formica and buried in clutter: junk mail, fast-food wrappers, Squatter's leash, and probably a couple of chew toys. His, not mine.

Simone pointed at the photo on Terri's laptop screen. Veronica, in her wheelchair, was talking to someone. Behind her, a few people sat on a couch. "On the couch, there, that's her boyfriend. And that's her cousin Sofia next to him."

I typed that down in my notes.

We were looking through all the photos we'd collected of the party where Veronica had died. We had over a hundred from various social media accounts, and several hundred more I'd gotten after tracking down the photographers that Apex had hired for the event. Both photographers claimed not to have been contacted by the police, and nothing in Girardeau's boxes of discovery said otherwise. I was appalled by how many stones our small-town police force had left unturned.

The crime scene photos Ruiz had provided, for instance, didn't show that the guest bedroom where Veronica had slept was about six feet up the hall from the side door. The whole house was on one level; it was something between a ranch and an updated shotgun shack, fully remodeled by Simone to be accessible and beautiful.

She obviously didn't mean "accessible" in the sense of easy to break into, but that was what I was thinking about. Simone's yard had what looked like a brand-new wrought-iron fence around it, but it was only about four feet tall. If the driveway gate was shut, climbing the fence might slow a man down, but it wouldn't stop him. And despite the guest room's location, the police hadn't dusted for prints on the exterior door or any nearby windows. In a way, that was good for our case —if I could come up with a plausible alternate story of how Veronica died, the failure to do such basic investigative steps gave me a good shot at convincing the jury there was reasonable doubt. But that failure was also part of the reason Simone was facing murder charges at all. It made me angry that anybody could face prison time just because cops got lazy.

"I'm curious." Terri clicked back and forth through the photos of Austin and Sofia sitting on the couch. "Did your mother ever meet any of these folks?"

"Well, she knew Veronica. Oh, and she met her boyfriend that day— she was over helping me get ready, and they got here early. Why?"

"I just wondered what she thought of them. Mothers sometimes have good instincts."

"Oh." Simone laughed. "Well, my mother pretty much doesn't like *anybody*."

Terri chuckled. "No exceptions there?"

"Definitely not. She never liked Veronica, so she certainly wasn't about to like her flaky-ass White boyfriend."

I didn't react—I didn't want Simone to get self-conscious—but I typed that down too. Why, I wondered, didn't her mom like that girl?

I still hadn't figured out what Simone was keeping from me about herself and Veronica. I hadn't confronted her about it because I figured if she got to a point where she trusted me, that information and maybe a lot more would come out on its own. I'd press the issue if I had to, if the courts opened back up and her trial got fast-tracked, but for now we had time; I was just building rapport.

A few photos later, Terri asked, "Do you know whose purse that is?"

Austin had a white purse on his lap. Terri went back a few photos to see the whole sequence: purse wedged between the couch arm and him, purse on his lap, him slipping his hand inside.

"I mean, it looks like Veronica's," Simone said. "I couldn't swear to it, but it does."

In the next photo, Austin had a phone in his hand and was glancing at Veronica as if to make sure she couldn't see him.

"That's definitely her phone," Simone said. "I know the case and the charms."

It was a flashy gold case with a strap that had what looked like a bunch of different earrings dangling from it. I typed a quick description in the notes I was taking. Terri noticed and told me the range of image numbers we were looking at, so I could note that down too.

The next photo showed him handing the phone to the cousin. Then the scene changed; the photographer must've turned to start snapping other parts of the room.

Terri said, "Did she use Venmo or any of those kind of things?"

"Oh, of course," Simone said. "I don't know if she used cash at all. Like, ever."

"More records for me to subpoena," I said, typing that down on my to-do list: *Venmo, PayPal, other payment apps. Austin handed V phone to cousin Sofia.*

Terri stopped at a video and clicked play. In it, Sofia was standing in front of Veronica and they were yelling at each other. Hands waved and fingers were pointed, but the music in the background was too loud to hear what they were saying. We watched it a couple of times but couldn't make it out.

"I don't remember that at all," Simone said. "I wish I did. The party was all over the house. I must've been someplace else."

Terri said, "The time stamp is—oh, it's not even 10 p.m. That's before you and Veronica argued, right?"

"Yeah. There weren't that many people left by the time we got into it."

"Write that down," Terri said, pointing at the file name on the video. "I know a place that might be able to strip the music out so we can hear what's left, if anything."

I did, and she clicked through more photos.

"Oh, I recognize that guy," she said, laughing. "That's the cute caterer. I don't remember his name offhand." The staff were in the background of the picture she was looking at, identifiable by their floppy gold chef's hats and black aprons with a gold lion logo. One of them was picking up a tray of hors d'oeuvres from the kitchen island we were now sitting at.

"Wait," Simone said. "Can you make that bigger?"

Terri obliged.

"Him," Simone said. "The guy at the oven."

Terri recentered the photo and enlarged it again. Another caterer was leaning down as he opened the oven door, lifting his glasses up to his forehead to look inside, and the oven light lit up his face.

"Oh my God!" Simone said.

"You know him?"

"Yeah, it's—I didn't think he wore glasses, but it's that guy, Shawn something. I can't remember his last name. The guy who was stalking Veronica!"

"Shawn Gifford?" Terri asked. "Are you sure?"

"Yes! How'd he get in here?" Simone was practically yelling. "How did I not know he was in my house? We had security at the gate, and we gave them his photo to keep him *out*! Oh my God!"

Terri shook her head slowly. "But they wouldn't be watching the staff, would they? If the caterer's van shows up with guys in uniforms, they might just wave them through."

"Jesus Christ," I said. There was not one mention of Gifford in what I'd gotten from Girardeau and Ruiz. "How did the cops not find that?"

———

Around lunchtime, Terri went home to run down what she could on Shawn Gifford, and I headed to the docks down by the marina. Restaurants were open again, for outdoor dining only, and I knew from Terri's reconnaissance that Sofia Lopez was a waitress at the high-end seafood place overlooking the bay. I'd never eaten there; when I'd first come back to Basking Rock, it was far beyond my budget. It was still more than I would ever spend on a meal, but the fried shrimp lunch I was envisioning was for the investigation, so Simone's retainer could take the hit.

It was well past 1 p.m., and the wooden terrace outside the restaurant had eight or ten tables on it, all with blue-and-white-striped umbrellas. Half of them were empty, a few still littered with dishes that hadn't been cleared. A waitress came out with bread for her customers. I heard gulls mewing and saw one try to land on the wooden railing beside one of the uncleared tables, but the restaurant had installed spikes to keep its kind away. A gust made the umbrellas flap, spooking the bird, and it took off down the beach.

I walked down the pier, stopping now and then to lean against the side, look at the water, and glance back at the restaurant. Eventually I saw Sofia, her long dark hair blowing in the sea breeze, come out with a bottle of wine for a table on the left side of the terrace. There were three open tables on that side, which I figured must be her section, so I moseyed back and sat down at one of them.

She brought me a menu and told me about the pan-seared scallops, the fried oysters, and the calamari. I asked her opinion on the shrimp and grits, which came dressed up with andouille sausage and various other black-tie items that, I guessed, were meant to justify the twenty-two-dollar price tag.

"Oh my goodness," she said. "Now, *that* is my favorite. It's made with local stone-ground grits and a garlic-parsley butter that is just *amazing*."

"You've sold me," I said, handing the menu back to her. "Man, it is great to see this place open again. The shutdown must've been hard on you folks."

"Oh, it was." Her bright smile disappeared. "I mean, I'm used to *seeing* people, you know? That's my *job*; I talk to people all day long! So to go so long with no friendly faces… And not to mention, no money? Yeah, it was hard on all of us."

"You know what, I was just going to have coffee, but we've all got to do our part to get local businesses back on their feet. Do you have any alcohol-free wines?"

"We sure do."

"Is there one you'd recommend with what I've ordered?"

"Um, you know, I am barely old enough to drink, but I do know that with shrimp and with something buttery like that, most folks like a chardonnay."

"Okay, then. One of those, please." I wondered if that was the first time in my life that I'd smiled while ordering a twelve-buck glass of wine.

"Be right out." With a wink, she turned away.

I looked at the bright blue water dotted here and there with white boats, and wondered what angle to come from when I started asking her what I was there to ask. She was a young woman with at least some ambition, judging from her hopes of becoming an influencer herself, and she'd lost her cousin, who was also her friend, barely a year ago.

I knew something about losing someone you loved.

When she came back ten minutes later with my order, I said, truthfully, "That smells incredible." She beamed. I looked out to sea and then back at her. "You know, I don't mean to intrude or anything, but I recognize you, and I know you're coming up on a tough anniversary."

She looked a little startled, and then her mouth moved like she was sad and trying to hide it.

I said, "Tomorrow it'll be a year since you lost your cousin, won't it."

She nodded and then glanced back at the restaurant, checking, I figured to see whether her boss was watching. She reached into the pocket of her apron, looking down at her order book and the menus she carried for desserts and drinks, and asked, "How'd you know?"

"Well, it's a small town," I said, "but also, I'm working on the case."

She looked at me, eyes wide. "I should've driven her home that night," she said. "I should've done a lot of things."

A busboy came to clear a nearby table, and she said, more loudly, "The key lime pie comes with a mango coulis, and it's drizzled with raspberry sauce. It's perfect for a sunny day like this." She handed me a dessert menu.

"It's not your fault," I said quietly, perusing the desserts, even though I hadn't tasted my lunch yet.

After a second, she said, "I think it was."

———

13

MONDAY, JUNE 1, 2020

I picked Terri up and headed to Charleston. We were going to meet with the head of Apex Image Management, not just to talk with him, but hopefully to get more footage of the party. Sofia had clued me in that they might have some. According to her, the company had its own videographer there in addition to the hired photographers, and what she and Veronica were fighting about in the five-second clip I'd seen had been Sofia's shameless efforts to get herself interviewed on camera.

It was muggy out. We drove with the AC on high, listening to music Terri had chosen to try to expand my horizons beyond Southern rock. It was Prince, Tom Petty, and other luminaries playing "While My Guitar Gently Weeps."

"This is good," I said. "And I don't know what you're thinking, but it's not all that different from what I'd normally listen to."

"Baby steps," she said. "I'm not going to drop Parliament-Funkadelic on you right off the bat."

I laughed. "I don't know what that is, but it sounds like a good call."

The country highway was a little more crowded now that the full shut-down was over, but it was still a nice drive, cruising past dense trees on either side.

"So," I said, "how d'you think we ought to approach the whole Gifford thing? I don't want them to get defensive about the fact he got in."

"If we mention it at all, we can blame the catering company. They should've done background checks, and so forth."

"Yeah. And let's definitely not get into whether Apex warned the caterer about Gifford. This isn't a civil case. We don't need to assign fault."

The car filled with a virtuoso guitar solo. "Dang," I said, "who's that? Is that Prince?"

"The one and only." We listened for a minute, and then she said, "So, what'd you make of Sofia?"

"She seemed genuine. Sad, you know, and still feeling guilty because if she hadn't stormed off after fighting with Veronica, none of this would have happened. She said she used to crash on Veronica's couch every time she was up in Charleston, and if she'd known Austin was so drunk, she would've driven her home—she never would've left her to stay the night with 'that bitch.' Which is apparently her nickname for Simone."

Terri nodded. I could tell she was adding that fact to the big pot of information she had on the back burner in her head, waiting for the few more ingredients she needed before whatever she was cooking would be done.

"She wanted to do this whole influencer thing too," I said. "Veronica wouldn't introduce her to her management company, so Sofia, I guess, took things into her own hands. Flirting with the photographers and the video guy, trying to get her foot in the door with whoever could help her."

"She say why Veronica wouldn't hook her up?"

"Well, she said something about not having enough followers yet, but it wasn't too clear. When we get there, I'll ask how they take people on. I don't think Simone had that many followers herself when they signed her up."

"I mean, she had several thousand. Which is a real good start for someone doing it all on her own. I was at her place yesterday, by the way, helping her mom weed the flower beds. That woman really knows her flowers and herbs."

"Huh. You find out anything useful?"

"Little by little. We're coming up on where she'll start talking to me."

"I thought *I* was patient," I said. "I got nothing on you."

"Oh, I grew up tending a vegetable garden. You learn to wait."

"No doubt. Oh, the other thing about Sofia is, she's got an alibi. Which is good—makes it easier to talk with her because she's not worried I'm trying to make her take the fall. She was a little embarrassed to tell me, but she did get around to saying that after fighting with Veronica, she went home with some guy she'd met at the party. Some *skateboarder*."

Terri laughed. "Your tone of voice! You might as well have said 'some homeless guy.' Or 'some convict.' 'Some pimp.' 'Some—'" She was cracking herself up so much she had to stop talking.

I smiled—she had a point—and said, "But I mean, skateboarder! How is that a profession?"

"You're just mad because you had to spend seven years in college and law school to get where you are now."

I chuckled. "Well, it isn't fair, is it? I don't even want to know how much some *skateboarder* can earn."

"If it's the one on the guest list," she said, "which I'm assuming it is, he got about two million in sponsorships last year."

"Goddamn! Since when is there all this money in Basking Rock?"

"Well, he lives in Atlanta."

"Still, though. Since when do millionaires come to parties in Basking Rock?"

"Times have changed."

Prince's solo faded to a close, and after a moment, the sound of New Orleans horns came through the speakers.

"Oh, man," I said. Anything that reminded me of New Orleans always reminded me of Elise. I sighed and shook my head. "They sure have." I wondered how much more the town and the world in general were going to change in my lifetime, and if at some point they would go from just weird, which was where things currently were, to barely recognizable.

"I can turn this off if you don't feel like listening right now."

"No, it's fine," I said. The horns had given way to thumping guitar and a rich female voice. "But this is kind of... country, isn't it? You listen to this?"

"It's Beyoncé," she said.

"Really?"

"It's called 'Daddy Lessons.'"

"Huh." I signaled for our exit. "I could use a few of those."

———

Apex was at the edge of the business district, a few blocks from Girardeau's office. I detoured past his building to see if his car was there—Terri thought commuting in a Lamborghini was so ridiculous she wasn't sure whether to believe me, so I wanted to show her—but to our disappointment, it was not.

We parked outside the address Simone had given me. The building was red brick with carved stone frames around the tall windows, a two-hundred-year-old former convent transformed into twenty-first-century office space from what I'd learned online. Inside, everything but the exposed-brick walls was sleek and either silver, black, or white. As we headed for the reception desk at the far end of the lobby, which was staffed by a young woman with ice-blonde hair who looked straight off the cover of *Vogue*, I whispered to Terri, "Think we should've dressed up a little before we came here?"

"We'd need a lot more than nice clothes," she said. "Plastic surgery, maybe?"

Behind the receptionist, three flat-screens on the wall were cycling through what looked like social media feeds. Photos and videos zoomed past too fast for me to make sense of them: gorgeous young people in some red-rock desert scene, an Asian boy applying makeup to his eyes, gorgeous young people dancing in a club.

She flashed us a big, bored smile—I thought we might also need cosmetic dental work to fit in here—and asked, "May I help you?"

"Yes, please," I said. "I'm Leland Munroe, and this is my associate, Ms. Washington. I called the other day and spoke with Mr. Legare, your CEO. We made an appointment to meet at eleven?"

"Oh," she said. Her smile disappeared. "I'm afraid Mr. Legare wasn't able to make it in today. His secretary told me this morning that she'd canceled all his appointments. He unfortunately learned of a coronavirus exposure on his recent trip to New York, so just as a precaution, he's isolating."

"Oh my goodness. I do hope he's okay."

The smile sprang back onto her face. "Oh, he is. We're all fine here. Everything's fine. It's just as a precaution—"

She stopped in mid-sentence, touched one finger to her ear, and nodded. She was listening to someone. I hadn't noticed before that she was wearing a little silver earpiece.

"Do you know what," she said to me. "Ms. Rutledge is actually able to see you instead! Our talent director! And I cannot believe she said that. She is a very busy woman. Let me just give you one of these." She handed me a plastic card. "You need that to make the elevator work. It's right around the corner there. She's on the second floor."

We followed her directions. The second floor had the same sleek color palette as the first, but I didn't have time to look around. A tall blonde woman who looked to be in her thirties met us as we stepped out of the elevator. We followed her down the hallway, which she took with long strides. With her old family name and sporty but elegant look, I figured she'd probably been a member of a local country club since the day she was born.

In her office, she gestured us to chairs and took a seat behind her desk. The pale gray walls were hung with photos of gorgeous young women and various framed awards.

"I do apologize," she said, "for not being as welcoming as we normally like to be here, but this is not a normal situation, as I'm sure you can understand. We were all just devastated by what happened to Veronica, and then to find it was another one of our own—it's a double blow. It's very hard. And with you being Simone's lawyer and all, I'm honestly not sure what to think."

"I understand," I said. Beside me, Terri was nodding sympathetically. "And I'm sorry to intrude, but I am duty bound to try to figure out what happened here and to help Simone."

"Of course," she said. "And it's— You know, I do understand there's a presumption of innocence, although it's a little hard to keep in mind when someone's been charged with murder. And I cared about both those girls." She shook her head, looking up at the wall behind me like she was imagining how things could've been different.

Then she switched gears and said, "I hate to be impersonal about something so—you know—personal to both those girls and their families, but I also have to consider how all this is affecting our business. So it's complicated, but I do want to understand what it is you're looking for."

"Well, I'd just like to know more about what all happened that night, and when I spoke with Mr. Legare, he indicated there might be some photos and videos here that didn't end up getting used on social media. And I thought coming up here and introducing myself would be a better way of going about things than sending you-all a subpoena or any of that."

She was nodding. "And we do appreciate that," she said, reaching down to pull a document out of a file drawer. "Mr. Legare asked me to have you sign this, just to make sure we can discuss what all we might have."

It was a contract. Skimming it, I saw they wanted me to agree not to use anything they gave me for any purpose other than Simone's defense, and not to release any of it to the media, Veronica's family, or any other third party.

Terri saw me reading and got to chatting with Ms. Rutledge.

I could tell from the contract that they were afraid not only of bad PR but of being sued by Veronica's family. Which I could well understand, since she'd died at an event they'd organized. What they were offering in return for my agreement to keep anything they provided confidential unless I was going to use it as evidence in court was an end run around the hassle and unpredictability of the subpoena process. Rather than wasting weeks fighting in court about what I should or should not be allowed to get from them, I could see what they had now.

If they were honest, anyway. If not, I might end up having to fight them twice over: first to get around this contract, and then to get access to whatever evidence I thought they'd hidden from me.

It was a calculated risk. I took it.

"Here you go," I said, signing on page three. "And could I get a copy of that?"

"Of course." She picked up her phone and said, "Marushka, honey, could you step in here and copy something for me?"

A tall young woman glided in on silver stiletto heels. I wondered if all the young women here looked like models. And where were they finding them? In my mind, people like that lived in New York or LA, not Charleston.

Ms. Rutledge handed her the contract, then stood up and said, "Now, let me show you what we've got."

————

14

MONDAY, JUNE 1, 2020

M s. Rutledge swept us out of her office, down the exposed-brick hallway, and to a white steel door that she opened with a security card. Inside was a photography studio: lights on stands, some with colored filters over them; a camera on a tripod, and several lenses sitting on a table nearby; a green backdrop hanging from the high ceiling. The room was full of light, but you couldn't really see outside; the windowpanes seemed to be made of what I thought of as bathroom glass, to block the view.

To the right of the green backdrop were what looked like props: unusual-looking furniture, a rack of clothes, a few old glass bottles in interesting colors sitting on top of a trunk. Off to the left was a bank of computers.

"That's where we do the editing," she said. "So these are the best ones to look at video on. Help yourselves," she said, pointing at a table that had goblets and a bottle of sparkling water sitting on it.

We went over, and I poured glasses for all three of us. I brought Ms. Rutledge hers and asked, "You folks edit everything before it goes out?"

"Well, not the livestreams, of course." She closed a drawer, locked it, and turned around with some sort of hard drive in her hand. "Those are… I would say managed and planned, for the most part, but the editing just comes down to deciding when to switch from one feed to another. So maybe curated is a better word? Here, I'll sit in the middle, and you two get on either side." She sat at a big iMac screen and plugged the hard drive into it.

I knew my office chairs—I'd bought one online when the shutdown order made everybody start working from home—and the black leather ones we were sitting in cost north of six hundred bucks, or six times what I'd paid for my own piece of junk. I remembered the ad I'd seen before the algorithm figured out I was a cheapskate: these chairs could do just about everything short of a chiropractic adjustment.

"So, after you called last week, Mr. Legare had this put together for you to save us all some time." She opened the drive onscreen; it contained a single folder whose name was the date of the party where Veronica had died. "All of these files are in chronological order," she said, clicking to bring up a long list, "so why don't we just click through? You can tell me when to stop."

She started clicking. Preparations for the party unfolded like a stop-motion movie; it looked like photos had been snapped every few seconds. Outside Simone's house, two gardeners planted full-grown red rosebushes on either side of her walkway. On the veranda behind them—her house had a veranda that ran across the front and down one side—a man cleaned the windows. A wheelbarrow containing another rosebush was pushed past Simone's mother, who pointed like she was directing the man where to go.

A man hosed down the driveway. Lights on tall stands were set up in the yard, and someone attached smaller ones to the underside of the veranda roof, between the hanging plants someone else was putting up. The catering van arrived, but windshield reflections kept us from seeing who was inside. In a later photo, we glimpsed it disappearing around the side of the house.

A red Honda appeared. Another click showed Austin McKrall pulling a folded wheelchair out of the hatchback and then Veronica wheeling herself up the walkway. In the background of another shot, we saw them going in the front door while someone pushed an equipment cart up the ramp. Simone's front steps must've originally been about seven feet wide, but she'd replaced the right half with a long wheelchair ramp.

Terri said, "Would you mind stopping there just a minute?" She peered closer, and I noticed what I thought she was looking at: Simone's mother at the far edge of the photo. As she watched Austin and Veronica go in, she looked... I wasn't quite sure what to call her expression, but to say the least, she did not look welcoming.

Terri asked, "Can you see what the time stamp is on that?"

Ms. Rutledge told her, and she wrote it down. If I knew Terri, she was hitting two birds with one stone: noting what time Veronica had arrived, which was information we wanted, and distracting our hostess from the fact that she'd also wanted to get a better look at Simone's mom.

The next batch showed Simone and Veronica in white robes, getting their makeup and hair done. They sat about six feet apart, didn't look at each other once, and only talked to their makeup artists, not each other; they might as well have been two strangers on a bus.

Then we got to a video. Someone asked Simone to stand, and when she did, her chair was pushed over next to Veronica's. As she sat back down, a woman offscreen said, "Okay, ladies, let's see some excitement!"

On cue, they gave the camera dazzling smiles and leaned close to each other. "This is my girl Veronica," Simone said, putting her arm around her. "Check out how gorgeous she looks! Look at the neon eye and the neutral lip! This girl is *on trend*, like always! And I am just so happy to welcome her, and all y'all, to my *home*!"

Veronica said, "Oh my God, *thank* you! And you too! People, if you click the link below, not only can you get this look yourself, but you can give back too. You know we *always* look for the products that are as good for the world as they are for your skin. And I just wish every one of you could be here with us! Tonight is going to be *lit*!"

They kept smiling until someone said, "And cut." Then it was back to the strangers-on-a-bus vibe, except for a look I didn't quite catch on Veronica's face.

I said, "Could you rewind five or ten seconds?"

She did. Veronica's expression, as she watched Simone walk away, was about one-third longing and two-thirds guilt. I wondered why. It was strange to think that the reason I couldn't ask was because not long after filming this video, she was dead. We were watching the last few hours of her life.

In the next video, Simone was leaning toward a mirror, dabbing at one of her eyebrows with a fingertip as she hissed to someone offscreen, "Why is she selling the makeup off *her* Insta? I thought we talked about that! She's taking money that should be mine, and I am *sick* of it! What would that girl be without me? I freaking *made* her! And this is my party! It's my damn house!"

She was still ranting when another voice told the photographer to stop filming.

———

We headed back to my car with copies of the hard drive and the contract in my briefcase. We'd been shown a few more videos in the same vein, but shot from a lower angle, like the guy had been filming secretly with the camera at his hip. When I'd asked about that, Ms. Rutledge said, "Well, we did get rid of him, of course—he was *not* hired to shoot footage that made any of our girls look bad! But there's no way to be sure he gave us back every copy of what he'd shot."

The sun was straight overhead. The palm trees lining the street cast a feathery, barely there shade. Inside my Malibu, it was hot as hell.

I put the AC on blast and told Terri, "If there's a lawyer who can make a jury still like Simone after seeing that stuff—or believe her when she says she didn't have a grudge against that girl—he's a better attorney than I'll ever be."

"Yeah, it's not good."

I checked my phone before pulling out. "Huh. Got a couple voice-mails from Girardeau while we were in there."

"Maybe he wants to show you his Lambo again."

I chuckled and hit play.

"Hey, Leland," his first message said. I heard wind noise in the background. "I found a thumb drive you might want. I'm heading to Savannah today, so I figured maybe I could drop it off to you on the way down or the way back. I'll be heading by Basking Rock in about half an hour and— Hey!"

The second message said, "Sorry, some asshole pulled in front of me and hit his brakes. Man who drives like that, I don't know how he's still alive. Anyway, I can drop it off at your office, or your home office, if that's what you're doing now. If lunchtime doesn't work, I'll be back through around six. Give me a buzz."

He'd left the messages over an hour before. I dropped the phone in the cup holder, pulled out into traffic, and said, "I do *not* want Girardeau getting a look at my house."

My rent, I figured, was probably less than what he spent on gas for his Lambo. And as for meeting up at Roy's office, even if it were on par with Girardeau's slick setup, which it wasn't, my name was conspicuously absent from the signage.

Terri said, "Wonder if he'd want to grab a bite at the truck stop. They're open again."

"Oh, maybe. Outside only, though, right?"

"Yeah, but they added that terrace out back. So it's not like you're staring at the gas pumps."

"Why do I get the impression you want to meet him?"

"Because I do." She smiled. "I've got a few questions, and I want to see his face when he answers."

———

A few minutes after six, we pulled into the parking lot between the Broke Spoke and the truck stop. The former strip club was still closed for renovations and still unchanged on the outside: pea green, rundown.

Terri said, "That work sure is taking a while."

"I guess they had to focus on one building or the other." I parked in a spot beside the truck stop. "And they chose this one. Maybe it's the bigger moneymaker—or it needed less work."

We went through the main room, which now had a bar along one wall to the terrace out back. It had been resurfaced with flat stone pavers and naturally fenced with saw palmetto and fan palms for a more gracious look than the former view of the parking lot would have provided. Around half the tables were occupied.

While we were looking at menus, Luke Delacourt came out with a big smile to greet us. "Good to see you again," he said. "I missed you at the grand opening."

"Well, you know. I figured you'd be full. Glad to see things are still busy on the day-to-day."

"Oh my God," he said, "I tell you, we are too. Look, I wanted to offer you folks a drink on the house. Just tell me what you'd like." He handed us wine and cocktail menus. "This year was about the worst time you could possibly open a new restaurant. Or reopen, but, you know, same thing."

"I can imagine. Thank you kindly." I spotted Girardeau in the doorway behind him and held my hand up so he could see us. He waved back and came over. He was dressed less casually than he had been the first time we'd met. Perfectly creased black pinstripe pants had replaced the jeans, and his shirt had the cut of a normal business shirt—button-down with collar and cuffs—but it was a kaleidoscope of about fourteen different colors, and he wore it untucked.

"Evening, Leland," he said. "Hey, Luke. And with whom do I have the pleasure—?"

Delacourt said hi to him and headed back inside. I hadn't realized they knew each other.

"Oh, this is Ms. Washington," I said. "Terri. She's my PI on the case. We just got back from some fact gathering up in Charleston, and I thought it'd be rude to tell her to go fend for herself, dinner-wise."

We'd been back about four hours and had already gone to our respective houses to shower and change, but he didn't need to know that.

"Of course! Of course. Well, pleasure to meet you, Ms. Washington."
He pulled his chair out, sat down, and crossed his legs so one knee
stuck straight out to the side.

Our waitress came with a drinks menu for Girardeau . She didn't offer
him one on the house.

After we placed our orders, he asked, "So, what took you up to
Charleston?"

Terri smiled, signaling a friendly joke, and said, "I wanted to see your
Lamborghini. Leland made a special trip."

He laughed out loud. "Well, little lady, you just peek through those
palm trees, and it's parked right there. Happy to give you a look."

She leaned back, pushed a couple of palm fronds aside, and looked.
"Oh my," she said. "What a *gorgeous* shade of blue."

"Had to special order it. Took six goddamn weeks to get it in."

I could not feel his pain. To avoid offense, I said, "My goodness."

"I know. But yeah, Charleston. You find something interesting up
there, for your case? Oh, before I forget, here's that drive." He pulled
a thumb drive out of his wallet and pushed it across the table to me.

I said, "We went up to talk with her management company. You
familiar with them?"

"Yeah, matter of fact, they're who referred her to me in the first
place."

"Oh? Just word of mouth, or did you work for them before?"

"Well, you know. They're basically in showbiz. I'm sure you can
imagine the kind of allegations that get thrown around against folks in
that industry." He pressed one nostril closed with his fingertip, letting
me know he meant drug charges.

The waitress returned with our drinks: white wine for Terri, club soda with lime for me. Girardeau took his whiskey on the rocks and said, "Much obliged, sweetheart." She gave him a polite smile and headed back inside.

When the girl was out of earshot, Terri smiled at him and said, "Oh, Mr. Girardeau, I think you're looking at the wrong waitress. It's that one over there who's been giving you the eye."

I stared at her. She ignored me.

"Really?" said Girardeau. She was pointing discreetly, and he looked over to a beautiful waitress serving a table across the terrace. The girl wasn't paying attention to him at all.

Terri said, "Aw, I think you made her shy."

"My goodness," he drawled, smiling. "My *goodness*." He shook his head like he didn't know himself how he managed to draw so much female attention.

Terri sipped her wine and asked, "So tell me, what took you to Savannah?"

"Oh, I had to meet with someone for a client. Going over some documents and preparing him to testify. Nothing nearly so fine as hanging out here with you-all."

"Well, *that* is client service," Terri said. "That's a long drive for one day."

I realized, a little late, that she was deploying skills I did not have in order to get him to talk.

"What is it," she asked, "another murder case?"

"I wish," he said. "That's always more exciting. Speaking of which, here's to your case." He raised his glass. "Wishing you the best on that."

We all toasted.

"I'll let Simone know you send your good wishes," I said. "I'm sure she'll appreciate it."

Terri nodded and said, "Mm-hmm."

"Yeah, please do. And I know you do *not* have an easy row to hoe." He shook his head. "Find out anything worthwhile up in Charleston?"

"Well, you know," I said, scanning the tables behind him to remind him we weren't alone. "Elevator rule."

He nodded.

"Oh, by the way," Terri said, as if the thought had just occurred to her, "I didn't realize you knew Mr. Delacourt. But I suppose up in Charleston, a man in your position must go out to fine restaurants all the time."

"I sure do," he said. He took another swig of his whiskey, looking at her over the glass. When he set it down, he said, "And in my line of work, you get to know folks. A lot more folks than most people might expect."

She smiled a bigger, prettier smile than I'd ever seen on her. "My goodness," she said. "You must have some *incredible* stories."

"Oh, I do."

"I'd love to hear some." She looked like she was hanging on his every word.

"I got some war stories, for sure," he said. "But—Leland, did you say she's a PI?"

I nodded.

"So you've seen some stuff," he told her.

"Well, it's mostly just run-of-the-mill. Folks trying to catch their spouse in an affair, or insurance trying to show someone's faking an injury. I *live* for cases like this, or the kind of thing you do."

Girardeau caught sight of something inside the restaurant, narrowed his eyes, and stopped talking.

I looked over. Delacourt turned—he'd been standing at a window—and walked away.

Girardeau seemed frozen, thinking about something. Then he tossed back the rest of his whiskey, looked at his watch, and said, "I hate to have to run, but that's life, ain't it." He smiled, peeled a twenty out of his wallet, and tossed it on the table. "Give me a call if you're up in Charleston again."

———

15

FRIDAY, JUNE 5, 2020

R uiz had finally dropped off the DVD I was waiting for—the police interview with Austin McKrall, which would be my first sight of him other than a few photos on social media—so Terri came by after lunch to watch it with me. I got my laptop set up on the kitchen table where we'd be able to keep an eye on our dogs romping in the fenced backyard. The sun was too bright for us to watch video outside.

She showed up wearing a purple face mask made of some sparkly fabric. People were starting to wear them now that it looked like the coronavirus thing wasn't going away. Once the dogs were out back, I poured us both coffee and got out a bag of Oreos just as she pulled a ziplock bag out of her purse and said, "I brought you something. My sister made them."

"Oh," I said, opening it and laughing. "Lawyer masks!" There were three, two in a pinstripe pattern—one charcoal, one navy—and one in blue and white seersucker. "Tell her thank you very much! Now I can keep safe without looking like a paramedic or something."

"Yep, that's the idea."

She still had her mask on. I didn't want her to feel awkward, so—with a pang of regret for that fresh cup of coffee—I put on the gray one and said, "Let me get a cross breeze going here. They say that helps."

"Thanks. You know, I worry about Simone," she said. "And her mom. I mean, she works in a nursing home."

"Yep. I would imagine she's taking proper precautions, though. Maybe the next time we go over, I'll suggest sitting out on the veranda instead of inside."

We got settled in with our notebooks and pens, and I started the DVD. Austin appeared, sandy-haired and tanned, a good-looking kid despite the police station's fluorescent lights. He looked nervous, like almost every other witness or suspect I'd ever seen in a police interview.

A cop offscreen introduced himself by name and rank. As I was writing that information down, Terri said, "Oh, I guess he's still who they use. He's, like, the opposite of intimidating, real good at establishing rapport."

She'd retired from the local police force more than a decade earlier, but things in Basking Rock didn't tend to change any too fast.

The cop, a Sergeant Battersfield, got Austin's name and age and then said, "I'm assuming you went to Basking Rock High School?"

"Yes, sir. I graduated in 2016."

"Oh, my Lord," the cop said with a belly laugh. "Thank you for making me feel old. I graduated more than thirty years before you did! My God. I might as well just roll over and die right now."

Austin laughed despite himself, then apologized profusely.

"Oh, don't mind me, son. It ain't your fault I'm old. Anyway, okay, I got what I think is your address right here. Or your daddy's address?" He read it out. "That's over by the old paper mill, ain't it?"

"Yes, sir." The kid looked a little ashamed. I figured it was because that was the dirt-poor side of town.

"Yeah, I know that neighborhood real well," the cop said. "My momma come from over there too."

Austin relaxed.

"Damn," I said. "You weren't kidding about how he builds rapport."

The cop went through Austin's background some more, nothing we didn't already know, and shared a few anecdotes of his own to grease the wheels of conversation. About ten minutes in, he gave a heavy sigh and said, "Now, son, I hate to do this, but you know I got to. So can I just ask you a few questions about your late girlfriend? Ms. Veronica Lopez, for the record?"

Austin gulped hard and blinked a couple of times. Then he nodded and said, real quiet, "Yes, sir."

"Okay, so tell me, how did y'all come to know each other?"

"Oh," Austin said, smiling at the memory. "She was a year under me in high school. But I never talked to her then. I mean— Well, you've seen photos of her, right?"

"Uh-huh."

"Okay, so she was— There wasn't no more beautiful girl in the whole town, far as I could tell. But she was a cheerleader, and I... well, you know." He looked down. "I mean, I wasn't nothing."

"I know how *that* feels," Battersfield said.

"Yeah, um, I didn't say one word to her all through high school. But I sure knew who she was."

"And so how did that come to change?"

"Oh, um, well, I got my associate degree—"

"You mean the boatbuilding diploma?"

"Yeah, it's called that, and you can do boatbuilding and repair with it. But it's really fine woodworking, all kinds, not just boats. Indoor, outdoor, anything. And so, when she had her accident, her daddy called the company I was with at the time, asking did we have somebody who could help build a ramp for her to get into the house. And you bet I jumped at that."

"Oh, man. Yeah, that poor girl. We all wanted to help her after that."

"Right? Yeah! I mean, this beautiful girl, and her whole life changed. So I got in with the master carpenter who was doing the job, and I just —like, I only ever billed for not even half the time I put into it. Because I wanted to make her the most *beautiful* ramp you could imagine, no matter how long it took. And real solid—it had dovetailed *everything*, you know? You could drive a truck up that thing. But I wasn't gonna bill her family for that. I just wanted to be there at her house, measuring stuff, building, talking to her…"

"So, now, is that when y'all started getting to know each other?"

"Yeah. She spent a lot of time out on that porch, watching me work, talking. Her momma would bring us lemonade. I asked her favorite colors and brought samples for her. And man, I learned so much about ADA design, I mean, you would not believe. I just wanted to make it *right* for her."

"And why was that?"

"I just—" He stopped talking and looked off to the side, blinking back tears. When he'd got ahold of himself, he said, "I really loved her." He shrugged, shaking his head, as if to ask what more there was to say. He was quiet for a few seconds, and then he said, "I still do."

I hit pause.

"Goddammit," I said. "Why does he have to sound so sincere?" I reached for my coffee. "I'm going to take my mask off and have a sip, if that's okay with you. We can take turns."

"Sure. Thanks."

I had a couple sips, put my mask back on, and said, "Okay, so, with this guy on the stand, we're going to need at least a box or two of Kleenex for the jury. A few of them might even want to line up and give him a hug." I sighed. "Dammit."

"Yeah, he is *not* looking like a great alternate theory so far."

I sprawled back in my chair and looked at the ceiling, thinking things through. I said, "Problem is, apart from him, I don't *have* an alternate theory. What's the other story? How the hell else could she have died?"

She shrugged and took a bite of an Oreo. "He could be lying. He's got the DV history with that other girlfriend. And there's no shortage of wife killers or girlfriend killers who can convince you they really loved the woman. Or who even believe it themselves."

"True enough. And it's not like he's being challenged on anything. This interview's about as far from an interrogation as I've ever seen."

"Mm-hmm. That was never Battersfield's style. If we wanted to do a good cop, bad cop thing, he was always the good cop."

"I can see why. He isn't even playing softball here. It's more like croquet."

She laughed.

"Okay. Back into the fray." I hit play.

Battersfield walked Austin through the day of the party at Simone's, how and when they got there, what he remembered. It all sounded about right, based on what we'd heard from Simone and what the photos and video had shown. He remembered when they'd arrived, where he'd parked, and who he'd seen when he went in, although he ran through those facts somewhat automatically. I couldn't tell if it was dishonest or not. His tone could've been because he was reciting a set of facts he'd rehearsed, but it could also just have been because he'd told the story a dozen times already.

He remembered Veronica's fight with her cousin Sofia, although he didn't recall where they'd all been when it happened: "It might've been the kitchen? Wherever the video guy was at because Sofia was, like… thirsty for this dude. She was all over him, and I think it kind of… embarrassed Veronica? Because, I mean, he was like, her colleague. And this—I mean, it wasn't really a party, you know? To Veronica it was a work event."

The cop said, "Uh-huh. Like a professional situation?"

"Yeah, exactly. And there's her cousin making her look bad."

"And do you recall where Simone was at that point? Was she involved in the, uh, dispute?"

Austin looked up to his left, then to his right, shaking his head slowly. "Sir, I just don't recall for sure. But I doubt she was close by, since she didn't spend a lot of time with us that night."

"And was that unusual?"

"Oh, no sir. Not at all. There was a, uh… I mean, I knew they weren't friends, and I knew why, but I just—I didn't realize how bad—I just wish I'd known. I wish I'd gotten her out of there." He ducked his face down and covered his mouth with one hand, trying to pull himself together.

"I'm sorry, son," Sergeant Battersfield said. "You take all the time you need."

"No, I got to do this," Austin said. "I owe it to her."

I noticed he still hadn't mentioned being drunk himself. Too drunk to, as he put it, get Veronica out of there.

"Son, can you help me understand what you mean when you say it was bad, or that them two girls weren't friends?"

"Yeah," Austin said, nodding. "It's—I mean, Veronica was always trying to be friends with Simone, but she told me Simone hated her."

"Huh. And did she ever tell you why?"

"Yeah, she— It was about high school. And I don't really remember this myself. I mean, I maybe remember just… hearing about it back then, maybe? But she told me her biggest regret in life was that in high school, she was part of this group of girls that tormented Simone. That's her word—Veronica's, I mean. 'Tormented.' I guess they, like, bullied her?"

"And did she say how? Or how long it lasted?"

"I don't recall. I don't know if she ever told me any details, except she did say it went on for years. Maybe all of high school?"

"My goodness. And what was your impression on how they got along?"

Austin sighed and shook his head. "I guess… I didn't take it serious enough. In my head it was just, you know, mean girls, whatever. People do shit in high school— Excuse me."

"Naw, son, don't worry. We can talk frank here."

"Okay, sir. Thank you. I just meant, like, that was high school. We're past that now. Right?"

"Well, I don't know. Did you ever get a sense that maybe Simone wasn't past it?"

"I don't know. They did have a fight over money that night, something about why was Veronica making any money from this party when it should've been Simone."

"Uh-huh."

I leaned forward, hit stop, and said, "Okay, if that's true, then I guess I know what Simone's been hiding from me. Did you know anything about this bullying stuff?"

"Yeah, I got just a hint of that last week, from one of my halfway house women."

"Huh. She a credible source, you think?"

Terri volunteered at the county's only halfway house for recovering female addicts. She'd gotten a key piece of information there the previous year, when she was helping me with Jackson's case, but she'd also mentioned that half the things she'd heard there fell someplace between tall tales and withdrawal psychosis.

"Yeah, a girl about Simone's age, and not as far gone as some of the others. It was nothing specific, but enough to make me add that to my list of things we need to ask Simone."

"For sure."

I scribbled down a note about that and hit play again.

"Now, son," Sergeant Battersfield said, "I want to hear everything you remember about that night. Everything from the fight Veronica had with her cousin, to whatever the last thing is that you recall before waking up in the a.m. and—you know."

Austin gave his account of the evening. As with what he'd said about their arrival, some of it checked out with what I'd seen on the videos or heard from Sofia, and none of it sounded implausible. He never got around to mentioning getting drunk himself, and the cop continued to play interrogation croquet. Sergeant Battersfield was treating this kid as a friendly witness, and from the discovery I'd seen from Ruiz, this was the only police interview the kid had ever done. I could understand why they might not lean toward seeing him as suspect number one after an interview like this: he was credible and seemed to genuinely care about the victim. But I still couldn't figure out why he hadn't been their focus from the start.

The kid said, "And so, the last thing I remember, I guess, is right before bed. We were in the living room, and, um, Simone had—uh, she gave us something to drink. Champagne, but, like, mixed with something? I don't know what. It was pink, anyway. Like a cocktail."

"You drink it? The two of you?"

"Yeah."

"And then what?"

"Uh…" He thought about it for a second. "You know, that's about all I remember. We went into the bedroom. And I guess we just went straight to sleep."

I hit stop, looked at Terri, and shook my head in disbelief.

She frowned. "Uh, that is *not* good."

"It is if you're the prosecutor," I said. "There is no way Ruiz isn't going to put him on the stand. And then he's going to say, 'Ladies and gentlemen of the jury, as the autopsy showed, when she died—which was shortly after she drank the champagne Simone had given her—Veronica had enough Valium in her system to knock her out.'"

"And Simone had a prescription for Valium, and it's a clear liquid that you could mix… Oh my God." She looked about as discouraged as I felt.

I went over to the back door and stepped out to watch our dogs. Buster was running circles around Squatter, who was jumping up and down in excitement. The sun was bright, and I could smell the ocean on the breeze. "Man, look at them," I said. "There is *nothing* wrong in their lives."

She came out onto what my landlord referred to as the "backyard patio," which was a fancier term than I would have used for a concrete pad with weeds growing through the cracks.

"Yeah," she said. "No pandemic to worry about. No worries at all."

"Nope. And no witness who just blew their case apart."

16

SUNDAY, JUNE 7, 2020

S imone had called to ask if we could come by, saying she'd found something out about Veronica's stalker. When I got there a little after lunch, Terri was already there. The sun was blazing down on the flower beds, where the rose bushes that Simone's management people had planted for the party grew alongside all manner of plants I couldn't identify: tall pink things that looked like wildflowers, dusty green leaves and dark needles that might've been herbs, and a carpet of yellow buds running down to the street.

"Hey there," I called out, waving up to the two of them sitting on the veranda. They were both wearing masks, so I put mine on.

"Come on up," Terri said. "You want tea or lemonade?"

"Tea, thanks." I hoofed it up the steps and said, "This is real nice. It's like an outdoor living room."

"Why, thank you." Simone had a set of modern-looking outdoor furniture: a gray sofa, which she was sitting on, and two chairs with red cushions, all arranged around a glass-topped coffee table that stood on a black-and-white rug. Hanging baskets of flowers dangled from the edge of the veranda roof.

I sat down, took the glass Terri handed me, and set it back on the table.

"Please, go ahead," Simone said. "I'll keep my mask on, but you go right ahead and enjoy your drink."

"Much obliged." I took a sip.

We hadn't told Simone yet about Austin's police interview. She'd been busy hosting a family birthday the previous day, and I didn't see any point in spoiling that with bad news.

Today was the day we were going to have to spoil.

"Simone was just telling me, before you got here, about this online friend of hers."

"I mean… online? That sounds weird," Simone said. "She's a friend, period."

"But you've never met, right?"

"No, she's in Florida. But we video chatted once or twice, at first. Mostly we just message back and forth."

Terri took a sip of lemonade and said, "So, wait, how'd she know Veronica had this stalker?"

"She followed Veronica too. She subscribed to both our channels. And I guess they messaged a lot with each other."

"What's her name?" I asked. "By the way, this is real good tea." The clinking ice cubes were perfect for such a hot day.

"I make it how my momma showed me. All credit to her. Anyway, this friend is Ilona Jones."

I pulled my little notebook out of my shirt pocket and wrote the name down, confirming the spelling.

"So, I hadn't heard from her in a while, but this morning Insta served up a memory, you know?"

Terri explained to me, "Some social media platforms have a feature where they'll randomly show you things you posted on that same date a year or two years or however long ago."

"Right, and it showed what I posted a year ago today, which was, um…" She looked down at her hands in her lap, and when she spoke again, I heard sadness in her voice. "That was the day of Veronica's funeral."

"I know it's hard, honey," Terri said. "Show him the post."

Simone pulled her laptop out from a shelf under the coffee table, turned it so I could see, and clicked through a bunch of pictures. The white coffin was open at the top, with the bottom half covered in pink flowers. What looked like at least a hundred mourners stood nearby, some hugging each other.

I said, "Oh, I don't think I knew you'd gone to the funeral."

"Of course I did. Everybody did. I mean, she was only twenty-two. It was tragic."

In one photo, I saw a fashion-model type in a black miniskirt suit. Her face looked familiar.

"Terri, isn't that the girl we met in Charleston? Not the director we met with—"

"Oh, her assistant, yeah. With the, I don't know, Russian name or whatever."

Simone was nodding. "Yeah, a lot of people from Apex came. But the thing about this post is, there was a lot going on, and I guess I was still kind of in shock at the time because I completely missed this comment."

She scrolled down. A user with the handle ilonajonz had written, *RIP sweet soul!!! SimoneBlkBeauty DM me! IMPORTANT!!!*

"So I checked my DMs," she said. "This morning, I mean. I was not in a good place back then, with what had happened, and I dropped the ball on a lot of things. So I didn't realize until today that Ilona had messaged me about this guy, Shawn Gifford. Which, I knew about him, as I told you. Ms. Rutledge at Apex had actually messaged both of us, Veronica and me, about him and sent these, like, guidelines on how to deal with stalkers. They were pretty good about that."

Terri said, "I'm glad to hear that. Seems like stalkers or online harassers must be an occupational hazard."

"Oh, like you would not believe. I've gotten just the nastiest— Even before any of this happened, there were always creeps who would message you. We were supposed to send screenshots to Ms. Rutledge so she could take care of it, or at least monitor them."

I asked, "So, what'd she say? I mean, Ilona?"

"She said he'd reached out to her. Shawn, I mean. The stalker. After Veronica died." Turning her laptop to face herself, she clicked and scrolled. "I guess he followed everyone connected to Veronica, just to… hear whatever any of us might say about her, or something. Or feel more connected to her. I don't know." She shuddered. "Okay, here it is. She sent a screenshot of what she got from him."

She turned the laptop back around so we could see. The message said, *Ilona this aint right. All her fake friends crying, they were the ones using her dragging her down, now I'm the loser they think?! I'm only one who understood her, if she would of known that, if she would of let me explain! But she wouldn't she put me thru HELL!*

I said, "Dang, that's not good. He didn't even know her, did he? I mean, they were never friends?"

"In real life, not at all," Simone said. "He just got obsessed. I don't know the details, but Ms. Rutledge must, since she kept track of all the weirdos. But us here in town, I mean, we all thought he was kind of a joke, showing up at every event and hanging back staring, never talking to anyone."

"Sounds like pretty much what he did at your party," Terri said. "Do we know when he left that night?"

I shook my head. "I need to talk to the other caterers again," I said. I'd called two of them to find out what they remembered, which wasn't much, but that had been before I knew to ask them about Shawn. "But unless they remember something they didn't recall before, our best bet is getting through the rest of that footage."

Terri explained, "That thumb drive Apex gave us had almost four gigs of files. We haven't been able to watch all the videos yet."

Simone nodded. "Okay. But read this next message. He sent her these two DMs and then just went silent."

The second one said: *It all went wrong everything. Alone in my oblivion, I can't watch and follow anymore, but now she will stay pure 4ever. I went to funeral home but turned around and left, would of killed that "boyfriend" if I saw him, would of got in her coffin and shot myself. You were her real friend not like Simone. I'm in hell 4ever I belong there, nobody can understand except maybe u.*

Terri stared at the screen, then looked around and asked, "You have deadbolts on your doors, don't you? And window locks?"

"Yes, ma'am, and I've got a top-of-the-line security system on this house. I installed it as soon as I could afford it, more than two years ago, because I was already getting some very creepy messages."

"Good. I've looked into that guy, and he doesn't have any arrests, much less convictions, so that's… something, I guess. Although it doesn't prove he's not dangerous."

"Oh my." I looked at Terri. What she'd said had given me an idea. "He was serving food, right? At the party? Was he serving drinks, do you think?"

"Oh." She got what I meant. "He could've—yeah."

"Uh, I'm a little lost," Simone said. "What are y'all talking about?"

It was time to deliver the bad news.

"Uh, so, Simone, I didn't want to trouble you with this when you were getting ready for that birthday party yesterday, but on Friday I finally got a piece of evidence from the prosecutor that had been delayed a while. It was a DVD of the interview the police did with Austin McKrall when he got back to town."

"Oh! And—" She seemed to register the look on my face. "Was it… bad?"

"Yeah, it… Well, I want to preface this by saying it wasn't an inter-rogation. They weren't treating him as a possible suspect, so they weren't asking him the hard questions that I think need to be asked."

When I didn't continue, she said, growing agitated, "But what did they ask? What'd he say?"

"Well, first off, he said Veronica bullied you pretty bad in high school."

I could see the truth on her face, but she didn't say anything. She looked down at her glass of lemonade and swirled the ice cubes.

I said, "The reason that matters is, the prosecution's going to see it as a possible motive. Their job is to tell the jury a story that makes sense

141

as to why this defendant, in other words you, would've wanted the victim dead."

She looked up at me. "I did *not* want her dead."

I believed her. But I also got the sense that if she'd been writing instead of talking, there would've been an asterisk at the end of that sentence. The thought was not complete.

"I'm so sorry," Terri said, "but could I use the restroom?"

"Oh, of course." Simone reminded her where it was, then picked up the pitcher to top up her own glass of lemonade.

As she stood up, Terri caught my eye and gave a little nod. She didn't actually need the facilities; she was excusing herself so that if Simone said something incriminating, I'd be the only one to hear it. That way, the attorney-client privilege would apply.

When I heard the screen door slam, I said, "Of course you didn't want her dead. But what *did* you want?"

She took a long sip of her lemonade, set it on the table, and sighed. She wasn't looking at me. "Okay," she said. "This is not something I'm proud of. It's not how a Christian should behave, but we all have some sin in us." She took a long breath. "I wanted her... destroyed. I wanted her to start making it as an influencer and then flame out and fail and watch me succeed."

"Okay," I said, feeling my shoulders relax a bit. "Well, thank you. I can work with that. And, if you don't mind my saying, I think that was an understandable way to feel, and we're none of us perfect."

Through the window behind Simone, Terri was looking at me. I nodded to let her know she could come back.

When she was settled back in her chair, lemonade in hand, Terri asked, "Did you get to what Austin said about the party?"

I shook my head.

"Okay, then, let me just… Simone, can you think back to that night?"

"Of course! I've been thinking back to that night every day since it happened."

"Okay, so, toward the end of the night, or whenever… Can I ask, how did it come up that Veronica needed to stay?"

"Oh, she was, um… I was a little surprised she was still here, actually, since almost everybody else was gone. A couple of people management had hired were taking down the lights, but… Anyway, she came up, and I think she was pretty embarrassed—I mean, she wasn't looking me in the eye. And she said something like, I'm really sorry to ask you this, but Austin is just wasted—or hammered, maybe? Something like that."

She turned and pointed through the window. "He was over there, sitting on one of the stools, sprawled across my—like, practically sleeping on my kitchen island. I figured she must've been waiting for him to sober up, but then he didn't. So I realized what she was asking."

"To stay, you mean?"

"Yeah. I mean, it's not like she had options. She's not going to Uber all the way back to Charleston, and you don't have to explain to me that finding an accessible hotel room that late at night is going to be hard."

"About what time was it?"

"It was maybe eleven thirty? Which, to me— I am not a night owl. To me that's late, and she'd gotten here around three or four in the afternoon to start getting ready. So it was a long day."

"Okay, and what happened after that?"

"Well, I— Nothing, you know? I showed her where the guest bedroom was and where the accessible bathroom was, right up the hall. And I went to bed. Or, I mean, first I used the bathroom, since I didn't want to wait for them to. And then I went in my room and closed my door and left them to it."

"And did you go right to sleep? Or come back out for anything?"

She shook her head. "No. I was *done*. I didn't want anything but bed right then. I think my head was on the pillow maybe five minutes before I fell asleep."

I exhaled, realizing as I did that I'd been holding my breath.

"Okay," Terri said, "so—just so we know, who set the burglar alarm? If you went to bed before they did, and there were still lighting guys or whatever taking stuff down?"

"My mom. She told me she'd take care of that so I could get some rest. And then I guess she drove home."

Terri looked at me. She didn't have to say anything for me to know what she was thinking. She needed to get that woman to trust her enough to talk. The fact she'd been there at the very end of the party but hadn't rushed to tell us everything she knew made me wonder— there was no way around it—if what she knew was harmful to Simone's case.

"Okay," I said. "Well, I'm glad to hear you went to bed first. I'm going to want to talk to whoever was left besides Austin, to see if they can testify to that, because he said something different. I don't know if he's just making things up to throw suspicion off of himself, or what, but he said you offered him and Veronica a nightcap. Said you served them some kind of champagne cocktail, and right after that, he fell asleep."

"I did *not*! Wait, drinks, and then he fell asleep? Is he trying to make it sound like I drugged them?"

Terri said, "Mm-hmm."

"Oh my God. I would never— Mr. Munroe, I don't drink. I'm Baptist. I do not touch alcohol. And I wouldn't know how to mix a cocktail to save my life! So we got him on that, right?"

"Well… that's helpful," I said doubtfully.

She stared at me, horrified. "Are you saying he could get away with this? Even though I don't drink, he could still get up on the stand and tell the jury I made them drinks right before they fell asleep?"

"He could. Yeah."

"And then they'll think that's where the Valium— Oh my God." She doubled over and put her face in her hands. I could hear her taking deep breaths, trying to calm herself down.

"Girl, do not give up." Terri leaned forward in her chair to put a hand on Simone's shoulder. "You haven't seen Leland here cross-examine somebody. I have."

I said, "And don't breathe one word of this to anybody, okay? Don't go posting on social media about this at all, or about the fact you don't drink. Nothing. I don't want him hearing your side of this until I have him under oath."

Simone, still bent over, nodded.

When she finally got ahold of herself, she sat back up and looked out at her flower garden. Then she said, "This is just… really *hard*." She sighed and asked, "When you say don't talk to anybody, is that— I mean, can I talk to my pastor?"

Basking Rock was too small a town for me to say yes to that, but before I could answer, Terri said, "Girl, you do not need a pastor to talk to God."

Simone looked at her and said, without words—with just an emphatic nod—*That is so, so true.* Then she said, "Okay then. Yeah. I guess that's who I have to take this to, every time."

Terri said, "It's all you can do. But it'll be enough."

Both of them sat back in the same position, arms crossed over their chests, looking out at the yard, shaking their heads in a resigned way. I had the sense they had both just stepped into the waters of a very old, very long river, one that countless generations of women like them had stood in before. They were carrying the weight of injustice but not letting it bend them. Somehow their faith was enough to keep their backs straight and their heads high.

It was not a river I had access to. I was glad they had it, but faith was not what I needed. A battle was coming, for Simone's freedom, and I had to get ready to fight.

———

17

FRIDAY, JUNE 12, 2020

Noah and I pulled into the parking lot of the strip mall that contained, among several other low-rent establishments, Freddy's Discount Furniture. It had been a week since retail stores were back to business as usual by order of the governor, and Terri had found out that Veronica's stalker was a salesman there. On Fridays, she told me, he had the floor to himself until 4 p.m. That meant I could give Noah a chance to tag along on a real investigation.

As I looked for a parking space, I ran him through our plan. "Okay, so what are we doing here?"

"Looking for a better office setup for me, since my summer classes are going to be online."

"And what are you studying?"

"Business."

We'd decided not to mention his PI career plans.

"What do you do if he starts getting weird? Or if I need to talk to him alone?"

"Back off and let you deal with it."

"Right." I pulled into a spot. "And how's that going to work?"

"If you put your hand in your jacket pocket, I act like I just saw something interesting somewhere else in the store and go look at it."

"Okay." I turned off the car and tossed my sunglasses into the center console. "Let's go."

Freddy's was lit by fluorescent tubes on the ceiling, plus about three dozen floor lamps and desk lamps, all of which had signs on them saying they were 20 or 30 percent off. Shawn was in the recliner section looking at his phone, but as we came in, he raised a hand to say hi and called out, "Afternoon! Y'all just make yourselves at home —we got plenty of good deals."

"Thank you," I said. "Just looking to upgrade a home office setup for my boy."

We went over to the office section and tried a few chairs. While we were discussing them, Shawn came over. He was a heavier guy in his thirties, dressed for work in a shirt and tie.

He pointed at the chair Noah was in and said, "Lot of folks like that one there. It's got the lumbar support, and that's fully adjustable."

"Oh, cool," Noah said.

"Leather, though," I told him. "For summer especially, you want something you don't stick to." I'd also noticed the $349 price tag, which I was not excited about.

"Yeah, I can't just wear boxer shorts on this."

Shawn laughed. "I hear you on that. I tell you what, I do a lot of gaming and social media myself, and I really like a mesh chair for that exact reason. It breathes."

"Yeah, you know what," Noah said, looking at the guy like he was about to tell him something fathers weren't supposed to hear, "officially this is for my schoolwork, since I'm doing summer classes, but I'm a big gamer too. So whatever you think is good for that, I'm interested."

Shawn took us over to the mesh chairs, chatting with Noah about some video game. I looked at filing cabinets nearby while the two of them hung out. If I'd been my son's professor, I would've given him good marks so far for establishing rapport.

When I strolled over after a couple of minutes, they had their options narrowed down to two.

Noah pointed to a chair next to the one he was sitting in and said, "Check it out, that one's only $99."

"Yep," Shawn said. "And it does adjust three ways. That one you're on adjusts six ways, and it has the three-point lumbar support. But it is more expensive."

"The cheap one's fine, Dad."

I said, "Well, good," and slipped my hand in my pocket.

"Oh," Noah said, looking across the aisle. "Just one sec." He got up and went to look at a desk.

The chair he'd just vacated had a $199 price tag. In a quiet voice I said to Shawn, "Sir, can you be frank with me and tell me which chair he liked more? I can spring for the more expensive one if it matters to him."

"Yessir, well, once he sat down in that one, he stayed there. And I have to be honest, it is a better chair. And a better deal—it normally retails for $299."

I smiled. "Well, thank you, uh—" I glanced down at his name tag, did a little double take, and said, "Oh my."

"What, sir?"

"Oh… no, nothing. Anyway, Shawn, you got that in stock so I can take it home today?"

"Yes I do. But, uh…" He looked down at his name tag. "Was there… I mean… Do I know you?"

"Well, you know, it's a small town." I looked around. Except for us, the store was still empty. "Okay," I said. "I wouldn't put you on the spot if there were people here, but I got to be straight with you. I'm an attorney, and I'm working on a case involving that tragic situation last year, where that young lady on the social media lost her life."

His face tightened. I sensed wariness in him, but also, if I wasn't mistaken, grief.

"I'm sorry," I said. "Maybe I shouldn't have mentioned it. I just wanted to be straight with you. I recognized your name because I had to look through all her posts and so forth, and you were one of her biggest fans."

He nodded slowly and said, "Yes. Yes, I was."

"A lot of people took inspiration from her." Something in his face made me add, "Course, a lot of people were jealous of her, too."

He blinked a couple times, very fast, and then said, "Sir, just so— Can I ask… are you law enforcement?"

"Oh, Lord," I said, laughing a little. "Hell, no. Hey, Noah!"

Across the aisle, he looked up from the desk he was sitting at. "What?"

Pointing at Shawn with my thumb, I said, "He asked if I'm law enforcement!"

Noah cracked up and said, "Dad, they got fitness standards in the police. And you can't even do a goddamn pull-up!"

"What the— I sure as hell can!"

He and Shawn were both laughing, but Shawn apologized when I looked at him.

"Naw, it's fine," I said.

"His whole workout," Noah said, still sitting behind the desk, "is scooting his office chair over to the printer."

Shawn cracked up again.

I shook my head, chuckling, and pulled out my wallet. "Okay, Noah, since you're so strong, you can push your own damn shopping cart."

He came back over while Shawn pulled a big box off the shelf and put it into a nearby cart. As we all went to the cash register, I said to Shawn, "Yeah, I'm in private practice now. And that means I'm usually facing off *against* law enforcement."

Shawn said, "Cool. Cool."

At the register, I paid and thanked him, and we left. I could tell Noah wanted to ask why, but he had the sense to wait until we got the chair in the trunk and were pulling out.

I swung around and headed for the road. "The last thing I want," I said, "is for him to think I had him on my list of folks to talk to. Today I just wanted to get him thinking I'm an okay guy, so when I come back and talk to him later, it's because I happened to meet him there today and then I wanted to run something by him."

Noah said, "That makes sense. I might be able to help too."

I looked over at him, then back at traffic to make my turn. He had a proud look on his face like he was about to score some points. "What're you talking about?"

"He's into OtherWorld," he said. "And I got his server and his character's name."

"What is that, a game?"

"Yeah. It's OtherWorld Saga, but nobody says the whole name. I'm going to meet up with him and play."

"Now wait a minute, don't you meet up with him anywhere," I said. "It's entirely possible our Mr. Discount Furniture Salesman killed a girl last year."

"Not meet up in real *life*," he said. "Online. Playing a game."

"Oh. Okay. What use is that, though?"

"I mean, you talk. You get to know people. You see what kind of person they are."

"In a game? Really?"

"Oh, yeah. You get a bunch of folks together and try to get something done, you see how they treat each other, how they operate… how they think, even."

"Huh. You know what, yeah, that might be useful." As we waited at a light, a thought occurred to me. "Are there women who play that game?"

"Yeah, lots."

"Okay. Well, can you pay attention to how he treats them? If he's… inappropriate, or aggressive, or, I don't know, anything else you notice?"

"You got it."

———

After dropping Noah off at home, I headed to Terri's so we could update each other. She lived in an updated shotgun shack with a big yard and a deck overlooking the fenced part at the back. Laptop in hand, I put my mask on and rang the doorbell. I'd never hung out at her place before the pandemic, and I still didn't now because we did everything outside. I got a glimpse of the interior as we passed through on our way to the deck: comfortable living room, nice kitchen with a farmhouse sink, the whole place spotless. Outside, her laptop and a pitcher of tea sat on a glass table shaded by a big yellow umbrella.

"This is real nice," I said. A line of sunflowers about six feet tall ran all along the back fence. Her dog was sniffing at something in the grass. I'd left Squatter at home for Noah to walk.

"Thank you. It sure is nice to live in such a gorgeous little corner of the world."

"Yeah. Shame about the people," I said, and we both laughed. "I wish all the murderers and abusers and so forth would go live on an island someplace and put us out of a job."

"Mm-hmm." She shook her head and then changed gears. "Okay, now, I know Simone doesn't want to take this approach, but you should be aware the officer who magically found that syringe in her van has a history of planting evidence. If she ever changes her mind and wants to get that evidence tossed, you should subpoena his disciplinary records."

"Why am I not surprised?" I typed that information into my notes. She could've emailed it to me, but we'd never worked that way. From the get-go, she told me stuff and I wrote it down. It was her habit, from working on insurance fraud and other civil cases; that way, nothing she uncovered was available to the other side in discovery.

"If you can put that spin on it, that might save her reputation on top of keeping her out of jail."

"Right," I said. "Because then she's not getting off on a technicality, she's getting off because he planted evidence. If I can connect the dots."

"Mm-hmm."

We both knew how courts worked. Proving that a cop sometimes planted evidence wasn't the same thing as proving that the evidence in your particular case was planted, and judges didn't like throwing critical evidence out unless you showed them that they had to. This information was a step in the right direction but not even close to a slam dunk.

I told her about my encounter with Shawn that afternoon, and she whistled to say she was impressed. But not with me: "I need to talk to Noah. Maybe I'll join him in playing with that guy."

"You do that?"

"OtherWorld? Yeah. It takes my mind off things."

I cracked a smile. "You just want to get paid to play games."

She laughed. "It's not much different from getting paid to scroll through Instagram. It's how we catch people these days. Speaking of which, I think you need to go talk to Austin's father and see if you can figure out where Austin is. None of his social media's been updated since he got back from Florida, and nobody I've talked to has seen him. His cell number, the one you got from Girardeau's files, is out of service."

"Will do," I said. "Although I'm happy to pay you to take care of that. Either way."

"Uh, *no*."

I looked at her, surprised.

"I drove by their trailer," she said. "I didn't see anyone, but I did see a Confederate flag on the porch."

"Jesus." I shook my head. "Understood." I added *Talk to Austin's dad* to my to-do list.

"You watch out too," she said. "If I were you, I'd go there armed, just in case."

I processed the fact that she thought a White guy might be in danger there in broad daylight. "What'd you find out about him?"

"Oh, everything. Child abuse. CPS has been there several times over the years. They even took the kids a few years ago, when the mother died, but then they sent them back. Firearms violations, DUIs, assault." She gave a little shrug, like there was more to say but no point getting into it.

"Okay," I said. "I'll be careful. Uh, as far as our checklist here, is that it, for now?"

"No. There's one more thing. It's… I don't know. Disturbing."

"What is it?"

"After we talked to Simone last weekend, I went looking for Ilona Jones. Online, I mean. Her Instagram and everything else I could think of."

"What'd you find?"

"Well, she's still posting… or someone is. And it *sounds* like her."

"But… what?"

"She's missing. Ilona Jones, of Tampa, Florida, has been missing since last fall."

———

18

MONDAY, JUNE 15, 2020

On Saturday I'd driven to a trailer park on the bad side of town, hoping to talk to Austin's father, but the only person there was a kid, maybe fourteen or fifteen—Austin's little brother, maybe. He had a sullen look on his baby face and was wearing what looked like some sort of heavy metal T-shirt. Noah would've known what band it was, but I didn't. When I rolled my window down and started introducing myself, the kid spat on the ground and went inside.

On Monday afternoon, I tried again. As I made my way through the trailer park, a few loblolly pines loomed over me, looking like Christmas trees on stilts. A solid minority of the trailers had Confederate-flag decor: drapes with that theme, a dirty flag draped over a porch railing, a sticker on a screen door.

As I drove down the gravel road that led to the McKralls' trailer, I saw two men sitting on chairs on the porch. Based on age, either of them could've been Austin's dad. A couple of kids' bicycles lay in the long grass outside. An elderly mutt was limping across the road, so I parked right where I was, gave him one of the dog treats I always had on me, and walked the eight or ten yards left between me and the men on the porch.

"Afternoon," I said, as I got close.

They looked at me, and one of them grunted hello. A curtain moved behind him, and I thought I saw a little girl's face duck out of sight.

"Mr. McKrall?" I asked.

"What if I am?"

The man asking was a big guy sitting in a plastic chair with a bottle of beer in his hand. His shorts and Lynyrd Skynyrd T-shirt allowed me to see which one of us was on the more muscular end of the spectrum. It wasn't me.

"Hey there," I said. "I'm Leland Munroe. I'm a lawyer working on a case where your son Austin's been helping out the police, and I had a couple questions for him, if he's available to talk."

"Austin is a grown man." He took a swig of beer. "He don't need my say-so."

"Okay, then," I said. "I just wanted to be respectful and ask you first. If he happens to be here, maybe I could ask him?"

"He ain't here. He's on his own. I told him when he was eighteen he could get a job or join the military."

His friend laughed. "Military? *That* boy?"

"Yeah, well, if he had, he'd have stayed out of trouble."

"Maybe so."

Austin's dad started peeling the label off his beer bottle with a thumbnail.

I said, "Understood. Well, you got a number for him, by any chance? Or an address?"

He didn't look up from his peeling. "You look in Florida?"

"Oh, he's gone back there?"

"A boy his age got better things to do than set here with us."

The last time I knew for sure Austin had been in town was on the day of his police interview, but with the delay there'd been in getting me a copy of the video, that was nearly six weeks ago. He could've skipped town at any point since then.

Out the corner of my eye, I thought I saw a kid grab one of the bikes and pedal off. I didn't want to disrespect Mr. McKrall by breaking eye contact, so I didn't look.

His friend shrugged and said, "He ain't here no more, anyway." He gestured to the trailer behind them. "That I can tell you right now."

"I hear you," I said. "Okay, well, thank you. Afternoon, y'all."

I crunched back up the gravel toward my car. As I pulled the door open, Austin's dad yelled to me, with a big smile on his face, "If you see him, tell him he ain't welcome here unless he's paying rent!"

He and his friend cracked up and clinked their beer bottles together.

I took my leave. My gas was low, and I cursed myself for not filling up before I'd headed over. Around here, I didn't know where the nearest gas station was. A man down by the trailer park entrance pointed west down the main road—the opposite direction from home. I went off that way and filled up. On my way back by the trailer park, at a stop sign, I heard a thump on the passenger side and a kid crying out.

I put the Malibu into park and jumped out. There was no traffic around. A little girl with dirty-blonde hair, maybe nine or ten years old, was standing on the other side of my car with her bike lying on the shoulder of the road.

She looked perfectly fine, but I asked, "You okay?"

"I'm sorry," she said, with a nervous glance across the road. "I'm real sorry. It's my fault." She was talking a little louder than it seemed like she needed to.

"You live over there? Let me get that." I picked her bike up, noticing as I did that there wasn't any mark on the side of my car. She clearly hadn't hit me very hard, and though it was a strange thing for a child to do, I was getting the sense she'd done it on purpose.

In a quieter voice, she said, "My brother ain't in Florida. He didn't go back there again."

"Oh?" I said. "Yeah, I didn't think so."

She said, "That was nice, how you gave that dog a treat." After a second, she added, "My daddy kicks it, mostly."

"Aw, he shouldn't do that to a poor old dog."

"I know." She took the handlebars of her bike back from me. "My brother's got some kind of construction job now," she said, "over the other side of town. At a restaurant, I think."

"Oh, does he? Well, thank you."

"He don't like my daddy," she said, "and neither do I."

"Well, I'm sorry to hear that, but I understand. Listen," I said, glancing at the trailer park entrance. "Let's get you home safe. I'll walk you over. Hang on."

I went back to the driver's side and grabbed the baggie of dog treats out of the console to give to her. Then I thought being caught with a bag of dog treats she couldn't explain might get her in trouble, so I took out one little bone-shaped cookie and brought it back for her.

"Here you go, if you want to give that dog something nice."

She smiled and pocketed it. I walked her back, then drove on home.

I stopped at a restaurant near the beach to grab shrimp dinners for Noah and me. Walking over to the building from my parking spot, I mentally ran through every restaurant in town. The only one I could think of that was under construction was the Broke Spoke. If Austin was working there, it made sense that no one had seen him: the place had no windows you could see into, and with COVID and whatever filth came out of the woodwork when a former strip club got remodeled, the workers were wearing dust masks on the rare occasions you did spot them.

When I got my take-out order, the smell of it brought home to me how good it was to be earning a decent wage. A few months earlier, I'd been subsisting on gas station sandwiches. Now I could get us whatever we felt like eating every night. I could pay my bills and start dragging myself out of the hole I'd gotten into.

But I didn't know how long these good times could last. How many rich clients with criminal cases were there around here? And even if there were enough to make a career out of it, I wondered how many of them could I take on. Unlike Girardeau, who I'd seen argue eloquently on behalf of rich pedophiles, I couldn't stomach representing any sleazeball who happened to have a checkbook and constitutional rights.

———

At home, Noah and I had dinner on the couch with our plates on our laps. I'd grabbed the remote, but we never got around to watching the news, because he had OtherWorld up on his laptop.

"So I met up with Shawn a couple times," he said, "and went on raids with him and Jackson. I told Terri what realm we were in so she could come on the second raid without it looking like I knew her."

"Uh-huh." I had no idea what he was talking about. I'd tried D&D in high school but never got into it, and my entire computer-gaming experience amounted to a couple of weeks playing Myst in college. "Wait, you haven't talked to Jackson about the case, have you?"

"Course not. I know it's all confidential."

His screen displayed some kind of *Lord of the Rings*-looking gateway with torches burning on either side. He logged in while I ate another shrimp.

"Terri's pretty badass," he said.

"Yeah, I knew that."

Unlike him, I wasn't thinking of video games. Terri and I had fought our way out of an ambush only six months earlier, and I felt lucky to be alive.

I hadn't told Noah about that. He'd already lost one parent, and I didn't see what good it'd do him to know how close he came to losing the other.

On the screen, a black pirate ship was speeding across the waves while a narrator told us we were a motley band of different races united in our pursuit of honor, freedom, and glory. Then we were on the deck of the ship with a band of ogres and medieval elves, or something along those lines.

I asked, "Which one's Shawn?"

"Oh, he's not here. I was just showing you. He's probably at work right now—he doesn't normally play until pretty late at night."

"And how exactly does that work? Can you talk to each other?"

"In chat, yeah. Just to each other, or to everyone." He logged out, set the laptop aside, and started in on his dinner.

"You been talking to him?" He nodded. "What's he like?"

"Uh… Well, one thing is, he has a lot of rules. He likes to call them principles, and he gets mad if other players don't follow them."

"That sounds fun."

He laughed. "Terri's been talking to him too. One-on-one. It's called Whispers. You can ask her if he said anything interesting. I had stuff to do for my classes, so I haven't gotten around to comparing notes with her as far as what he's talked about. Although she did tell me he hit on her almost as soon as she joined."

"He— People do that? You can do that in a video game?"

He looked at me like I was stupid and then wolfed down a couple of shrimp. "Terri's like this Valkyrie," he said, wiping cocktail sauce off his chin. "I mean, her character."

"A Valkyrie? Really? What's she look like?"

His eyebrows jumped up, and he gave me a smile. "Don't *you* get all interested, now!"

"No, it's— I mean, I'm curious—"

"Whatever, Dad. Her character wears this, like, leather armor. It's pretty cool. She told me she plays as a girl because it brings out all the creeps. Folks say stuff to her they'd never say if they thought she was a guy."

"I can believe that," I said, "unfortunately. And I can see where that'd be useful for a PI."

"Yeah. I might try it myself, if I'm playing to investigate something."

"Seems like a good idea." I nodded. "Although what could you really investigate? How many people play these games?"

He shrugged. "Pretty much everyone I know."

"Huh." I looked at his laptop. The screen was back to the *Lord of the Rings* doorway with the flames on either side. I felt my brain start rearranging itself to accommodate the fact that, apparently, there were whole worlds inside the internet that people could escape into. Did escape into.

I was still thinking about that when my phone dinged. It was an email: Venmo, responding to my subpoena.

"Dang it," I told Noah, "I got to go log in."

I took the plate with my last two shrimp to my office and started up my laptop to see what Venmo had to say about Veronica's account.

When I saw it, I picked up my phone and closed the door so Noah wouldn't hear.

"Terri," I said, when she answered, "Venmo responded to the subpoena. On the night of the party, at 9:56 p.m., she sent—or I should say, someone using her phone sent—$2,500 to Austin McKrall."

She said, "Ha! *Yes!* Hang on. Let me get my notes."

While she was getting them, I skimmed the rest of the document Venmo had sent. Simone was not kidding when she'd said Veronica never used cash. The list of one month's transactions was two single-spaced pages long, with dozens of small purchases at coffee shops and drugstores.

She'd also received three payments of $250 each over the course of the month. The sender's name was Ilona Jones.

———

19

TUESDAY, JUNE 16, 2020

Terri and I went over to Simone's in the morning. It was cloudy, for once, and on the chilly side for June, so we brought coffee and muffins from a local shop. Simone met us at the door in a silky purple outfit and matching mask, and we went around to her sitting area on the side porch.

"I've got a purple one too," Terri said, taking off the gold mask she had on. She was smiling. "I should've worn it."

As I set the cardboard tray of lattes and a cappuccino down on the coffee table, I said, "We come bearing gifts. And more pieces of the puzzle, which I'm hoping you can help us put together."

"I sure hope so," she said. "It got my curiosity up, what you said on the phone."

I handed her the zucchini muffin she'd requested and said, "You check the time stamp on those photos?"

"Thank you," she said, taking off her mask and reaching for her coffee. "Yeah, that whole sequence with Austin on the couch was between 9:54 and 9:57 p.m."

"Well, that checks out. The $2,500 payment went to his account right in that time frame."

She sipped her coffee and said, "The memo just says 'J.' What's that?"

Terri said, "We don't know yet."

"Oh."

"What's shocking to me," I said, "is that this Venmo information wasn't in the discovery I got from the solicitor's office. I should not have had to subpoena this from the source. Money is a motive so often that the police should've pulled it as part of the initial investigation, just as a matter of course." It occurred to me as I spoke that Girardeau should've subpoenaed it too.

"I told you," Terri said, shaking her head like this failure was no surprise to her. "The Columbos and Sherlock Holmes types are not on our local force. Nothing here's up to big-city standards. Not the police work, not the coroner, nothing."

"Oh, speaking of the coroner," Simone said, "there was something in the autopsy I didn't understand."

"You read that?" Terri looked from her to me. "You let her look at that? With the *photos*?"

"He did warn me," she said. "Several times. But I went to nursing school, remember? I observed an autopsy when I was nineteen! And I wanted to fully understand the evidence they're going to put up against me."

Terri nodded like she was impressed.

"I had two questions," Simone said. "The first one is the time of death. Is it bad that they couldn't determine it?"

"Well… I don't know if it's bad or good. It just means they're not sure enough about when she ate. What did it say? It looked like she'd eaten about ten hours before she died?"

"Yeah, she wouldn't have eaten at the party. She didn't like eating in front of people."

"Oh, okay. Well, so, because of that, they can't narrow down her time of death too precisely."

"Okay. I guess that's too bad. Then my other one was, it didn't actually *say* she died of a heroin overdose. It didn't find heroin at all. It said levels of morphine *consistent* with a heroin overdose. Can we, I don't know, argue that maybe there's reasonable doubt she died the way they're saying?"

"I hate to burst your bubble," I said, "because that's good thinking. But that's what a heroin overdose looks like on autopsy. Heroin's got a half-life only a few minutes long, so unless the person dies instantly, that's not what they're going to find. Heroin metabolizes real fast into a couple of other things, including morphine, so what they check for is blood levels of those other things."

"Oh." She deflated a little.

"I'm real sorry," I said. "But you're doing exactly what we've got to do, which is ask every question, leave no stone unturned. About that, did you get a chance to look at those two medical experts? I want one of them to read that autopsy report and give us his thoughts."

I'd asked around for recommendations and gotten a couple of names.

"Yeah. They both look solid. I ran them by my doctor, and she said she doesn't know either of them, but they both seem good. So if you want to just get whoever's available on board, that's fine with me."

"Will do. I'll call them this afternoon."

Both the experts charged upward of $300 an hour, twice my own billing rate, which I'd purposely set on the low side so as not to burn through too much of Simone's money. The fact that she could afford all this gave her a fighting chance. I tried not to think about folks in her shoes who couldn't.

I took a bite of my Danish and looked out at the yard. At the far edge, past the roses and the carpet of yellow, a row of sunflowers stood like a fence guarding her land from the neighbor's.

"Your mom help take care of all this?" I asked. "I know how much work a beautiful yard like this is. My wife used to keep ours in Charleston like this."

"She did?" Simone looked at me. "How about when you moved down here?"

I winced.

Terri said, "She passed away. A year and a half ago."

"Oh! Mr. Munroe, I am *so* sorry."

"It's okay." I shrugged and gave a little smile; I didn't want to make her uncomfortable. "I mean, it's not, but… it's life. Everybody's got their tragedies."

"Yeah," she said, nodding slowly. "I guess they do."

Something had settled in her attitude toward me. I got the sense she trusted me more because now she felt we were at the same level. Instead of being like a doctor and patient, me high and mighty in my white coat trying to save her, we could stand side by side and compare our scars.

"Okay," I said, "well, getting back to these transactions, there were a few others I was curious about." I handed her the Venmo document. "I know you said Veronica knew Ilona Jones, but do you have any idea why Ilona would be sending her $250 every week or so?"

"Oh. Wow." She nodded as she looked at the transactions. "You know what, I wonder if that's the OtherWorld stuff."

"The what? Are you talking about that video game?"

"Yeah. You can buy and sell things within OtherWorld, and some people—influencers, mostly, and models, DJs, that kind of thing—they sell what's called an Experience. It just means you can play with them. Like, a person can pay to get into their guild for a night and go on a private Journey with them. Apex asked me to do it, and I tried it once, but I didn't feel like it was a fit for my brand. Veronica did it, though."

Terri said, "Why would Ilona pay through Venmo, though? I thought you paid for that within the game."

Simone shrugged. "Maybe she didn't have enough Agility?"

Terri must've seen my baffled look because she explained, "Agility is like points or credits. It's basically the currency within the game."

"Yeah. A player who doesn't have enough, if they want an Experience, the player granting the Experience can send them a key. So you pay outside the game and get a key within the game, which lets you into the Experience."

"Dang," I said. "That's pretty amazing. Sorry for putting on my lawyer hat here, but it sounds like a whole *other world* people can get into trouble in. I wonder if law enforcement's on that yet."

Terri said, "Not like you mean. I know a cop who plays, but the game has its own law enforcement. It's got algorithms that escalate problems to resolution teams and a reporting system and so forth."

I said, "I bet those algorithms would've pulled Veronica's financial records right off the bat. Unlike our local police force."

They laughed.

Terri took out a pen and the little notebook she took everywhere. "Simone, can you tell me your character name? And Veronica's, if you know it?"

"Yeah, let me text them to you." She picked up her phone and started typing. "Hers had numbers in it, and they're both spelled a little... like, uniquely." When she was done, she added, "I don't know what you can find out about the OtherWorld stuff, but just so you know, Apex sometimes played for us. I mean *as* us, using our avatars."

That surprised me. "They did? Why?"

"I mean... like if someone had paid for an Experience, but it conflicted with something else we had scheduled. Or, I don't know." She shrugged. "It was a way of making more money. For us, and for management."

"Wow, that is really interesting," Terri said, in a tone that indicated *interesting* meant *messed up*. She took a bite of her blueberry muffin, then raised a finger, chewing and swallowing quickly. "Sorry, I forgot to ask: do you happen to know Ilona's character name?"

"Not offhand. I might have it somewhere, or I guess I could ask her."

"Well, um..." Terri took a sip of coffee. "Leland, I don't know if you've mentioned the other thing about Ilona?"

"No, not yet." I leaned forward, getting ready to deliver the bad news. "I didn't want to tell you this on the phone, but Terri did some digging and she found out something a little strange. Your Ms. Jones has been missing since late last year."

Simone's eyes went wide. After a second of shock, she said, "Do you mean literally missing? Like… suspiciously?"

Terri said, "I don't know if it's suspicious, exactly. Her mom filed a missing persons report, but it didn't go anywhere because she was twenty years old and there was nothing indicating foul play."

"But she's *gone*? How is that not foul play?"

Terri shrugged. "Adults are allowed to disappear. That's what the police say, anyway, to explain why they're not investigating something. And, I mean, it's true, but it doesn't really account for the fact that when a young woman disappears, she's usually not okay."

"Wait, when last year? Because I talked to her, or at least…" She stopped to think. "I mean, we chatted. We were in touch. Not, like, regularly, but…"

Terri said, "Do you remember the last time you actually *saw* her? I mean, FaceTimed or anything like that?"

Simone shook her head slowly, still thinking. "No, I… we only video chatted maybe twice? Two or three times, toward the beginning of when we were in touch. The rest was just text, you know, chats. Just a second." She opened her laptop.

I asked, "What date was it she disappeared?"

Terri said, "Well, the missing persons report was filed on October 19." She flipped open her notebook and scanned a couple of pages. "Her mom said at that point she hadn't heard from her in four days."

"And what were the circumstances?"

"She lived alone, and she'd quit her job, so there was no way to know exactly when she went missing. It could've been anywhere in those four days."

"What was her job?"

"Retail. Women's clothing. She'd just finished training to be a bartender, though. That pays a lot better, and the police thought maybe she quit to take a bartending job someplace."

Simone, staring at her laptop screen, said, "Did you say October 19 of last year? Because I've heard from her… it looks like at least half a dozen times since then."

Terri said, "On what platform?"

"Insta, and also in OtherWorld. The last time was not even a month ago. Do you want screenshots?"

"Yes, I do. I'll see if I can find out what IP address those messages came from. Do the DMs sound like her?"

"I mean…" Simone started reading. "I guess? Nothing's jumping out as being weird, at least." She read for a few seconds more. "She wished me good luck for my case. So I guess she's following it?"

Terri and I exchanged a look. I could tell we were thinking along the same lines: that this weirdness with Ilona might have nothing to do with Simone's case, or it might be important somehow. On the off chance it mattered, we wanted to know more.

Terri said, "Would you mind sending me all of them? I mean, every message you two ever exchanged? I don't mean to pry into your business—"

"Oh, no problem," Simone said. "It's not like she was someone I told my deepest, darkest secrets to. This is weird, and I want to know what's going on with her. Even if it's just to make sure she's okay."

———

As I was driving home, I got a call from Terri.

"I didn't want to say this in front of Simone," she said, "because I know she's worried about her friend. But when a young woman's been missing that long…"

"Yeah, I know." There was a very good chance Ilona was dead.

"What I want to know," she said, "is who Simone has been talking to. Because if it's *not* Ilona, who is it, and why are they talking to her about this case?"

"Yup. How do you want to run that down?"

She thought for a second. "Well, the simplest, if she goes for it—I mean, if *they* go for it, whoever this is—would be to get them to click on a link that scrapes whatever data we can get. IP address, GPS coordinates if they're clicking from their phone… Or if we can get them to send Simone a photo, there might be enough metadata in it to track them down."

"Okay. Let's get it done."

———

20

THURSDAY, JUNE 25, 2020

I'd driven past the Broke Spoke a few times a day for the past week, hoping to see workers going in or out. I was still looking for Austin, and all I had to go on was his little sister's hint that he might be working there. Terri had looked for traces of him but come up dry. He had no credit, no traffic stops, or criminal record more recent than his marijuana arrest in Florida two months earlier. And he'd stopped posting on social media. In my experience, witnesses didn't lie low for no reason. I wanted to know what his reason was.

A couple of times I saw the workers' van outside the club, so I pulled in and knocked, but nobody answered.

It was Thursday evening, getting toward sundown, and I was trying again. I knocked, waited, and knocked some more. Across the lot, the truck stop terrace was open for dinner. I could hear folks eating behind the decorative screen of fan palms, saw palmetto, and stands of pale gold pampas grass that Delacourt had recently added.

I headed over. Maybe Delacourt was working, and I could find out something useful from him.

When I got there, I saw he'd added a handsomely made wooden tiki bar and some stools along one side of the terrace. It struck me that a tiki bar without people around it was a pretty sad sight. Three of the eight tables were occupied, all attended by one frazzled waitress.

I took a stool at the empty bar and nodded to her. After she'd gone inside and come back out with another table's appetizers, Delacourt appeared in the doorway and raised a hand to say hi. I did likewise, and he headed over.

"Leland! What can I get you?" He went behind the bar.

"Didn't know you were a bartender, Luke."

"I am a master of hospitality," he said with a hint of humor. "And it's a good thing because sometimes folks don't show up for their shifts. Like my bartender tonight." He picked up a towel and wiped a glass down with it. "Care for a whiskey? Or just a beer?"

I shook my head. "The thing is, I'm on medication, and it doesn't mix well with alcohol." That was a lie, but it was an easier explanation than the truth: my wife had died from driving drunk, and since then I'd lost the ability to enjoy drinking.

"I'm sorry to hear that. I feel for you."

"Tell you what," I said. "I don't want to take up space at your bar without paying you for it. How about I flip the bird at my condition by drinking something ridiculous? Can you do some kind of virgin cocktail with umbrellas and cherries and stuff like that?"

He laughed. "How about a piña colada? I can serve it inside of a real pineapple, even."

"Perfect."

He rinsed a blender out, stuck it on its base, and poured in a scoop of pineapple chunks and some coconut cream.

"From scratch!" I said. "Nice."

He nodded as he buzzed the blender. "I'm not a big fan of mixes. They have their place, but this ain't it."

"I don't know how you have the *time*," I said. "Making drinks from scratch, and running this restaurant, and overseeing the renovation over there? How do you do it?"

He laughed, glancing in the direction of the Broke Spoke.

And I saw something. I'd learned, as a prosecutor, about a thing called microexpressions. That's what I'd just seen on his face: a flash of fear, as if the Broke Spoke were an abuser that he thought might hit him again. Microexpressions go by so fast that most people miss or ignore them, but I'd been trained to know what they were: the truth peeking out for an instant.

As he added pineapple juice to the mixture in the blender, I asked, "Things not going so great with the renovation?"

"Well," he said, shrugging it off. "Renovations never do, really. I don't think I've ever seen one that went smoothly."

He was busying his hands on the counter, looking down as he wiped at something that wasn't there. Not making eye contact. I needed to get him comfortable again.

"My God, I hear you," I said. "You know, a guy I worked with up in Charleston, he and his wife redid their kitchen a few years back, and after the contractor installed the wall cabinets, tiled the whole backsplash, and installed those— What are they called? Like brackets under the cabinets, but fancy, and made of wood?"

"Oh, you mean, uh, corbels?"

"That's it! Yeah. Decorative corbels, the whole shebang. And it's beautiful, I mean, this was, I think, *marble* tile on the backsplash, you know, close to thirty bucks a square foot."

He whistled and said, "Damn. I don't think I want to hear where this is going."

"Yeah, well, at least it's his house and not yours. Everything was done. Except there was supposed to be like four outlets along this wall —this was where their coffee maker and coffee grinder and everything else was supposed to go—and he hadn't installed a single one!"

"No! Not *one*?" He looked at me, horrified.

"No electricity at all. They had to rip the whole thing out and start over. Backsplash, countertop, everything."

"God*damn*." He shook his head and laughed. As he poured my mocktail into a hollowed-out pineapple, he asked, "You really want umbrellas in this?"

"It ain't complete without them. If you got 'em, give me three or four!"

He laughed, grabbed a handful from under the bar, and started poking their toothpick handles into the pineapple. The sunset was lighting the sky pink behind him, and he was looking relaxed again.

When he was done, he slid it over and I took a drink. "That is excellent," I said. "Feels like I'm relaxing on a beach someplace. You should make yourself a real one. Might help you deal with the stress from that renovation. Who you got working on it?"

The look flickered across his face again—that sense of him cowering and then a flash of wariness. "Aw, nobody. Why do you ask?"

"Lord, I just want to know who not to hire!" I took another sip of my drink and then said, like it had just occurred to me, "I hope you didn't get your contractor recommendations from the, uh, family? The folks who own the place? They're— Well, I shouldn't say."

I played with one of the paper umbrellas for a second while he fought his curiosity and lost. "Why not?"

"Aw, well, I'm sure you know the background, at least. Father in jail awaiting trial on homicide charges, clueless pothead son now owns the place."

"He doesn't own all of it," he said, a little smugly.

"Oh, you got in on that? On paper and everything?"

His little smirk said yes.

"Good," I said. "'Cause that boy couldn't manage a restaurant to save his life. I'd be surprised if he can manage much more than picking his own nose."

Delacourt snorted with laughter.

"And so what I was afraid of," I said, "was if the kid was calling the shots down here, he'd have got you to hire all his pothead friends and nothing would get done. Although obviously that's not what happened over on this half of the property." I raised my pineapple and gestured around the terrace with it. "This side moved pretty fast, considering the pandemic hit halfway through. And it looks great. You use a different company over here? Or different crews?"

"Uh, yeah, matter of fact, it was a Charleston outfit I brought down with me for this side. They're real good. I'd recommend them any day."

He was speaking faster than he had before. I had the sense he was steering me to talk about this other contractor to get me off the previous topic.

"You would? That's good to know." I pulled a pen out of my pocket and got a napkin from the dispenser two feet away. "Okay, what's their name?"

He told me, and I wrote it down, then tucked both napkin and pen away. "I know there's nobody of that caliber down here. You must have some local boys ripping up the carpet and doing demo."

His eyebrows moved in a way that I read as, *Yep.*

I shook my head sympathetically. "No wonder it's taking so long. Oh, matter of fact," I said, screwing up my eyebrows like this recollection had just come to me, "I thought I saw Austin McKrall heading in once when I drove by."

I could see he knew who I meant and took what I'd said to be true. So the kid was indeed working for him.

"You got a lot of fine woodwork to do in there?"

He gave a polite chuckle. He did not want to say more, and figuring out why got added to my to-do list.

I looked around. Two more tables were now occupied. "Glad to see the place filling up. It'll be even better when this pandemic is done with and you can put a few more tables in here."

"Oh, hell yes. This distancing thing is killing me."

"Yeah, I hear you. Girardeau was saying, up in Charleston, some of his favorite restaurants are really struggling."

His face tensed at the mention of the name. Girardeau had said no such thing; I hadn't discussed restaurants or social distancing with him at all. I just wanted to check if my previous impression that Delacourt didn't like him was correct.

"Apart from that piece of wisdom, though," I said, "he's kind of a jackass, ain't he."

With gusto, Delacourt said, "Yes, he *is*."

I laughed and raised my piña colada to toast that sentiment. After a sip, I said lightly, "But have you *truly* seen his dark side? I mean, have you catered an event at his home?"

His eyes flicked to me and away again: an off-balance look. I was getting to him, and I didn't want to. It wasn't useful to have a person wary of you.

"I'm just joking," I said. "I can't resist making fun of Girardeau. I mean, the crocodile shoes, and all that." I rolled my eyes.

"You ever see his blue snakeskin boots?"

"Aw, he does *not* have— Are you serious?"

He nodded. "To match his car. That's what he told me. Had them made in the same shade."

"My God."

We marveled at that for a second. He started lining up some glasses on the bar, preparing, I supposed, for the dinner rush.

"To be fair, though," I said, "he's pretty damn good in a courtroom."

"Oh, I'd hire him as a *lawyer*."

So it wasn't some unfortunate legal run-in that had made him dislike Girardeau. It was something personal.

Figuring that out was going to have to wait. I'd already come too close to making Delacourt feel like I was interrogating him, and the dinner rush was starting. I finished my drink, pulled my wallet out, and put ten bucks on the bar. "Keep the change," I said. "This place is kind of an anchor for Basking Rock, and I'm glad to know you're in charge."

It was nearly dark as I walked back across the parking lot. The workers' van was gone; they must've left while I was chatting at the tiki bar. I swore under my breath. I'd wasted a week trying to collar Austin in a way that could seem casual and not confrontational. It wasn't going to work. It was time to play hardball.

As I turned my car toward home, my mind went back to Delacourt and Girardeau. Something about them kept bothering me. I didn't know why I cared that they didn't like each other, or how it could possibly matter to anything, but for some reason I couldn't let it go.

———

Late that night, as I was working on the case in my home office, I got a text from Terri: *You up?*

Yep.

In a second, the phone rang. I said, "Burning the midnight oil, are you?"

"Yeah, takes one to know one. But I wouldn't call so late if it wasn't something weird. Simone finally sent those DMs with Ilona today, and something's up."

"Yeah? What's that?" I leaned back in my chair and started swiveling it from side to side. The rhythm helped me think.

"I'm going to start from the beginning. The not-weird part. So, they're friends, they talk about life and a little bit about God. They're both... spiritual, I guess. Ilona asks for advice because maybe she wants to be an influencer too—this was, like, two years ago, almost, when they first started talking."

"Okay..."

I felt Squatter nuzzling my ankle and pulled open my desk drawer to get him a treat.

"And it starts getting a little weird. Not crazy, just, like, Ilona kind of thinks of herself as psychic, and Simone's supportive, but she lays some religion on her. As in, 'Don't go overboard with that. As long as you're right with the Lord, yeah, sometimes He sends you signs.'"

"And this is all before she disappeared?" Squatter licked my fingers, looking for more.

"Yeah. And Ilona sends her these supportive messages after Simone got arrested, 'Have faith' kind of stuff. There's a couple more like that in late October, November—"

"So, after she disappeared?"

"Right. Then, around Thanksgiving, she sends a DM saying she's got a bad feeling about Simone's case. She says, 'I know this isn't what you want to hear, and it's not my business, but I truly believe Mr. Girardeau is right about the plea thing.'"

"Huh." I picked Squatter up and set him on my lap.

"That's not the weird part. The weird part is that her last message, which was two weeks ago, was about you—"

"*What?*"

"It was along the same lines, but it said, 'Mr. Munroe would probably make a lot more money losing your trial than winning by getting that syringe thrown out. Maybe, like Mr. Girardeau said, you should try to make that evidence go away.'"

"What the heck?" I didn't know what to think. "So Simone's talking to this random person online about... what, my strategy?"

"No. That's the thing. Simone said she sent me all the messages, to and from, and if that's true, she never told Ilona—or whoever this is— what you're doing. She never even said your name."

"Well, my name you could get from the news." I petted Squatter, trying to think. "But—"

"But not the rest, right? Nobody should know you're not planning on moving to exclude that evidence until, what, right before trial?"

"Exactly. Who the hell are we dealing with, here? And how are they — Like, where's the leak?"

"I'm on it," she said.

————

21

WEDNESDAY, JULY 1, 2020

I parked not too far from the Charleston waterfront and headed for the restaurant. Terri—or, rather, her online alter ego, Kayleigh—had convinced Austin's former girlfriend to talk with me, and we were meeting her at a swanky rooftop place for dinner.

The city still wasn't nearly as crowded as it normally was. I was glad not to have to share the elevator with anyone, and glad again when I got to the roof and saw the socially distanced tables, more than half of which were empty. The lack of potential eavesdroppers, not to mention the pop music playing through speakers by the bar, made delicate conversations easier to have. I nodded to Terri, who'd driven separately, and headed over to meet her at the far edge of the terrace.

"Good choice," I said, sitting down. "This is a hell of a view." We could see the water on one side and the setting sun on the other.

"Yeah, it's wonderful."

I didn't know if it was the sunset light or something else, but it felt good to look at her.

"I just noticed that a minute ago," she said, pointing inland. "Isn't that Apex?"

I turned and saw the brick building on the other side of a small park. "Oh yeah. Funny."

We chatted about our drives up, and then I saw a young blonde woman coming across the terrace. She looked like an imperfect version of her airbrushed profile photo: pretty, and about twenty-two. She smiled tentatively. I got the sense she wasn't used to being in such a fine establishment.

I stood to greet her. "Great to meet you in person, Madison. Thank you so much. This is private investigator Terri Washington, who I mentioned on the phone."

They said their hellos. The waitress had followed Madison over, so we got menus and ordered drinks. We chatted about nothing, and then about Madison—she was a tour guide on one of the city's walking tours while working part time toward a degree in hospitality management. We sympathized with how the COVID shutdowns and plummeting tourist numbers had affected her. When the drinks came, we ordered our food. She just got a salad, maybe because she felt awkward eating on a stranger's dime, or maybe because, like so many other young women, she suffered from the delusion that she needed to lose weight.

Terri and I made eye contact. I could see she agreed that the mood was now relaxed enough to get to the point.

"So, Madison," I said, "I truly appreciate that you're willing to talk with us about this case. And before I get into my questions, I wanted to check with you: is there anything you're wondering about, or any questions you have about why we wanted to meet with you?"

"Well, um…" She looked away, uncertain. "I mean, I want to help…"

"And that's *so* important," Terri said. "Thank you."

Madison nodded and took a gulp of her wine. "I mean, I guess… *my* thing is… or what I'm wondering is, do you really think Austin *did* it?" Her eyes were wide. She looked like a little kid trying to wrap their mind around something that was beyond their comprehension.

"We don't know," Terri said.

"Right," I said. "And we're not prosecuting him. We're not cops at all. We're just trying to understand what happened—and hopefully stop an innocent young woman from going to jail."

Madison nodded, seeming reassured. The waitress returned with our food, and we ordered another round of drinks.

Madison said, "Okay, so, I really don't think Austin could kill anyone, except maybe by accident. He was never a violent person." She took a bite of salad.

Terri said. "Do you mean, apart from that one domestic violence incident? Or—"

Madison was shaking her head. "That was, I mean, honestly, a mutual fight. That was the night where he said, um, you know, he was leaving, and I kind of freaked out. He did shake me, like—" She gestured, elbows bent, hands out in front, like she was holding some imaginary person by the arms. "But that's all."

Terri and I exchanged a look. We were both wondering, I could tell, whether this girl was minimizing a violent incident, as abused women often did.

"I'm so sorry that happened to you," Terri said.

"Could I just ask," I said, "what the fight was about?"

Madison finished her wine, set the goblet down, and sighed. "It was… basically, as soon as he saw that girl, I mean Veronica, he was gone.

We were done before they even got together. And it was like he was dumping me for nothing, for this, like, *fantasy*, after all that I'd, like, done? I supported him through so much, for two *years*."

"You felt like you deserved better," Terri said.

"Right! Yeah, exactly." Her tone was getting angrier.

I said, "That's hard. It's unfair."

"Right? I mean, I'd let him move in with me because his dad— Things were just really hard at home, and he wanted to get away and live in the city. He wanted to somehow get his little sister out, too, and we were talking about how to do that."

"His sister?" I said. "The— What is she, about ten years old?"

"Yeah. I think she must be going on twelve now. She's real little, though. But he was saving up, and…"

I saw a flicker of something she didn't want to say.

"About how much had he saved up?" I asked.

"Oh, uh…" She looked down at her salad, speared a few leaves, and took a bite.

Terri said, "You know what, when I was your age, I had a boyfriend who convinced me to give him money. A lot of it. Did that happen to you, too?"

A flash of anger crossed her face. "Yeah. Out of my freaking student loans, you know? And on top of that, I didn't even ask him for rent, just his share of utilities. I was trying to help because we had all these plans."

"That doesn't sound fair."

"Right? It's not!" She looked around—checking, I thought, whether anyone was close enough to hear—and then said, "I never went to the cops with this, and besides, I figure now he's punished enough, with her dying and all, but he was dealing. He was getting out of it, toward the end of— Like, when he broke up with me. It was getting too weird, so he was getting out. But that's how he was saving money, besides his regular job."

I shook my head in sympathy. "Dang." I did not say what I was thinking, which was that it was utterly astonishing for a drug-dealing boyfriend to not be charged with the manslaughter of a girlfriend who died of an overdose right beside him. Why had they passed him over in favor of Simone?

"We're not the police," Terri said, "and nothing you tell us can get him convicted for dealing."

She was right, in the sense that if he did go to trial for that, we couldn't testify about what she'd told us. It'd be secondhand information. In other words, hearsay.

Madison nodded. She looked around again; there was still nobody sitting nearby, and the restaurant's piped-in music put a veil over each table's conversation. "He just sold party drugs, though. Not, like, the hard stuff."

"Oh, like ecstasy?" I said.

"Yeah. And weed. He said he didn't even want to know the guys who sell hard drugs. They'd kill you for nothing, and he—I mean, obviously he didn't want to die, but he especially didn't because he wanted to be there for his sister."

"Does he just have the one sister?"

"Yeah, one little brother, and then the youngest is the sister. Her name's Jodie."

As I wrote that down, I wondered if the memo on that Venmo transfer had something to do with her.

After dinner, Terri and I ambled along the waterfront. We chatted about everything but Simone's case—a dark street with who knows what passersby was no place to discuss that, even though the traffic and the rush of water from a nearby fountain did make things harder to overhear.

We passed a glitzy restaurant, and then a blue car parked up a side street caught my eye. "Hey, here's your chance," I said, starting toward it and beckoning Terri to follow. "You can admire Girardeau's Lambo in all its glory."

She laughed and caught up with me. "My goodness," she said as we got close. "It doesn't look *real*. How much does one of these things cost?"

"Probably a quarter million? Maybe more."

She shook her head in amazement. "I mean, if I had a quarter million to spare... I just can't picture any situation where *this* is what I'd spend it on."

"Yeah, and I don't even want to know how much insurance costs. Or what it'd run you for repairs if it got dinged by a shopping cart or a baby stroller—or a pebble, for that matter."

We walked around it, checking it out from different angles and chatting about all the things we'd rather do with that much money. We were enjoying ourselves, and I was enjoying the feel of the night air after the sweltering day. Then I heard yelling from the corner and looked up to see a familiar figure twenty or thirty feet away, waving his fist in our direction. His face was lit up by the corner window of a restaurant, and a woman teetered on high heels behind him.

I called out, "Girardeau? That you? Evening!"

"Oh," he said, and his fist fell to his side. "Leland?"

"Yeah!"

His tone turned friendly. "What the hell!"

He slipped an arm around his lady friend, who slumped against him, and they headed toward us. When they passed under a streetlight, I saw she was wearing a silver minidress so short that it would've been only slightly more revealing if she'd just wrapped a piece of duct tape around her bikini area.

"Remember Terri?" I said. "We were in town for dinner, and I spotted your car. Thought I'd show it to her, since she didn't have a chance to check it out last time."

"It's beautiful," she said. "Looks like something out of a video game."

He laughed. "It sure does. I like that. Oh, this is, uh, Marushka? Baby, say hi to my friends."

"Oh, yes," I said. "Hello."

Marushka had seemed fine when I'd met her at the Apex offices, but tonight, her glazed eyes made me think of the Stepford wives. Her teeth, in their fixed smile, were perfect. She raised a floppy hand in greeting but didn't say anything.

"You want to hear it?" Girardeau said, reaching into his pocket. "The engine sound is like nothing else," he said, bleeping his key fob. The car roared to life. In the flare of the headlights, I thought I saw a streak of blood at the corner of Marushka's mouth as she wavered at Girardeau's side. It wasn't lipstick; hers was pink.

Terri looked at me. She'd seen it too.

"Damn," I said. "You weren't kidding about that engine. What is that, a V8?"

"You kidding me? This is a V12. Six hundred and ninety horsepower."

I whistled like I was impressed. "What's the zero to sixty time?"

"Two point five seconds."

"Well, I'll be goddamned. Mind if I take a look at the—are those gauges, or a digital display?"

"Be my guest. It's all digital—that's where it really looks like a video game," he said, giving Terri a smile.

She smiled back. "Here," she said, holding out an arm to support his dazed, slow-blinking date. "We girls can just step over here while you show him."

"Thanks." Girardeau slung his door open while I went around to the passenger side. Over the top of the car, Terri, with Marushka leaning on her, gave me a jerk of the head to indicate they were going up the street.

I got in the car. I wasn't sure what she was up to, but whatever it was, I figured she'd need me to buy some time. We slammed our doors, and I admired every facet of his Lamborghini, asking about the engine and its performance, the leather seats, the sound system, and every other detail I could think of. He was happy to talk about all of it. I guessed he didn't normally get to show off his car nearly as much as he wanted to.

A few minutes later, when I was running out of questions, he said, "You want to take a spin?"

"Oh, hell yes!"

"Let me just tell—" He looked out the window, saw nobody there, and twisted to look up and down the street. "Did you see where they went?"

"Uh-uh." I looked out my side.

We both got out and looked around. "What the *hell*?" he said.

"I wonder if your girlfriend might not have been feeling so well. Is there a ladies' room around here they might have gone to? Maybe back at that restaurant?"

Girardeau was making a phone call. He paced back and forth with the phone at his ear. Nobody answered, I guessed, because he swore and hung up. While he was texting, I pulled my phone out and did the same.

I said, "I'm going to check in the restaurant," and headed back down the street. He came with, and we were looking in the corner window when my phone dinged. "Oh my," I said, reading Terri's text. "Yeah, she got sick."

He pulled my hand over so he could see the text. As he read it, I felt him relax a little. "Huh," he said. "Goddammit. Where are they?"

As he watched, I texted, *You in the restaurant?*

In a few seconds, she answered, *No. BRB.*

"What's that?" he asked.

"Oh, my son tells me it means 'Be right back.' I wonder where they went."

While I was texting Terri to ask where to meet them, Girardeau phoned his girlfriend again. She didn't answer, and he hung up with an angry sigh. "This was going to be a great night," he said, "if you catch my drift. You see the legs on that girl? Goddamn. If I didn't know better, I'd think you were bad luck."

I laughed. "Oh," I said, looking at my phone. "She says to meet back at the car."

We headed back. As we approached, Terri emerged, alone, from a little park up the street.

"What the *hell*?" Girardeau demanded. "You *leave* her someplace?"

"Oh my goodness," she said. "Of course not." As she got under a streetlight, I saw her dress was all wet down the front. "That poor girl," she said. "She must've had way too much to drink. She got sick all over me! I cleaned her up as best I could and sent her home in an Uber."

"God*dammit*!"

"Well," I said, "at least she didn't get sick in your car."

"Aw, hell," he said, wide-eyed at the thought. "Yeah, goddamn!"

"I am *so* glad," Terri said. "I don't know if you'd *ever* get the smell out."

"Yeah, that's— Damn," he said. "That would *not* have been worth it." He laughed and shook my hand. "I guess you're good luck after all."

We said our goodbyes. Terri and I walked back down to the corner, and then she took me around the block and back up to the other side of the little park, where we found her Subaru.

"Hop in," she said. "I'll take you back to your car."

She had tinted windows, so it wasn't until we got in, shut the doors, and she pointed back between the front seats that I noticed Marushka sprawled on the back seat, asleep.

"Holy shit! Excuse me." Then I started laughing. "*Man*, that was smooth, the way you— Wait, why didn't you get her an Uber?"

"Things can happen," she said. "I don't know who the driver is. I'm not going to take this poor girl out of the Girardeau frying pan just to throw her into the Uber fire."

She plugged an address into her GPS, explaining that she'd managed to get part of it from Marushka before she passed out but ended up having to look in her purse for her driver's license. A few blocks into the drive, I realized the car smelled fine and asked, "Did she really throw up?"

"No. I emptied my water bottle down the front of my dress for added realism."

"Wow," I said, shaking my head in admiration. "You are weapons-grade. Girardeau has no idea what hit him."

When we pulled up at Marushka's house, Terri said, "Put your business card in her purse. I already left mine. Maybe she'll have something interesting to say."

"Yeah. I was wondering," I said, pulling out my wallet, "if there's some kind of a conflict here. I know Girardeau's represented folks at Apex. I don't know if there's a rule against it, but I'd feel weird dating a young girl who worked for a business I got a lot of work from."

"That's because you're a decent human being."

I scribbled *Hope you feel better* on a business card and stuck it in Marushka's purse. Then we half carried her up the steps and delivered her into the arms of her roommates. One said "Thanks," but the others didn't speak. They shared her high-cheekboned, long-legged look, and they did not invite us in.

———

22

FRIDAY, JULY 3, 2020

I was on my third cup of coffee of the morning when Terri called. When I congratulated her on the other evening's heroism, she said, "That's what I was calling about, sort of. Yesterday I checked the title on that house where we dropped her off, and it's owned by Apex, which I thought was a little weird."

"Huh." I thought about it for a second. "That is odd. And you know what else, I know one word isn't much to go on, but did it sound to you like the girl who thanked us might've had an accent?"

"Actually, yeah. I don't know what kind, but she didn't sound like she was from the South."

"Right. Not at all." The word, as she'd said it, had a crack to it, not the elastic twang we had down here.

"So," she continued, "Apex runs Simone's career, they ran Veronica's, they hosted the party. And that Ms. Rutledge, her assistant—or whatever Marushka is—lives in a house that they own, which... I don't know what that means, but it doesn't seem like a normal setup to me. I want to know more about them."

"Yeah. Tell you what, I'll give Roy a call. He's been doing business and property law for, what, thirty-plus years now? He'll know how to run this down."

———

Two hours later, Noah finally dragged himself out of bed. Once he'd achieved consciousness through caffeine, he came into my office, still in his boxer shorts, and sat down in the armchair. He looked like he was thinking something through.

I quit working and said, "What's up?"

"I was just wondering… I was playing OtherWorld last night, and after Shawn went to bed, I went looking for Veronica and Simone."

"Veronica? She's still—her character's still in there?"

"Oh, yeah. Just because a person dies, that doesn't mean their character does."

"Well, did you— Is she still *playing*?"

"Somebody is. I mean, I didn't play with her last night, but I've found her before, and this time she was in a different realm. So somebody moved her. But that's not what I came in here to tell you. The *weird* thing is, I thought Simone didn't play anymore, right?"

"That's what she told me."

He nodded, eyebrows raised. "Okay, so then I want to know, why'd this girl I play with a lot get offered a private Journey with her?"

"What, you mean one of those paying things?"

"Yeah. It must've happened after I logged off because this girl I was on a raid with last night messaged me at like 5 a.m. I just saw it now. She said she got an offer, and she thinks Simone is really cool, but she was asking if I thought it was legit. You know, because of the case and stuff. She wasn't sure if Simone was still playing."

"Why's she asking you? Please tell me you haven't been discussing Simone's case online."

"Course not. This girl doesn't even know who I am in real life. She does know I live in Basking Rock. She once mentioned Simone, and I was like, oh, yeah, I know her, I used to see her around."

I wondered why he'd lied, or at least slanted the truth. Maybe that was just how people interacted online. "Huh. So, when she asked if it was legit, what'd you say?"

"I didn't answer yet. I wanted to check with you."

"Good call. Thank you. Listen, I'm going to check with Simone, so give me a minute. I'll let you know what to do."

After he cleared out, I texted Terri to see if she could talk, then dialed Simone. Once we were all on the line, I explained the situation.

Simone was outraged. "I haven't played since before Veronica died! And I *told* them, I could not have been more clear that I didn't want them playing for me anymore. My whole brand is health, you know? Physical health. The *body*, right? What does that have to do with some avatar jumping around medieval castles in an online game? But wait a minute, let me go check something."

When she came back, she told us her statements showed that she hadn't been paid anything for online game play since the previous spring. She was livid. She wanted to call Apex right away, to demand that they send her whatever they owed and stop selling these Experiences, but I talked her down. I did not want to alert the company to anything yet.

"Did Noah's friend say how much a key would cost?" Terri asked.

I leaned out the door and hollered the question. Noah looked up from the toast he was buttering and told me, "Fifteen hundred Agility. And the window's only open from... I forget what time exactly, but it's next weekend."

I didn't understand much of that, but I repeated it into the phone.

"Okay, that's about a hundred and fifty dollars," Terri explained. "And the window's probably two hours—that's how it works. They make it a little hard for you. It's got a cost, it's short, and it's not necessarily at a convenient time."

"Yeah, they told me that," Simone said. "It's a psychology thing. It makes it seem like a rare opportunity, so people get invested in it. I thought that was... kind of gross, you know? Like, manipulative."

"Tell her to do it," Terri said. "Wait, can I talk to Noah? Speakerphone is fine."

I went and got him. She asked what he knew about this girl. She was nineteen, or so she'd said, and she lived outside Atlanta.

Terri said, "And it sounds like she's worried she's being catfished. Smart girl. Okay, Noah, what if you tell her you're worried too, and you'll... well, since you can't go with her in the game, maybe you could be on the phone with her. We'll get you a burner phone, you give her the number, she'll see it's in Basking Rock. And she can tell you what Simone says, or if that's too distracting while she's playing, maybe we can set up a way for you to watch it on video."

"I like this," Simone said. "I want to know what they're telling people in my name."

After we finalized plans and hung up, I called Terri back. I'd learned enough about the game from their discussion to have an idea in mind.

"Hello again," she said.

"Hi there. It sounds like I ought to subpoena some records from this game company. Can you find out the contact info for that?"

"Yeah, definitely. You'll need to decide which approach to take. I helped a friend get these kinds of records a couple years ago, for a different game. There's a statute that covers it, the Electronic Communications… something. I don't recall the rest of the name, but all the game companies have rules and procedures that parallel it, so you have to pick which route to go."

"What are the routes?"

"Well, there's subpoenas, of course, and that'll get you one level of information. The account holder, IP address, that kind of thing. Court orders will get you more, and if we were law enforcement, search warrants could get more too."

"I'm guessing chat records require a court order?"

"I would think. But there's also another route… I don't recall the details, but you can send them a consent form signed by the user. I think it needs to be witnessed or notarized too, or verified somehow. And with that, you can get everything."

Toward dinnertime, I got a Zoom invite from Roy with the message, *Got some info*. I logged on at the appointed time, expecting to see him looking tanned and relaxed. He was in the Outer Banks with his daughter and her family. Instead, I found myself face-to-face with a unicorn wearing a polo shirt and muttering in frustration.

"You look different, Roy. Is that what a beach vacation does to you?"

"Goddammit," the unicorn said. "I let my granddaughter use my laptop to Zoom with her daddy, and now I don't know how to turn this thing off."

"Well, I'm fine with it if you are. I can try to put a filter on myself, if you don't like being the only one. Maybe a pug or something?"

"I do not need another ridiculous thing on my screen. Anyway, my daughter's about to put dinner on the table; I don't want to waste any more time trying to fix this. So, listen, I had Laura look up what you asked for. She's going to send you some documents, but she gave me the gist."

He pulled something toward him on the desk. When he looked down at his notes, the unicorn's rainbow mane fell gracefully forward.

"She ran down the ownership on that company. And I don't know how much I need to explain—maybe you've mastered all this now, since you took that business law CLE?" The unicorn gave me a deadpan look.

I chuckled and said, "Roy, I defer to your expertise."

He laughed. "Okay, so what we found is a whole lot of very deliberate *nothing*. Apex Image Management is an LLC inside of a shell corporation inside of a holding company—the list goes on, from here through Delaware, and then the trail ends in the Caymans. That's where the parent company is, or at least the highest-level company I could get to so far."

"The Cayman Islands?"

"I'm not aware of any other Caymans, yeah. So, offshore, tax haven, money laundering haven. It's only been less than a year that it's even been possible to get the names of a Cayman company's current directors. Which Laura is working on, but that takes time."

"Why would this management company in Charleston—"

"Exactly. This is an awfully sophisticated setup for a company operating out of a single office in Charleston, which is all they *appear* to be. And I don't know how it works in the Caymans, but on the US end it's a pain in the ass to run all those different entities, with all the corporate filings, the minutes of shareholder meetings, the tax forms, and so forth. If I had a client running a business like this, I'd tell them to form an LLC or an S corp, period, end of story. Or, depending on their funding situation, maybe a C corp at the most."

"Well," I said, "this sounds shady as hell."

"It is," the unicorn said, nodding hard. "Not only do you not need this level of complexity to run a business like that, you don't *want* it. Not unless you're trying to hide something."

———

23

SATURDAY, JULY 18, 2020

W e'd found Austin, or Terri had. After lunch, I was planning to drive down to where he was staying and see if he'd talk to me. It was about a forty-minute drive, in a rural area outside Bluffton. Two weeks earlier Terri had seen him leave the Broke Spoke in a silver Accord—"one of the commonest cars in America," she reminded me. He'd sped off before she could get the full plate number, so it took a while more before she could track him down.

"I wasn't going to walk up to it in the Broke Spoke parking lot in broad daylight and slap a tracer on it," she'd said. She'd had to wait until she spotted the car someplace more crowded and anonymous.

When the tracer told us where Austin seemed to live—the place the car ended up most nights—Terri looked it up and found an old ad for it online. The landlord was an older guy who lived in Bluffton; the house was a two-bedroom in the woods renting for $600. Noah called the number, pretending he was looking for a place, and the man told him, "Sorry, son, I got a boy there right now."

We hadn't been able to watch Noah's online friend in OtherWorld as she had her Experience with whoever was pretending to be Simone.

Noah had learned the hard way that asking questions sometimes scared folks off. You had to learn that several times, I'd found, screwing up in several different ways, before you could even start to get competent.

Terri had started trying to get herself invited on a private Journey, but it seemed like a long shot, so in the meantime we'd gone to plan B. I helped Simone submit a notarized consent form so she could get a copy of everything OtherWorld had on her account: login dates and times, messages, chat transcripts, all with the IP addresses that she and anyone she was talking to were posting from. She could've gotten the transcripts herself just by logging in, but knowing where the messages were being posted from was at least as important as knowing what they said.

As I headed toward Bluffton, I thought through what talking with Austin might be like. I'd known lawyers who prepared bullet points of topics they wanted to hit, but I only did that in the courtroom when I had limited time to get the information I needed from the witness's mouth to the jury's ears. If the jury needed to hear points A through E in order for me to win, I'd jot down those points on my legal pad and glance at it while examining the witness.

But outside the courtroom, looking at a human being who had no duty to talk to you at all, much less any sworn obligation to tell the truth, I'd never had any success in proceeding according to plan. You had to respond to whatever was in front of you: a flash of fear, a sidelong glance, a muscle clenching in someone's jaw. You had to see it—that was the first art on which the rest depended—and then you had to respond.

So I wasn't thinking, as I drove, about what to say to Austin. Feeling the humidity, putting the window up and the AC on, I was just thinking on who he was.

What I knew of him was that he was a hard worker who worked with his hands. He made things, beautiful things, but he hadn't been good in school. I'd reached out to a couple of his teachers early on, but they remembered him vaguely: just another local boy who didn't much like to read.

He liked money, and for his age he did pretty well with the fine carpentry, but for some reason, he needed more. He'd dealt drugs, so he was willing to break rules, and he'd done it with enough luck and discretion not to get caught for anything serious. I wasn't sure why a young man who was working a good job—and maybe still earning more by dealing party drugs—would pull $2,500 out of his girlfriend's account behind her back. That could be nearly half a year's rent around here. Did it have something to do with his sister? And if so, what?

The foliage got thicker and darker as I headed south. Austin had stolen from Veronica, it looked like... but I did believe, from watching him testify and from talking to his ex, that he loved her. I'd driven by her parents' house, and the ramp he'd built was still there. The house was a pretty Victorian, and he'd made the ramp look like something off the *Titanic*, like the ship's grand staircase with its carved curlicues. It wasn't some modern accessibility add-on; it was a fine feature that looked like it could've been original to the house.

There was no way the man who spent untold hours making that did not love Veronica.

I turned from one small road onto an even smaller one. I checked my phone; it had one bar of reception. When I turned again and got a ways down the long gravel road that Austin lived on, that one bar started flickering. How'd a kid his age survive out here, I wondered.

I slowed as I came up on a silver car parked in front of a shabby little house that I recognized from the ad. I parked and crunched across the gravel toward the porch.

The front door opened before I got to the steps, and a shadow behind the screen said, "The hell you doing here?"

I stopped. "Austin? That you?"

"Don't fucking lie to me," he said. "Don't pretend you don't know. I don't have to say one word to you. I know my rights."

"Yeah, you're right, you don't have to." I nodded. "You absolutely do not have to. But is it stupid of me to wish you would?"

He thought that through but didn't answer.

I said, "I guess I should've realized, a man who lives way out here is not a man who takes kindly to company."

From behind the screen door, I heard a snort that might've been a laugh.

I waited for him to speak again. More questions seemed pointless; I'd never met anybody who liked to be interrogated. I looked up at the trees. They were so thick I could hardly see the sky.

Finally, he said, "Now that you know you ain't wanted, what the hell are you still *doing* here?"

I wanted him to come out. I was at a disadvantage, having a conversation with a shadow fifteen feet away, a man who could see my face when I couldn't see his.

"Yeah, I can go," I said with a shrug, starting to turn. Then I looked back at him and said, "Oh, I talked to your little sister the other—"

He burst out the door and shouted, "You stay away from my sister! If you go near her again, I will *end* you!"

He was a little taller than average and built strong. With his left hand he'd pointed hard at me as he was yelling, but his right hand was held at hip level, a little to the rear. It was a position I took to mean he was ready to reach for a gun stashed in the back of his waistband.

I said, real calm, "I know you've been trying to help her."

"You don't know *nothing!*" He stepped closer to the edge of the porch. His right hand stayed at the ready.

"I don't know nothing?"

"You don't know me, or my family, or nothing!"

"Well," I said, "I met your dad. And I can see why a man might want to get his sister out of there."

His arms relaxed a little, and he looked off to the left—just to stop looking at me, I thought. He was breathing hard, but not too fast. I sensed the temperature of our conversation going down a degree.

I gave him a minute and then said, "It's hard, getting a kid out. But it can be done."

He sighed. "You don't know my business." But he said it more softly, and he was looking at the ground.

"No, I don't," I said. "But keeping a child safe, I kind of think that's everybody's business."

He looked up for a second, like he was checking me for bullshit, and then down again. "*You* can't keep her safe."

My tone, I knew, was important. This was no place for defensiveness. With nothing but mild curiosity, I said, "I can't?"

"You keep criminals out of prison," he said. "That's *your* job."

"I keep crooks out of prison?"

"Well. Sometimes, I guess." He cleared his throat and spat off the porch. He still wasn't looking at me, so I studied him for a minute.

The bravado, or really the fear, that had sent him snarling out the door at me was mostly gone.

"Can I just tell you two things, and then I'll get back in my car and leave you be?"

He shrugged like it made no difference to him.

"I'm sorry," I said. "Three things. Because the first one is that I came here unarmed. Just so you know. And I'm getting a card out of my pocket, that's all."

He watched while I slid a business card out of my chest pocket, slowly, with my fingertips.

"I'm just going to put this on the ground there, under that rock. You do what you want with it, or leave it there to rot."

I leaned down real slow and tucked the card under a fist-sized rock.

When I stood back up, I said, "Okay, the second thing is, I got a good friend who's in social work. If there's a way to get your sister out of that house, she'll know it. I can't promise nothing, because I don't know what's possible, but I can tell you she will try."

The air was getting heavier. I felt a raindrop hit my shoulder.

He still wasn't talking or looking at me, but I didn't expect him to.

"And here's the third thing," I said, "and then I'll go. The third thing is, if your daddy got arrested for what he's done to you kids, I would not take his case. Not for $10 million. Not for nothing on this earth."

I gave him a nod, and then I walked to my car.

———

24

FRIDAY, JULY 31, 2020

Terri and I were at Simone's, eating brunch on the veranda while we looked through what had just come back from the company behind the OtherWorld game. That morning, Simone had gotten a set of PDFs totaling more than a thousand pages. She'd forwarded copies, and we were sitting with our laptops and our coffee, each of us looking through a different section page by page.

Terri said, "The players 'you'"—she made air quotes—"are messaging with are all over the Southeast. I've got IP addresses in twenty-one different cities and towns so far."

"Does that seem normal?" Simone asked. "I mean, I do have more followers in the Southeast than in other parts of the country, but they're not *all* down here."

"That's a real interesting question," Terri said. "I don't know." She made a note, adding it to her running list of things we'd noticed or wondered about.

"How many players, total?" I asked.

"Uh, so far, 168. And the Atlanta area has the most."

"My goodness, 'I've' been chatting back and forth with nearly two hundred people?" Simone looked incredulous. "And going on raids with all of them? How can the players believe that? How would I even have the time?"

"Would they all know each other?" I asked. "Or know about each other?"

"I guess not. Well, apart from whoever was on the raid with me. And I guess that wouldn't normally be more than... eight or ten people at a time."

Terri nodded, then asked me, "What do you have on the Journeys?"

"Well, let's see." I counted. "Okay, in the past six months, 'Simone' invited eighty-three players on private Journeys, and twelve of them accepted. The prices were anywhere from, uh, what is Agility right now? About ten to a dollar? So I guess it's from about fifty to three hundred bucks."

Terri cocked her head like that didn't make sense. "Is there any pattern to that? I mean, were there more takers at the lower prices, or...?"

I scanned the page. "No, it doesn't look like it. There's four at two-fifty or three hundred, and then another four at fifty or a hundred... Yeah, it's all over the map."

Terri thought about that a minute. She picked up her cheese Danish, took a bite, and chewed it slowly, looking off toward the sunflowers. I smiled to myself. I'd noticed her habit of chewing on a snack when she was trying to figure something out, as if it would kick-start the gears turning in her brain.

It worked. She turned to Simone and said, "You remember what you said a while back about the psychology of this? That Apex made it inconvenient and a little expensive to make people feel like it was important?"

"Yeah, of course. And I thought that just wasn't right."

"Did they ever tell you how they set the prices?"

She thought, then shook her head. "No. But I think I know where you're going with this."

I didn't, so I sipped my coffee and listened.

Terri was nodding. "The price they offer to any particular player isn't random. Because that wouldn't work, right? To some folks, fifty bucks is a stretch, but to others it's nothing." She turned to me and added, "There's a huge age range of folks that play this game. Everything from thirteen-year-olds to, you know, professional people in their fifties, folks who'd drop fifty bucks on a tube of lipstick or two hundred on earbuds for their phone."

"Thirteen? They let kids play this?"

"Well, they don't stop them. How would they? Although unless kids use a parent's credit card, they have to earn Agility through gameplay alone."

"Yeah," Simone said, "and that takes *time*. I played in high school. Not for stuff, but... honestly, because I was lonely. OtherWorld gave me a community. Anyhow, I don't remember if they had all the Experiences available back then, but whatever they had, there would've been no point offering me something that cost two hundred dollars."

Terri laughed. "Right?"

"Right! That's not how you sell things! Like now, when my followers see products, it's targeted. I mean, I don't put different prices on the exact same product, like they're doing with those private Journeys." She shook her head, her mouth pressed tight in disapproval. "But the products I sell, the only ones a follower even *sees* are the ones that we think —or, you know, the data thinks—they would want and can afford."

"Huh," I said. When they looked at me, I said, "Oh, nothing." I was recalling that when I was online I only ever saw ads for Fords and Chevys. The algorithms somehow knew I was not going to buy a Cadillac, much less a Lamborghini.

"What I don't understand," Simone continued, "is where are they getting the targeting data? I don't know why I didn't wonder about that before, but..." She shook her head. "I guess because I was never all that into the idea of selling Journeys to begin with, I didn't research it as much as I should have."

"It's not your fault," Terri told her before turning to me. "Leland, the reason this isn't blowing your mind is that you don't play OtherWorld. Its whole *thing* is that they don't collect much information. They don't track you; there are no in-game ads. Unlike most everything else online, they don't live off ad revenue. They make money with subscriptions and with selling... uh, virtual equipment, basically. Like, if you want to ride a horse in the game, you've got to buy one."

"A picture of a horse?" I said. "A cartoon? People pay for that?"

They both looked at me like I was the slow guy on the relay team.

"Sorry," I said. "Forget I said that. I hear your point. But like you said, if the folks running OtherWorld don't collect that info, how would Apex target Experience prices to certain players?"

"Right," Terri said. "Where'd they get the information they'd need to *do* that? Because it's not coming from the game, or it shouldn't be."

Simone nodded. "The fact they don't collect that is central to their brand."

"It's a huge part of why it feels like a community," Terri said. "People feel *safe* there because you know you're not being tracked." She was shaking her head slowly, as if she'd been personally betrayed.

"Could they be using IP addresses?" I asked.

"That just gives location," she said. "Like my list of cities, here. So that could be *part* of it, but..." She took another bite of Danish and chewed. "Okay," she said, putting the pastry down. "I think we need to skip to the chats."

———

A half hour later I was pacing circles in Simone's living room, on the phone with Cardozo. I'd stepped inside, leaving Terri and Simone out on the veranda, to have a private call. The one-on-one chats, or the few we'd had time to read so far, were alarming. They started out sounding authentic—that is, sounding like Simone in her public mode, being friendly and inspirational for a fan. As they went on, over days or even weeks, they asked for more and more information, but always in the same friendly, "You go, girl" tone.

Send me a pic, one of them said. *Girls get all these messed-up messages about how we're supposed to look, don't we? But we each have our own unique beauty! I want to look right at you and tell you I see yours! I see u!*

The photo sent in response was a White girl, maybe thirteen, with braces and a goofy, self-conscious smile. To me—maybe this was the prosecutor in me, or maybe the father—she looked vulnerable as hell.

Cardozo kept jumping in and out of the call depending on whatever minor crisis was unfolding around him. He was on vacation at his new summer place, a cabin he'd had built up in the Blue Ridge Mountains of North Carolina.

I explained, "So, Roy said the corporate structure—I mean that whole series of shell companies leading back to the Caymans—he thought it sounded pretty shady."

"Yeah, it does." Cardozo said that casually, as if half the things he saw in an ordinary day were shady as hell. Since he was a federal prosecutor, I had no doubt that was true.

"He didn't see any reason a little management company in Charleston should be set up that way."

"Yeah, well, no, he's right. I'm not saying he's wrong. Hang on."

He yelled something to one of his kids, then returned to the line and said, "Management company, did you say? Managing what?"

"Uh, influencers? Entertainers, basically. People who are famous on the internet. And, I guess, people who wish they were. Every secretary in there looked like she walked right off the cover of a magazine."

"Huh." He laughed. "I wonder if that's one of the new red-flag terms. You know how certain things trigger—like if you put on your tax return that you're taking a home office deduction, you're basically asking for an audit? Some business types are just *begging* my office to put surveillance on them. You know: modeling agency, massage parlor—there's a whole list of businesses where I basically assume there's at least some illegal immigrants in there, probably rampant labor violations and tax fraud, maybe even human trafficking. And on top of all that, maybe it's run by the mob. So, for instance, the massage parlors caught on to that and started calling themselves day spas."

We both laughed.

"You realize," I said, "most people get to go their entire lives without looking at the world this way. Whereas me, I can't see a van with out-of-state plates without thinking it's smuggling drugs."

"Yeah. They didn't tell us in law school that becoming prosecutors would turn us into freaks."

"I guess recruiting would be harder if they did."

"Or they'd attract the wrong kind of guy. But, no, I hear what you're saying about this place. And if they're who's behind this whole scheme of ripping fans off by pretending your client's playing the game with them, then assuming it crosses state lines, you could be looking at wire fraud. Maybe not something I'd prosecute all by itself, given how low the amounts they charge are, but you know how it works. If you can link those offers solidly to them, it's an easy rack to hang them on if there's also a bunch of other nefarious shit going on that's harder to prove. Uh, hold on."

He yelled at somebody to get the dog out of the pool. While he was solving that problem, I looked out the living room window. Terri and Simone were looking at each other's laptop screens, talking animatedly, and beyond them it was a bright, beautiful day.

When he came back, we chatted a minute more and then got off. It was nice to know that somebody at Apex might be committing a federal crime by bilking Simone's fans; that would give us a lot more leverage if the goal was to get them to stop. But it did nothing to help me keep her from going to prison for murder.

I called Terri during the drive home. When she answered, I could hear wind noise; it was a nice day to have the windows down.

"I got a meeting on Monday afternoon with the medical expert," I said, "and was hoping you could be there. It's remote—he's in Atlanta."

"Sorry, I can't do Monday. Any idea yet when the trial might be? I heard the court system was gearing back up for in-person everything."

"Yeah, there's supposed to be pilot trials in a couple of other counties starting next week or the week after. They're working the kinks out as far as sanitary procedures, distancing, and whatnot. If they go smoothly and don't end up being superspreader events, I'd be surprised if things weren't back up and running by mid-September or so."

"Wow. That's not a lot of time. I guess we should assume we've got six or seven weeks and prepare accordingly."

"Yup. Oh, by the way, did you hear anything back on the Austin situation?" That was our shorthand term for what I'd told her about Austin trying to get his sister away from their dad.

"Yeah, I talked to my friend Lisa at CPS. Why, did he call you?"

"No, and I don't know if he ever will. I was just curious if he has a shot. I don't know what's going on with his dad, but, uh, he freaked out on me like I have rarely been freaked out on. So I got the sense it must be *bad*."

"Yeah. Damn, anyone who hurts a child, I just want to push them off a cliff."

"That makes two of us."

"Although finding a cliff in the Lowcountry," she said, "that's going to be a challenge."

"Probably a good thing. Otherwise we might be in jail."

"And not even the same jail," she said. "That would be a bummer. Anyway," she said, "Lisa walked me through it. And he definitely has a shot."

"What did she say?"

"Well, I'm assuming he wants to take his sister in. That'd be easy if his dad consents. He can petition for guardianship, and with him being twenty-three, working in a solid trade, and so forth, I can't see why they wouldn't grant it. That marijuana charge in Florida isn't great for him, but compared to his dad's CPS history, not to mention the DUIs, they still might grant it even if the dad fights it."

"That's good."

"Yeah. And even without him petitioning, if things got bad with her dad and they took her into foster care, he'd have priority as a kinship placement. They don't like placing foster kids with strangers if they don't have to."

"That sounds... actually, more promising than I was expecting. Can you send me Lisa's email? Or her number, whatever she prefers? If he does get back to me, I'm going to send him straight to her and be done with it. I want to help that little girl, but not to the point where Ruiz— or not Ruiz, I guess; it would be Ludlow—might accuse me of witness tampering."

"Yeah, going to jail is not a good look for a lawyer." She laughed. "I'd come visit you, though."

———

25

MONDAY, AUGUST 10, 2020

On my computer screen, Simone looked more scared than I'd ever seen her. She'd sent a Zoom invite to Terri and me half an hour earlier.

"It's my mother," she said. "I don't know if you recall, but she works in that nursing home over by Sheldon Corner?"

"Oh, of course we remember," I said.

Terri nodded. "How're they doing?"

"Um, not good. They're having a coronavirus outbreak." She put her hands to her face in something like the prayer position, closing her eyes and breathing deep like she was trying to get ahold of herself. "They've already lost four of the residents, all in the past few days. One of them was just the nicest old lady—my mama loved her."

Terri said, "Oh, I am so sorry."

"Thank you. But that's not even— The thing is, my mama's sick."

"Oh, Simone," Terri said.

"I don't know if folks weren't tested, or if the results took too long, but—whatever it was, staff weren't even told there was an outbreak at all until, I think, Thursday? And my mama had woken up feeling like she was coming down with something, so she got tested. And... I'm just scared. I'm so scared. She got her results today and called me right away."

I said, "That's real hard. Please give her our best."

"I will. Thank you. I hadn't— I was *wondering* what was wrong because she hadn't come around in five days, and she, you know, she never goes that long without a visit. But today she told me she got sick four days ago, and she was waiting on her test results before she told me."

"If you need anything," I said, "or if she does, you let us know."

"Has she got a good doctor?" Terri asked. "And does she have all the groceries she needs?"

"I had some delivered. She's good on that. But I'm, uh... I'm scared." She closed her eyes and pressed one hand to her chest.

Terri said, "Yeah. It's a lot. What you've had on your plate this year is just..." She shook her head.

"Yeah, it is. And I—I really want to thank both of you for being there for me. And Terri, I am so sorry, but when you were over here last week—"

Terri, nodding, said, "Mm-hmm. She was there. So I'm going to have to isolate for, what is it? Ten days?"

"Terri, I am *so* sorry."

"It's not your fault. And don't worry. It's been, what, five days now? And I feel fine."

Ten minutes or so later, when I was making a sandwich, Terri called.

"I was going to tell Simone this today," she said, "but not now. She's too upset."

"Tell her what?" I tucked the phone between my shoulder and my ear so I could scrape the bottom of the jar for the last bits of mayonnaise. "You get some news?"

"A couple of things, yeah. I've been in touch with the police down in Tampa, trying to—"

My phone clattered to the counter, then to the floor. I swore and picked it up.

Terri was laughing. When I apologized for my inability to multitask, she said, "Do *not* put me on speakerphone. I am not dealing with that today. Get your laptop, and we can talk on Zoom."

She hung up. She hated my speakerphone, and most other features of my cheap, ancient smartphone.

I put my laptop on the counter, clicked the link she sent, and we got back to talking.

"Oh," I said. "I got a text from Austin this morning."

"You did? Wow. What'd he say?"

"Hardly anything. It was about six words long. Just that he wants help with his sister. So I wrote back, 'This is who to call, best of luck,' and gave him your friend's number and email."

"Lord, I hope that little girl is okay. It tells you something about how bad I know her dad is that I feel excited about helping a possible killer get custody of her."

From her tone, I could tell she was mostly joking; she was pretty convinced Austin hadn't killed Veronica.

"Yeah," I said. "For the sake of Simone's case, I hate to say it, but at this point, I don't think he did it. At most, if his ex was wrong when she said he stayed away from hard drugs and the folks who deal them, and if he somehow got Veronica into heroin—"

Terri shook her head, dismissing that idea. "I've talked to a whole lot of people and looked at every record I could get my hands on. I haven't seen even a hint that either of them was ever into that."

"Well, that's good for that little girl. Not so good for Simone."

"Yeah. So, speaking of, why I called in the first place is, I've been talking on and off to a policeman down in Tampa, trying to light a fire under them to really look for Ilona."

"That's... I mean, it's important," I said, pouring some chips onto my plate, "and I know Simone cares about her, but we've probably only got five or six weeks before the trial—"

"I know, I know. That's why I haven't been giving you the blow-by-blow on this. You've got enough on your mind. The reason I'm telling you now is because I convinced that policeman to subpoena Instagram and Ilona's cell provider. And those just came back. According to both the IP address and the cell-tower stuff, Ilona, or whoever's been messaging Simone from that account since Ilona disappeared, is in Charleston."

I was heading for the table with my plate, but I stopped dead and said, "*Charleston*? Why?"

"Well, I am not God," she said, smiling, "so I cannot peer into the heart of whoever this is and answer that question. But..."

I nodded, getting her drift. "But it's a hell of a coincidence that Simone's friend from Florida disappears, and then she, or her phone, anyway, somehow ends up here in South Carolina."

"And in the same city where Simone's shady management company is."

"That too." I put my lunch on the table and came back to get the laptop. "How far back did he subpoena the records? Can you see when the phone got here? And what route it took?"

"Back to October 1, since that was the month she disappeared. It went to Tampa over to Jacksonville, then up to Savannah—following the highways."

"Sure. You mind if I turn off my video? It feels weird to sit here eating my lunch on camera."

"Course not. Anyway, there were also a few logins from Basking Rock IP addresses."

"Really? Which ones?"

"Just the courthouse Wi-Fi and the truck stop. Which, you pick those up anywhere within a block."

"Yeah, I know. I get the courthouse one in the diner across the street." I chewed my ham sandwich, thinking things through. Then I laughed at myself, realizing I'd picked up her habit of almost literally chewing on thoughts.

"What's funny?"

"Oh, it's... nothing. Uh, but that's real interesting. It makes you think it must have been Ilona still using that phone, or why would she have gone straight to this little South Carolina town where her idol lives? Or her online friend, or whatever Simone was to her."

"Well, she went to Charleston first." She picked up her laptop and said, "I'm taking you out on the deck."

"That's where the highway runs, though. To Charleston. If she was in a car, she could just take the Basking Rock exit, but if she came up in a bus, she'd have to go to the city first."

"True." She slid her patio door open, went out into the bright, sunny day, and set the laptop on her table. I saw her go over to the side of the deck, yell her dog's name, and hurl a tennis ball into the yard. When she came back, she said, "I think Buster's in love with the neighbor's dog. I have to keep an eye on him."

"Man, Squatter's going to be sad."

She laughed. "Buster will still make time for him."

I finished my sandwich and turned my camera back on. She was watching Buster play. I said, "I wouldn't want to get Simone's hopes up before we know more, but what you found is a little encouraging, at least, don't you think?"

"Oh, hi," she said, noticing me on the screen. Then she looked away again, sighed, and said, "Yeah... I guess. I don't know. Maybe I spent too long as a cop."

"How come?"

"Because... I look at this phone stuff, and all it says to me is that it looks like Ilona didn't die *in Florida*."

In other words, she must've died somewhere else.

———

That afternoon I talked with the forensic pathologist I'd hired to review Veronica's autopsy report. I was still debating whether to put him on the stand. He was eminently qualified, but whether to put a medical expert on at all was a strategic decision I hadn't made yet.

Some of the best defense lawyers I'd faced when I was on the prosecution side were the ones who put on few or even no witnesses. Since the government had to prove its case beyond a reasonable doubt, sometimes the most effective approach was to rip the government witnesses apart on cross. Then, with the state's case lying in tatters on the courtroom floor, you simply pointed to the biggest and most dramatic shreds so they'd stick in the jurors' memories during deliberations.

If I did put him on, it helped that this guy looked the part. When Dr. Chisholm joined the video call from his office in Atlanta, I'd been pleased to see he was a little older than his website photo, closer to fifty than to forty. The gray hairs mixed in with the brown conveyed expertise.

Things like that shouldn't have mattered, but "should" was not a useful word when it came to juries.

We chatted a bit and got to know each other better than we had on our initial calls. Dr. Chisholm scored some more points in my book by speaking in a relaxed but confident way, with a solid dose of gravitas.

I asked, "Can you tell from the amount of drugs in her blood how quickly she died?"

"No. In fact, I can't even tell you *that* she died. The only reason I'm certain she's dead is that I'm looking at an autopsy report." He picked it up off his desk and gestured with it. "There's a significant overlap between fatal and nonfatal doses because different people metabolize drugs differently. And her numbers fall within that overlap, although the diazepam, or Valium, certainly increased the likelihood that her dose would be fatal."

"Huh," I said, jotting that down. "So would there be room for me to argue that she might've been conscious long enough to move the syringe herself?"

"That strikes me as highly unlikely. Particularly when you factor in the diazepam, it's unrealistic to think she remained conscious for any significant time."

"Okay. And does it seem reasonable to you that they concluded she likely died of injecting heroin when they didn't find an injection site?"

"Well, from the prosecution's perspective that's not ideal," he said, "but then, real life rarely is. That blood draw she'd had a few days earlier, for her anemia, created a site in the arm that could be easily reused, and with the examination they did, there's no way to prove that it was or wasn't."

"Are you saying they should've done a better examination?"

"No. This was a competent autopsy," he said. "For a garden-variety overdose, which is what her death looked like, they did exactly what they should have. This coroner proceeded through the external examination, internal examination, and so forth, just as he ought to have done. I've seen instances where that was not the case," he said, grimacing at the memory, "but this was not one of those."

I nodded. "Well, that's not what I wanted to hear," I said. "But it is what it is."

"Oh, Mr. Munroe," he said, lifting his index finger to signal that he wasn't done. "I haven't gotten to the part that you might want to hear."

"My apologies."

That wagging finger was a bit condescending, but if I did put him on the stand, maybe I could coach him not to do it. Or maybe we could play up his professorial demeanor and emphasize that he was a professor at an Atlanta medical school. The jury might see him as an expert with a capital E and overlook his occasional condescension.

"Now," he said, putting on his glasses and picking up the report, "here on page fifty-seven, your local coroner has written that— This is the section on the testing of bodily fluids. He goes through what he found, diazepam, et cetera, and he concludes that the levels of morphine he found are 'consistent with' a heroin overdose."

He looked at me meaningfully over the top of his glasses. I realized, from the eye contact, that he had to be looking at the camera, not at my face on his screen. He knew how to use the technology. I liked that; I suspected he'd know how to use a courtroom to his advantage too. "And what about that catches your attention, Dr. Chisholm?"

I hoped it was good. Simone was going to love it when I told her that the one sentence in the entire report that made her think twice was also the first one our expert mentioned to me.

"Well, the problem with that conclusion, Mr. Munroe, is that it ends there. It doesn't go on to say that it's also consistent with an overdose of morphine."

"Huh," I said. "Are you saying it could be either one?"

I didn't love that argument. It was better than nothing—anything that could raise doubts in the jury's mind about what the prosecution claimed had happened was good. But common sense told you that a suspicious death of a young woman at a party was more likely to be from a street drug than from something you mostly found at hospitals.

"It could be either, yes. But—first off, you're familiar, I assume, with the fact that blood tests for heroin usually don't find heroin itself? Because heroin metabolizes so quickly that within a few minutes, it's no longer heroin?"

I nodded. "Yeah, it's about six minutes, tops, as I understand."

"That's right. One of the things it metabolizes into is morphine, but finding that in the blood could also mean the person took morphine—or opium, though that's rare these days. So what I would call the gold standard for concluding that a death was due to heroin is something else: namely, test results finding a metabolite known as 6-acetylmorphine, or 6-AM for short, in the blood. In a heroin death, usually we find both morphine and 6-AM. That latter metabolite is a unique biomarker that conclusively points to heroin. Tests for it have only been in wide use for about ten years."

"Oh. So… has that technology not yet reached the coroner's office in my neck of the woods?" I was not looking forward to basing my argument on that. I'd do it if I had to, but I didn't think my small-town jury would like being told that the facilities in our area weren't as good as what folks had in big cities.

"Oh, no, Mr. Munroe," the doctor said. "It has reached you. He tested for it. And it wasn't there."

26

WEDNESDAY, AUGUST 19, 2020

I set the groceries down on Terri's front porch, knocked twice, and texted for good measure to let her know they were there. She'd been down with coronavirus for about a week, although she insisted it wasn't bad enough to head to the hospital.

I'd been dropping things by every day: canned chicken soup, Pedialyte for fluids and electrolytes, and a pulse oximeter, with instructions that I'd printed off some website saying to call 9-1-1 if her oxygen got down below 93 percent and stayed there. If I wasn't doing something for her, a door inside me cracked open and let helplessness start creeping in. There was no worse feeling.

As I trudged back to my car, my phone dinged with a text from her saying *Thx*. Then the thing rang. Ruiz's number showed up onscreen.

"Hello?"

"Hey, Leland. This a good time? I got something to run by you about the Baker case."

I pulled open my car door and said, "Good as any other."

"Okay, good. Hey, I heard Terri's got the COVID. That's rough. I'm sorry to hear it."

"Well, thank you, yeah. She's hanging in there."

"She's a tough one. Based on past experience, I think it might take a direct missile strike to remove her from this earth, so I wouldn't worry too much."

I laughed and started the engine. Ruiz had known Terri when she was a cop. And, more recently, he'd arrived on the scene the previous December as she emerged from the near-death experience she and I had shared. When he got there, she was covered in blood and carrying all sixty pounds of her injured Rottweiler pup up a hill. He'd watched her stand there, deadly calm, telling paramedics what to do. He was no stranger to her toughness.

"Okay," he said. "Don't shoot the messenger, but being as how we'll probably be in trial late next month if we don't get this figured out, I got a plea deal to discuss."

I pulled out of my parking spot. "I doubt she'll listen, but I know you got to run it by me."

"Yeah, I told Ludlow she's unlikely to go for it. I know that. But anyway, we're prepared to drop this to manslaughter and recommend a thirty-month sentence."

"Huh," I said. That was only six months more than the bare minimum for manslaughter. Still, with how hard Simone had fought to avoid spending even one night in jail before her bond hearing on the murder charges, I was sure she'd reject it out of hand.

"I pushed Ludlow for that," he said. "He started off drawing a hard line at three years, minimum."

"Well, thank you. I'll talk with her and let you know."

We hung up.

At a red light, I checked my phone and saw another text from Terri: *Blood ox up to 93% from 91% last night. Doing ok I think.*

"Dammit." I gave the steering wheel a whack. Since she'd gotten sick, I'd become a Google expert in oxygen levels, and she was not out of the woods yet.

———

Noah wasn't home when I got there, which was just as well. It meant I could call Simone about the plea deal from the comfort of my couch.

When she picked up, I started in on my spiel about how she'd been offered a deal, and although she'd made clear before that she wasn't interested, I still had a duty to advise her of it and explain the pros and cons. Before I could get halfway through, she interrupted.

"I'm so sorry," she said, "but I don't even—I can't even think about this right now. I got a message this morning from Ilona, and I just—I don't understand."

"What'd she say?"

"Let me pull it up." I heard her laptop slide across a table. "Okay, here it is. She said, 'I had a weird dream last night. Something about morphine. It just gave me a bad feeling about you and your case. What does it mean if there's morphine in the house? Isn't your mom a nurse?'"

After a second of shock, I said, "What the *hell?*"

Then I apologized. She didn't like anybody cursing, and her definition of a swear word started at a far milder threshold than mine.

"Don't worry. But what is this? How does she know anything about this?"

"Just to check, I assume you didn't tell her, right?" I'd emailed Simone after talking with Dr. Chisholm to let her know what he'd said about morphine. She'd been less excited than I'd expected.

"Of course not! Like you said, I don't even talk to my preacher about any of this. And I haven't messaged her back at all since, I don't know, May? Early June? Whenever it was that you warned me it might not really be her."

I stared at the blank screen of my TV, trying to figure out what the hell was going on. It could not be a coincidence that somebody was warning Simone about "morphine in the house" right after I'd told her what Dr. Chisholm had said and how it could improve her chances before the jury.

Then I looked at my phone. Was that where the leak was?

"Uh, Simone… How about I come by? I think this is something we might want to discuss in person. We can sit outside. I'll wear a mask, obviously, since I saw Terri right before she got sick."

"Sure. Of course. I'm so sorry, I should've asked: how is she?"

"She's holding up. How about your mom?"

"A lot better. She never did end up having to go in the ICU, thank the Lord. It looks like in two or three days she might be able to come home."

"Well, that's a relief."

We chatted another minute, and then I hung up and grabbed my keys off the table. As I walked out to my car, I realized I hadn't set the burglar alarm. I never did in the daytime, but I was feeling a little spooked. I went back in and set it.

———

At Simone's, I left my phone in the car. When she answered her door, I suggested she leave hers inside. As we went around to the side of the veranda, I said, "There's always a chance something weird could be a coincidence, but I think we ought to be careful. I'd rather be paranoid and wrong than be too careless."

"No, I completely agree."

"Until I figure this out," I said, sitting on the far side of the long coffee table from her, "I think we ought not to say anything, uh, sensitive, or important, electronically. You're ten minutes from me—if either of us has something confidential to say, I can swing by."

"Yeah. I think that's a good idea. And thank you. I know it's not as convenient for you."

She set her laptop where I could see the screen. I read the message. "You mind if I scroll up a little?"

"Not at all."

I skimmed the thread and said, "Huh. So it looks like she, or whoever this is, hadn't even messaged you in over a month?"

"Nope. Nothing. And then out of nowhere, she's talking about morphine and my mother."

Those last two words caught my ear. I'd wondered about that part of the message on my way over.

I said, lightly, "Your mother?"

She broke eye contact and looked down. That did not strike me as a good sign. I gave her a minute.

When she didn't speak, I said, as gently as I could, "If there's anything I don't know yet, you really can tell me. There's just about zero exceptions to the fact that I'm legally bound to take your secrets to the grave."

232

Her eyes flicked up to mine, then back down. I saw her hands were kneading each other on her lap, twisting up the sky-blue silk of her pajama-style pants.

"Mr. Munroe," she said at last. She still wasn't looking at me. "I think I mentioned how because of the MS, I have all sorts of—well, muscle spasms, back pain, that kind of thing."

I nodded. "Yes, I recall. Maybe not in that much detail, but you did mention some of that before."

"And my mom is a nurse."

"Mm-hmm. It's more than twenty years she's been a nurse, isn't it?"

"Yeah. My whole life." She looked up at me. "It's... I truly believe it's her calling."

I'd learned, not on my own steam but through good mentoring when I'd first become a lawyer, that echoing back what someone said could help draw them out. So I said, "Mm-hmm. Her calling?"

"Yeah. I mean, she knows so much, and cares so much, and—she's just my *rock*. And she's that way for all her patients too."

"She's your rock?"

"I mean, until this case, getting my diagnosis and dealing with all of this has just been the hardest thing I have ever been through. You and I, we've talked a little about how Veronica bullied me in high school, and it was bad, but it was *nothing* compared to this. And I could not have gotten through either of those things without my mom."

"You got through because of her?"

She sighed and looked down again. I heard the wind rustling through the flowers in her garden.

When she looked up again, she wouldn't look right at me—she turned her face a little toward the yard—but she had tears in her eyes.

"All these things I've done," she said, "the fact I'm able to make videos and talk to people and—and even *think* straight, is because I'm *not* in constant pain. And she— A few years ago, my doctor at the time prescribed oxycodone for when the pain was bad. But my mom tore that prescription right up and threw it in the trash. She worked in rehab when I was little, and she's just—she's seen the worst things addiction can do. She said she was *not* going to let that happen to me."

I nodded real slow. "Well, she's your mom," I said. "Course she's not going to let that happen to you."

"Right?" She looked me in the eyes. "Yeah, you're a father, you understand."

I understood a little too well, with what had happened to Noah before we moved back to Basking Rock, but I wasn't about to tell her that.

"So what she did," she said, "was— She's not going to get in trouble, is she, Mr. Munroe?"

I shook my head and told her, "Simone, I could not betray your secrets even if I wanted to. It's not allowed."

She looked down. Then she said, "My mother and me are so similar, Mr. Munroe. We both get springtime allergies, we're both a little allergic to strawberries. And we're both real sensitive to any kind of anesthesia."

"Uh-huh."

"Apart from her not having MS, it's almost like we have the same body. So she told me she knew how to help me with the pain. How a smaller dose would be enough because we don't metabolize it as fast as most people do. She thought those pills that doctor prescribed would be too much for me. So what she did…"

Her voice got quieter. I had to lean forward to hear.

"What she did was, she, uh, brought home morphine from work. In those, you know, those injector pens?" She made a little stabbing motion.

"Oh, yeah, the pens."

"She said, 'If you're hurting, I will know what dose you need. And I'll give it to you.' And she did. And it *worked*, Mr. Munroe. She was right. She's the reason I've been able to accomplish so much."

"She was right?"

"Yeah, she— The idea was, if I'm popping pills, you know, you can get those prescriptions from any doctor. You can get three bottles at a time. You can take more than you should. It's real easy to get addicted. But if *she* had the medicine, then I couldn't take more than I ought to. I wouldn't take it every day—she wouldn't let me. And I can't get it someplace else because these pens, and morphine in general, that's not something you would normally get for MS. The doctors want you popping pills."

My poker face must've failed me for a second because she said, all in a rush, "She did not *do* this, Mr. Munroe. That's not what I'm saying. Whatever happened to Veronica had nothing to do with her. All I'm saying is, this is why I was a little nervous about Dr. Chisholm's morphine idea, and it's why Ilona's message freaked me out so much."

"Yeah," I said, taking it all in. "I hear you. That makes sense." I started forming a mental checklist of what to do. First up: see if Simone's mom had any record for this because if she did, Ruiz would find it.

"I'm sorry if it complicates things."

"Well," I said, "thank you for telling me this. I truly did need to know."

"Yeah," she said. "I'm real sorry. Maybe I should've told you earlier, but…" She shrugged.

"Oh, just so I understand, how do those pens work? Is she injecting it into your veins?"

"No, the pens are intramuscular. You know, shoulder, thigh… it's real easy."

"Okay. Thanks." I slapped my hands on my knees like I was fixing to go, but then I remembered the reason I'd called in the first place.

Talking with Ruiz about the plea offer seemed like it had happened days ago instead of an hour earlier. What Simone had told me dwarfed everything else. But I still had to run it by her.

"Oh, like I was saying when I called, Mr. Ruiz offered a new plea deal today."

Her eyes widened. "The man who's prosecuting me?"

"Yeah. Which is pretty standard before a trial. And taking the deal would avoid the risk of a much longer sentence."

"And what'd he say?"

"He said they can drop it to manslaughter and a two-and-a-half-year sentence."

She closed her eyes and sighed.

"You know I can't do that," she said.

———

In the car, I had a text from Noah apologizing for setting off the burglar alarm and giving me a hard time for turning it on in the first place. I chuckled, started texting him back, and stopped, wondering if somehow my phone was under surveillance.

If it was, I figured what I had to say was harmless. I typed, *This'll teach you to be as paranoid as me.*

I added a smiley face.

Heading home, I wondered about what Simone had said. Could a churchgoing nurse kill a girl with morphine? Nurses had murdered hospital patients before. And the dead girl had tormented Ms. Baker's daughter all through high school.

But if she'd done it, why would such a dedicated mother let her child go through a criminal prosecution without speaking up?

When things didn't add up, I'd found it could help to set your thoughts on a shelf and leave them there a while. So I did that and got back to wondering about Terri. How was she doing, and what would she think of all this? I couldn't text her, not until I figured out where the leak was.

I parked outside my house. Through the front window, I could see Squatter sitting on the back of the couch. He looked up and barked a couple times to say hello.

I went in and passed by Noah coming out of the shower, wrapped in a towel. He ragged on me in a friendly way about the burglar alarm as I ducked into my office to plug my phone into the charger. My laptop was on the desk, and the sight of it gave me pause. It was in an email from that laptop, not from my phone or my desktop computer, that I'd told Simone about Dr. Chisholm's morphine idea.

Nobody touched that laptop but me. I couldn't even get into it without typing a fourteen-digit password that looked like something a cat might type by accident if it killed a mouse on the keyboard.

I went to the desk and pulled out the top drawer. Sitting there among the pens and paper clips was the little black thumb drive that Girardeau had given me. The one he'd driven through town specifically to drop off.

I'd run my antivirus program on it before copying it over to my laptop, but maybe that wasn't enough.

———

27

SATURDAY, SEPTEMBER 12, 2020

Terri had recovered fully, thank God, and trial was eleven days away. The court clerk had told us at the end of August that in-person trials were starting up again on September 21, and we were first on the docket. Right after getting our trial date, Terri'd received her first negative COVID test since getting sick, and it felt like a lottery win: it meant we could work in person again, and I wouldn't have to go to trial alone.

We were sitting on Simone's veranda going through our pretrial to-do list. Simone was inside editing a video for her TikTok feed, and her mother, who was still on the mend, was due to drop by shortly.

"Maybe I should thank Girardeau for making me get rid of my old laptop," I said. "This one's so much better."

"Cardozo would kill you."

"Oh, I'll wait till he's done."

Cardozo had pointed me to a computer forensics guy, who confirmed that a keystroke logger had been installed on my laptop and that it came from the thumb drive Girardeau had given me. That flashy

lawyer had been spying, for some reason, on every damn thing I typed
—which had put Cardozo on high alert about everything relating to
him, Simone, and the management company that employed them
both. I didn't know the details, but some kind of investigation was
underway.

For the first week or so after getting my new laptop, I'd used the old
one to send fake messages to Terri and Simone. Girardeau was
presumably still spying, and I wanted to make him think our trial
strategy was different than it was. I sent lists of evidence I wasn't
planning to use and sketched out old ideas that in reality I had long
since abandoned. But when I got notified our trial date was coming up
fast, I no longer had time for that. I wondered what Girardeau thought
of my sudden silence.

"Will you look at that," I said, turning my laptop around to show
Terri. I'd just gotten an email from our litigation services vendor with
drafts of some of our trial exhibits attached.

"Wow," she said, clicking through the slides. "*Showing* the jury how
many people could've done this is a lot more powerful than just
telling them."

The vendor had gone through the party photos we'd provided, as well
as the guest list and real estate records showing how Simone's house
was laid out. Their first slide had three shots that made her place look
like a packed New York City nightclub. It took five more slides just to
show the names and thumbnail images of everyone who'd been there
that night, and the next three showed the floor plan of her house with
headshots indicating who'd been where at three different points in the
evening. On each, the side door near the room Veronica had died in
was colored red so I could point out how easy it would've been for
someone to sneak in or out that way.

I said, "My good Lord, going to trial with *money* behind you is a
whole different experience."

"Mm-hmm." She took a sip of the lemonade that Simone had set out for us. "She would have *no* chance without it. So, what are we going to do about Dr. Chisholm?"

"I don't know. That all depends on what Ms. Baker has to say."

———————

About an hour later, after we'd sent the vendor some comments on the slides and I was outlining the issues I wanted to hit when I cross-examined the police detective in charge of the case, Ms. Baker's blue Ford Taurus rolled up at the curb. When she got out, she saw us and waved.

Terri poured her a glass of lemonade while I carried our phones and laptops inside and then went to meet her at the steps.

"How you feeling, Ms. Baker? It's good to see you back up and about."

"Well, I can't complain," she said, "since the Lord saw fit to pull me through."

She was gripping the railing as she climbed the steps, moving more slowly than she had before. When she reached the top, she waved through the screen door to her daughter and then came around the corner to sit with us.

"Here you go, Ms. Baker," Terri said, patting the chair beside hers. "Thank you so much for taking the trouble to come out."

Terri had gone to visit with her twice while they both were recuperating, and while those conversations hadn't unearthed any critical facts, she told me she thought Ms. Baker now trusted us as much as she was ever going to. Terri had asked Simone to have us all over so we could try to get whatever Ms. Baker was willing to share about the morphine. Without that, I didn't know if Dr. Chisholm's morphine-or-heroin argument would risk causing more problems for Simone than it solved.

Terri hadn't found any troubling background on Ms. Baker; she had no criminal record and no disciplinary issues with her nursing license.

But Ruiz was not stupid. He would know as well as I did that if a person overdoses on a pharmaceutical drug that nobody on the streets is dealing, and that neither they nor anyone close to them was prescribed, you look at the people around them who work in pharmacies or healthcare.

And the only person at that party who fit that description was Ms. Baker.

Simone brought out some snacks and another pitcher of lemonade. She did not partake; she kept her mask on, but I pulled mine down when I took a sip, and left it that way. With Terri and Ms. Baker recently recovered, I figured I wasn't likely to catch the virus from them. And for this conversation, I wanted Ms. Baker to see my face.

When Simone sat down, Terri said, "If it's all right with y'all, I feel called to do a prayer circle before we start. This is an important moment. We've been running a marathon for Simone's freedom all this time, and now we're coming up on the very last stretch."

"Amen," Simone said, and her mother followed suit. We all held hands. They bowed their heads, so I did the same.

Terri said, "First, Lord, we give thanks for the abundance you've given us. We are rich in so many ways."

"Thank you, Lord," they all said. I said the same, at a slight lag.

"Lord," she continued, "we are here for Your daughter, Simone. We pray for justice. We pray for her freedom. We pray for the wisdom to understand how best to walk this path You have set before us."

I echoed their amens.

"She has been challenged, Lord," Terri said, her voice growing more urgent. "She has been walking the steepest hill she's ever walked in her life, and we are walking with her."

"Yes, Lord!" her mother said.

"Please, Lord," Terri said, "please tell us how best to deliver this young woman to the future we're all praying for. In Your grace, Lord, please show us the path to her *liberation*!"

"Praise Jesus!" Ms. Baker declared, her eyes closed. "Praise the *Lord*!"

After more amens, they all let go of the hands they were holding. I settled mine on my lap, waiting to move until I could see what the etiquette was.

Terri made sure everyone's lemonade was full, and then she began.

"Now, Ms. Baker," she said, "please go ahead and get us started whenever you like. I apologize that I didn't have time to fix any of this food myself, but Simone told me where to shop."

Ms. Baker nodded and reached for a biscuit. "I know what you're doing for my daughter," she said. "I know you don't have time to cook."

When she'd taken a bite and was having a long sip of her lemonade, that seemed to be the cue for Terri to start eating. I waited until she'd begun before reaching for my glass.

A few bites in, Terri said, "So, Ms. Baker, as I had mentioned the other day, Simone told us about something you had been doing for her, to help with her pain. And we've got a decision to make, as far as the trial goes, about what we've got to say."

"Mm-hmm," Ms. Baker said. "I know."

"And to find the right way forward for Simone," Terri said, "we need to know whatever you can tell us about that night."

Ms. Baker nodded and took a sip of her lemonade. When she set it down, she turned to me and said, "Now, Mr. Munroe, it's my understanding that we are in a holy circle here." She gave me a long look. "You are bound, I believe, to hold every word said here in confidence. Is that correct?"

I nodded slowly. That wasn't how the ethics rules phrased it, and those rules had a few exceptions, but it was close enough. I could see in her eyes that I had not convinced her yet, so I found words that I thought might speak to her. "I consider this a covenant."

She looked satisfied.

"And I don't know if you saw," Terri told her, "but Mr. Munroe put all our phones and computers inside when you got here. There is nothing here to record any of this, and he's not even going to write any of it down."

"Mm-hmm," Ms. Baker said. "I left mine in the car."

"Thank you, Momma," Simone said. "I don't mean for that. I mean for everything."

"Of course, baby girl."

While the two of them exchanged what I could only describe as looks of fierce love, Terri had a sip of lemonade.

Then Ms. Baker turned to her and said, "Now, you tell me, Terri, what is it that you need to know?"

"Well… what we need is just to hear whatever you recall about that night." She looked at me.

"Right," I said. "We've seen a lot of video and heard a lot of stories about what happened during the party. We know about some arguments and fights, and we got a good sense of who all was there. But we don't know what happened when things were winding down."

Terri added, "And I don't think we know anything about what may have happened after Simone went to sleep."

Ms. Baker took that in, squinting thoughtfully off into the distance. "All right," she said. "I think it might be best if I just walk through it in order."

"Yes, that makes sense," I said.

"And, so you know, I was there to watch over my daughter. She knows I don't think highly of those people. *Any* of them. They drink, they use drugs—it is Sodom and Gomorrah with them. And, you know, also, we'd put away a lot of her things to protect against stealing and snooping, but I still wanted to keep watch."

I said, "Very understandable." And it was. I still wished I'd been that protective when Noah'd been younger.

"So I was going to watch until the last person was gone and I knew she was safe. But then that girl ended up staying, and with her *boyfriend* too." She shook her head in disgust.

Terri asked, "Apart from them, do you recall who were the last folks still there?"

"Oh, um… Well, there were still some of the company folks, wrapping up their lights and electrical cords and so forth. And the caterers were coming in and out. I think they must've left last, since they had to clean everything up."

"Did you talk to Veronica or her boyfriend at all?"

"Oh my goodness, no. That girl did terrible things to my daughter when they were younger. I had no time for her."

"Did you happen to see anybody offer them drinks?"

"No, I did not. But since you mention it, there were two… goblets, I guess you'd call them? I saw two of those on the kitchen counter. Which I noticed because those caterers had cleaned up real well otherwise."

Terri and I locked eyes. Then I looked back at Ms. Baker. "Uh-huh," I said. "And about when was that?"

"Well… it must've been toward the very end, since I don't recall anyone else around."

"Do you recall where Veronica and her boyfriend were at that time?"

"Oh, they must've gone to bed. Like I said, there was nobody left. I was about to leave, myself."

"Uh, Simone," I said, "you told us you went to bed around eleven thirty, is that right?"

"That sounds right, yes. I showed them where they could sleep, and then I used the bathroom and went to bed."

Her mother was nodding.

Terri said, "Ms. Baker, do you happen to recall who all might've still been there when Simone went to bed?"

"Apart from that girl and her boyfriend? Well, like I said, there were still—not guests, but maybe two or three of the workers. But they were all out of there before I finished my last walk-through. You know, down to the garage, and then I checked her studio. And before I left, I bolted the side door."

"No, Momma, I did that right before bed."

Ms. Baker looked at her. "Well, I don't know, baby, but it was unlocked when I checked."

246

"My God," Terri said. "That has to be how the killer got out. I wonder if he heard you coming and fled."

I asked, "Ms. Baker, do you know which workers were still there? Caterers, or…"

"I'm sorry. I just don't recall."

"And which way did you go out?"

"When I left, I went out the front door."

She fell quiet. She was holding something back.

"Ms. Baker." Terri paused. "Ms. Baker, all truth is known to the Lord."

"Yes, it is," Ms. Baker said. "Yes, it is." She looked at her lap and sighed. "Baby girl," she said, "There's one more thing I never told you."

"Momma," Simone said. "What?"

"I looked in on you," she said. "And you were sleeping. You were fine. And then I went back up the hall and saw the door on the guest bedroom wasn't closed. So I looked in, and those two children were sleeping. In their street clothes, I remember. And in the light coming in their window, I saw—" She was shaking her head, looking near tears. "Baby, I thought it was your Solamorph. Which made no sense, but that's what it looked like, and I just… panicked a little, I guess. I even thought, did they get it out of my *purse*, somehow?"

Terri said, "Ms. Baker, where was it?"

"On the bed next to her. Right by her shoulder. The blanket in there was purple, and the pen was white, so I saw it. I grabbed it and put it in my purse."

"Oh, Momma."

"But she was breathing when I left, baby. I checked them both. I was so angry. I thought they'd taken your medicine to get themselves high." Tears were running down her cheeks. "Baby, if I'd stayed a few minutes longer, if I'd seen she was in trouble, that child might still be alive."

We let her cry for a minute. Terri pulled a Kleenex from her purse and passed it over. When she'd cleaned herself up and blown her nose, Ms. Baker said, "And, baby, if I'd just left it there, none of this would've happened to you. Because it wasn't even one of yours. When I got home and looked at it in the light, it wasn't a Solamorph. It was another brand."

———

28

FRIDAY, SEPTEMBER 18, 2020

On the morning of the last business day before trial, Ruiz called with another plea offer.

"I got Ludlow down to twenty-eight months," he said. "He's not willing to come down more, and honestly, I'm with him on that. Even if all your client meant to do was help a friend get high, there's got to be some kind of real penalty when that ends up killing someone."

"I hear you," I said. "And I'd agree, if I thought that was what happened."

He let that sit there.

"Ruiz," I said, "can I just ask you one thing?"

"Course. Shoot."

"Why is it, with *thousands* of photos of this party and I don't know how many dozen hours of video footage, why is it that you've got nothing against my client but a few-minute spat?"

That was a stab in the dark; maybe he had photos I hadn't seen.

"We got witnesses," he said. "And besides, that's ridiculous. She only died after everybody else had gone."

"Witnesses to what? Their spat? And something about those cocktails?"

"Look, we got trial coming up. I've got to prepare, just like you do. We need to know what your client says about my offer."

I wasn't sure why he'd said "witnesses," plural, but I felt a little more confident he didn't have any photos that would be devastating to my case.

"I'll run it by her. But you and I are both busy, so I'll only call you back if she's interested."

After we hung up, I sent Laura an email asking what time Dr. Chisholm was arriving. I was having him fly in, at a cost to Simone of nearly $3,000 a day, to sit in court and watch the state's coroner testify in case he said anything we could catch him on.

I still wasn't sure if I was going to put the good doctor on the stand. We were in a catch-22: an accomplished and persuasive doctor could make the jury doubt the state's case by showing them that there was reason to question whether Veronica had died from heroin at all. If the state couldn't even get that right—and on top of that, they hadn't properly investigated the boyfriend or the stalker—the jury, I thought, would not get past reasonable doubt. For that alone, they might set Simone free.

But if I raised the morphine defense, I couldn't put Simone on the stand. No prosecutor worth his salt would let that go by without asking Simone if she'd ever used morphine. It would be one of the first questions out of Ruiz's mouth.

Even if Simone could lie about that convincingly, which I doubted, I could not allow her to do it. Under the ethics rules, if she got up on the stand and committed perjury, I would have to withdraw as her attorney then and there. And if the judge asked me why, I'd have to say. Her case would be done for, and she'd go to prison.

I was sure some lawyers didn't abide by that rule, but I wasn't one of them. I wasn't about to put myself at risk of disbarment to save a client who lied on the stand, no matter how convinced I was that she was innocent. And looking at the bigger picture, the justice system had enough trouble as it was. Rich people won and poor people lost more than they should. Without clear rules, the whole system would go completely to hell.

And if she told the truth? Then my murder defendant was admitting that she regularly made illegal use of a Schedule II drug. Not just any drug, but one of the only two drugs on earth—morphine and heroin— that could've killed this victim.

But I wanted to put Simone on the stand because the jurors needed to see who she was. There was nothing shifty about her; she spoke with absolute conviction. I wanted to stand in front of the jury box and ask her the questions that would let her tell them that she was a church-goer, that her mom had been at this party as her chaperone, and that she'd never touched an alcoholic drink, much less heroin.

And when it came to it, I wanted Ruiz to accuse her of killing Veronica over years-old high school bullying and make her cry, make her hang her head in shame as she admitted her own conflicting feelings: that she thought Veronica's message for disabled young women was important and good, but at the same time, because of the pain of the bullying, part of her wanted Veronica to fail.

When she'd told me that, I'd seen a flawed but honest human being. I thought the jury would too. Seeing an upright young woman reduced to tears on the stand might even turn them against Ruiz. And then it'd be my turn to question her again, on redirect. I'd ask her if she killed

Veronica, and she would lift her tear-streaked face and say no like she was talking directly to God.

―――――

I was eating leftover pizza for a very late lunch when my phone rang. It was the main courthouse number, the same one that showed up no matter what office was calling. I put my professional voice on and said, "Afternoon, Leland Munroe speaking."

"Mr. Munroe," a familiar voice said, "Pat Ludlow here. How you doing today?"

It was Ruiz's boss. He'd never called me before.

"Doing well, Mr. Ludlow. How about yourself?"

"Pretty good, pretty good. Except I want to make sure your client is aware of the consequences of not accepting what I think is a more than fair plea offer."

I'd called her, and she'd said no. "Yes," I said. "She is indeed."

"Uh-huh. Well, as we've disclosed today, we've got two witnesses now saying your client served those tainted champagne cocktails to the murder victim. Not just one."

"Yep," I said. I wasn't about to let him know he'd surprised me. I brought up my email. There was a new one from Ruiz. "Well, thanks for letting me know." I opened the attachment.

"We are not backing down on this," Ludlow said.

"I hear you." Scanning Ruiz's email, I got to the part where he said Delacourt would be testifying. Delacourt? I didn't know what the hell to make of that. I said, faking nonchalance, "Seems cumulative to me, but—"

"Cumulative? That's your argument? I should mention that if she declines, we'll be seeking thirty years. And when you present this offer to your client, please add that it expires at five o'clock today."

He hung up without saying goodbye. I looked at the phone in my hand and said, "What the hell was *that*?" Maybe things were different down here, but when I'd been in the solicitor's office back in Charleston, I'd never known my superior to call any defense counsel directly. Discussing plea deals was not his job.

I called Simone to do my duty and convey the offer, and she again said no.

I didn't have time for this. Trial was starting in less than two and a half days. I had exhibits to review, witness outlines to prepare, and an opening statement to write. What I needed was caffeine… and maybe some sort of conveyor belt to drop a piece of hot pizza on my desk every few hours.

I worked on. Terri called. I talked to Chisholm. I wrote.

Noah got home at some point, dropped a box of take-out shrimp in front of me, to my profuse thanks, and headed to his room to play video games.

I put one of the sets of slides up on my laptop, stood, and practiced how I'd walk the jury through them. When I noticed Shawn the Stalker on one slide, with his photo and full name alongside those of the other caterers and workers, I called the vendor and had them make the photos smaller and take the names off.

Now it just said *The Caterers. The Technical Staff. The Business Staff.* No names. So far, Ruiz had given no indication that he realized Shawn had been there. If there was a chance this news might surprise him or his witnesses, I didn't want to blow it.

It was past 3 a.m. when I finally decided to wrap it up and go to bed. I went to the kitchen and put away what remained of my snack. I walked through the living room, yawning, and clicked off the one lamp that was still on. Noah had left the hallway light on, it looked like, or maybe just the light in the bathroom that opened onto the hallway. I padded toward it and froze.

There was a man in the hallway. With a gun. Just outside Noah's room.

I couldn't speak. The man was looking at me with a little smile. I'd never been so cold. He put a finger to his mouth to say, *Quiet.*

He pulled Noah's door shut, real gently, and walked a few steps toward me. He was a big guy, fiftyish, and vaguely familiar.

I tried to erase any sign of recognition from my face.

"Your son's sleeping," he said, in not quite a whisper. He shrugged. "I thought I'd give him a chance."

My gut fell through the floor. I breathed, "Just tell me what you want."

He made a face like he was thinking about it. "Well, you know," he mused, "we all want something."

I nodded.

"You wanted the money," he said with another shrug. "I understand that. But you don't have to keep fighting this case."

My mouth was trembling. I remembered what Girardeau had said once: "It's a dog," I whispered.

"Yeah." He smiled. "It's a dog."

After a second, still smiling, he gestured with the gun like he was asking me to move. I moved. He took a few more steps, then stopped at the front door and turned to look at me again.

"We good?" he asked.

I nodded. "Yeah. We're good."

He opened the door and let himself out.

———

When I unfroze, I lurched to the door and deadbolted it. I turned on the goddamn burglar alarm, cursing myself for thinking I only needed it when we were sleeping or gone.

Noah's window might be open. The man might come back. I opened the bedroom door. "Noah," I said. "Noah, we got a problem. I need you to wake up."

Squatter looked up from beside Noah's leg, where he'd been sleeping.

"Noah!"

I didn't want to turn on the light. That man might be out there, watching.

I went over and shook Noah until he grumbled and came round.

"What the— Dad? What?"

"Noah, you got to get up. Quietly."

———

I never did turn a light on. I told him we were in danger and had to get out. We stumbled through the dark house, gathering up what we needed: phone chargers, dog food, our laptops, extra shoes. We packed two bags, I made sandwiches, and less than half an hour later, we left.

At a gas station outside Charleston around 5 a.m., while Noah filled the tank, I checked all the wheel wells and under the bumpers for tracers, since Terri had once told me that's where they usually were put. I found none, so I turned my phone back on, got in the car, and called Cardozo. I gave him a minute to wake up and get to another room, so his wife could sleep, and told him what had happened.

I also told him who the man was. When my brain had calmed down enough, about halfway to Charleston, I'd placed him: Pete Dupree. I'd seen his mug shot the previous year, when I was investigating the murder charges against Noah's friend. Dupree was an old-school mobster, part of the drug cartel that case had blown wide open. I had no theory, though, as to why he cared about Simone.

"I know you had a warrant out for him," I said. "Well, two hours ago, he was in Basking Rock."

"Shit."

Cardozo never swore, so that reverberated.

"Okay, Leland, I'll deal with that in a second. But right now, where are you going?"

"I don't know. I just couldn't leave my son there. I thought I'd see if you had any ideas."

I heard him pouring something. "Uh… yeah," he said. "But listen, I'm not going to say it on the phone. Come by here."

When we got to his place, he brought us into the kitchen and served us coffee. He was still in his bathrobe. He made sure our phones were off, and for good measure, he took them and tossed them, along with his own, into the fridge.

"You want bagels?" he said, taking some out and shutting the door.

"Sure, thanks."

As he started slicing them, he said, "You know my cabin up in North Carolina? If you got time to drive there, I'll give you the key."

"How far is it?"

"It's a little before Asheville." He dropped the first two bagels into the toaster. "At this time of day, maybe four and a half hours."

"That'll work. Is there a car rental place around there, do you know? That'd be open on a Saturday morning?"

"What for?"

"Well, Noah's going to need a car."

Noah looked at me. "What, you're leaving me there?"

"My trial starts on Monday."

"You're *doing* it?"

Cardozo and I looked at each other. He understood.

To Noah, I said, "I can't just not show up. I'm lead counsel. *Only* counsel. She's got no one else."

"But—this— Can you at least *postpone* it?"

Cardozo shook his head.

"It doesn't work that way," I said.

Cardozo explained, "If we postponed trials every time a lawyer got threatened…"

"What? This *happens*? This— People *threaten* you guys like this?"

"No, no," Cardozo said reassuringly, buttering one of the bagels. "Not that often. But if we postponed trials when it did, it would happen a whole lot more."

———

I drove all morning, stopping outside Columbia to get Noah five hundred bucks from an ATM, then in Asheville to get groceries and rent him a car. We pulled up outside the cabin around eleven. It was perched at the top of a steep road with a view down over the rolling blue hills.

We went in, and I got him and Squatter situated. It looked like they had everything they would need. I bent down and petted the dog.

Back outside, as I was leaving, I said, "You take care of yourself."

He just looked at me for a second. Then he nodded, not saying anything, and held out his hand to shake. In his clenched mouth and big blue eyes, I could see a flash of him when he was six or eight years old, and scared, and being brave. I grabbed him around the shoulders and pulled him in for a hug.

He waved from the porch as I drove away.

———

29

MONDAY, SEPTEMBER 21, 2020

At 8:30 a.m., jury selection began. Due to COVID, the fifty prospective jurors were divided into groups of ten, with most of them in different rooms connected to us by video link and ten sitting in the courtroom with us, widely spaced across the jury box and the spectator seats. Terri and I were side by side at the defense table with our laptops, and everybody was wearing masks making it impossible to try to get a read on any of them.

There were no spectators, and there weren't going to be. That was the only reason I was able to stay calm on the outside. If outsiders had been allowed, like they were before the pandemic, then every time I heard the courtroom door open I'd wonder if it was one of Dupree's men coming for me. Logically, the idea of someone attempting to shoot me in the middle of a busy courtroom was ludicrous, but my emotions were a jangle and I kept having to remind myself that I was safe here.

We'd been assigned Judge Calhoun. He did voir dire himself, reading the jurors the questions Ruiz and I had submitted. Had they heard anything about this case? Did they know any of the people involved?

Eight jurors were dismissed for obvious conflicts, as was a mother who'd brought her breastfed infant to court due to lack of childcare. The next to be dismissed were six young women who'd followed Veronica or Simone on social media.

On our laptops, Terri and I texted back and forth about which jurors to use our peremptory challenges on. I wanted a racial mix, to reduce the impact of conscious or unconscious racism. There were not, unfortunately, many Black people in today's pool. But there were quite a few women, and I wanted them. I was going to throw both Austin and Shawn under the bus if I had to, so I needed folks who knew in their bones that a perfectly nice-seeming White boy could be dangerous behind closed doors.

And because of the syringe found in Simone's van, we needed to somehow figure out which of these folks, if any, would believe a police officer might plant evidence. That wasn't a question we could ask. Anyone who answered yes would get dismissed by the prosecution. All we could do was go by proxy: folks who were poor, or not White, were more likely to have seen the bad side of cops.

Keep #14, Terri texted me. *DV victim.*

That was another question we weren't asking. Ruiz wouldn't want any juror who'd be especially likely to suspect the boyfriend. Instead, I was relying on Terri's deep knowledge of virtually everything any human had done to another in Basking Rock.

It was almost eleven before we had our jury. Two were Black, four were women, and two of the White guys were related to police officers. It wasn't great, but it was the best we could do.

Judge Calhoun announced that, after a fifteen-minute break, the trial would begin. The prosecution would give its opening statement, and after lunch I'd give mine. Then the first witness, Detective Davis, would take the stand.

Opening statements told each side's story. The evidence came afterward, and each side's goal was to use that evidence to show that their story was true.

Ruiz started big. After thanking the jurors for their service, he said, "I know this has been a challenging year. To protect folks' health, the state of South Carolina closed our courts down for months. We've just opened back up again today. This trial, the one you are serving on, is the very first one. And the reason it's the first is that it involves the most heinous of crimes." He paused before saying, "Murder."

Veronica's smiling face filled the large screen on the wall facing the jury. She looked like what she'd been the night of the party: a healthy, happy, beautiful girl.

"This is Veronica Lopez." Ruiz's assistant clicked to the next photo, a zoom-out so we could see she was in a wheelchair. "Veronica was a local girl, graduated from Basking Rock High School in 2015. She was a talented cheerleader. She was well liked. In 2016 she was in a terrible car crash, which put her in the wheelchair you see here. As you can imagine, that was very challenging for her. But she overcame it. She decided to become a voice for young women like her. She spoke for the disability community. She spoke to other young women going through similar challenges, and she helped them stay strong."

The next photo showed two messages, apparently from Veronica's social media. The first one, from a user called Ashley240, said, *My life is over I can't live like this, my BF dumped me bc of the chair.*

Veronica's reply said, *U can do this!! Ur strong! I got U and U will make it!! FAITH!!!!* Below her words was a line of heart and flower emojis, and several sets of praying hands.

Ruiz said, "Veronica was so good at inspiring people that she was able to make a living off it. As you heard in the voir dire, she was what's called a social influencer, which means that folks all across the internet listen to you. They listened to Veronica because what she had to say *meant* something to them. She had found her community, and her voice."

As he spoke, his assistant clicked through more photos: Veronica smiling in an evening gown at a gala event, another inspiring message, Veronica leaning over the side of her chair to hug a cute little girl in her own tiny wheelchair.

"But then," Ruiz said, "her voice was silenced." A photo of Veronica's flower-covered coffin appeared. "On the morning of Saturday, June 1, 2019, police responded to a 9-1-1 call from the residence of the defendant. When they arrived, they found Veronica's lifeless body in the defendant's guest bedroom. Her boyfriend was distraught, and the defendant appeared, to quote the police report, 'in shock.'"

Ruiz looked at Simone, and the jurors looked too. She looked in shock right now.

"Veronica's death," he said, "was immediately suspicious. She was a young, healthy woman. She had no history of illicit drug use, not even rumors. But six weeks later, when the coroner's report came back, it indicated that she had likely died from a combination of Valium and heroin. And the coroner determined that the heroin was likely given to her by injection, due to an injection mark on her arm and the lack of some telltale signs that you find when it's administered in other ways.

"But, ladies and gentlemen, that's not the reason this is a murder trial. That's not the reason we know this was no ordinary overdose. We know that for two reasons. First, what was there: Levels of Valium so high that that alone would've knocked Veronica unconscious. She would not have been physically capable of giving herself the heroin.

"And the second reason is what *wasn't* there. As you'll see in the crime scene photos and hear from the police detective, no syringe was found at the scene. No drug paraphernalia of any kind.

"And that means, ladies and gentlemen, that somebody moved it. Not Veronica. She was already unconscious. She was dying. Somebody else moved it, to cover their tracks." He was looking back and forth, making eye contact, I figured, with each juror. Every one of them looked totally absorbed. "And, ladies and gentlemen, there were only two other people in the home that night."

He went on for a couple of minutes about what a dedicated boyfriend Austin was. His assistant displayed photos of the happy couple, Austin at Veronica's family Thanksgiving, Austin and her mother hugging at Veronica's funeral. I couldn't look at the jury while he talked but Terri kept texting me her thoughts on how they were responding and it wasn't looking good for Simone.

"We investigated Austin," Ruiz said. "Of course we did. A police investigation has to be thorough. But that investigation raised no concerns. In *contrast*, ladies and gentlemen…"

He turned to Simone. In unison, the jurors turned their heads and I kept staring at my laptop.

"What we found when we investigated the defendant, Ms. Simone Baker, was very different. On the surface, she did not appear suspicious. Like Veronica, she had no drug-use background. Like Veronica, she's an internet influencer—in the health field, even. Matter of fact, she helped Veronica get started down that path. But she did not do that out of the goodness of her heart. The evidence will show that, during high school, before her accident, Veronica had fallen in with a little bit of a bad crowd. Many of you will recognize the term 'mean girls.' These girls bullied other girls, and for a little while, to her everlasting regret, Veronica joined them in that."

A photo appeared of Veronica in high school, looking slightly uncomfortable as she stood beside a few other girls as good-looking and well-dressed as herself.

"The defendant was one of the girls that crowd bullied. And years later, *years* later, she still had not found it in her heart to forgive. When Veronica was first injured in her accident, she felt like her life was over, and, like most of us would, she looked on the internet for help. She found Simone, who isn't disabled but does suffer from multiple sclerosis, and what Simone talked about online helped Veronica get through her challenge and find her path in life.

"But when she reached out to Simone—to *apologize* for the bullying and to ask for guidance—Simone did not forgive her. Oh, she pretended to. She even introduced her to the management company that had enabled Simone to succeed as an influencer herself. But what Simone was doing, ladies and gentlemen, was luring Veronica in. What Simone had on her mind was revenge. By the time Veronica was killed, the evidence will show she was getting to be more successful as an influencer than Simone was. What drove Simone, I believe you will conclude, was envy, greed, and the desire for revenge."

He went on that way for another ten minutes. The temperature in the room was changing and I could feel the jury's righteous indignation and their commitment to do right by Veronica. I knew Ruiz believed Simone had done this, or something close to it. And, because he was good at what he did, he was making the jury believe it too.

———

30

MONDAY, SEPTEMBER 21, 2020

At lunch, Terri and I holed up with Simone in a windowless office beside the courtroom, sharing sandwiches and getting ready for my opening statement. The two of them barely ate; most of Terri's time was spent talking Simone down from the ledge that Ruiz's speech had put her on.

"Honey," she said, "opening arguments are a roller coaster. The whole trial will go from the highest highs to the lowest lows. But we've got you. It's going to hurt, but you'll get through this. Have faith and stay strong."

"Are you sure? I know you warned me about what to expect, but listening to Mr. Ruiz talk, I'd believe him," Simone said. She kept rubbing her arms as if she were cold.

Terri reached out to take her hands and squeezed them. "I'm sure. Now. I know it's the farthest thing on your mind, but try to eat something. We have a long afternoon ahead of us and it won't do to have you passing out from hunger."

That got a whisper of a smile from Simone and both she and Terri did manage to eat something. I kept quiet during their conversation. Input from me wouldn't have helped and I had my own demons I was battling and it was making me edgy.

After lunch, we went back into the wide hallway with its stone floor, and I took a long look up and down. The courthouse was much emptier than it had ever been before the pandemic. I was glad of that and glad of the metal detectors at the entrances, which allowed me to breathe easier. Cardozo had told me he'd text immediately if Dupree was arrested, but so far, there'd been no news.

When the judge had returned to his bench and the jury was seated, I stood and walked around the defense table to face the jury box. I could feel they were already against me. Ruiz had been too good. A story had been told, and it was terrible, and now I had to convince them that it wasn't true.

After thanking them for their service and acknowledging how important the case was, I said, "Now, I have to tell you, ladies and gentlemen, when I got to court this morning, I had a different plan for talking to y'all. I had it all written down." I held up my yellow legal pad with its scribbling.

"You may have seen shows on TV," I said, "*CSI* and that kind of thing, where there's a whole lot of evidence that somebody's death was a murder and that a certain person killed them." I walked alongside the jury box. "There might be DNA evidence, fingerprints, or witnesses who saw a crime happen with their own eyes. There might be video footage or confessions." I stopped and faced them. "But there is none of that here. There is absolutely none of what we in the law call 'direct evidence.' None at all. What little the government has is purely circumstantial."

I had their attention. One juror, the Black lady in her fifties or so, had her head cocked a little to the side with a look of concern.

"So that's what I was going to tell you," I said, heading back to the table and setting my legal pad down. "But then Mr. Ruiz got up here, and he said a lot of terrible things about Ms. Baker. What he said wasn't true, and it wasn't fair. And I cannot let that stand. So if y'all will excuse me a moment, I need to ask my associate to put up some different slides from what I was originally going to show you. You'll see the other ones later, as the evidence comes in. I just want to make sure you see these too."

I leaned down to Terri and whispered, "Family photos."

A second later, we were all looking at a photo of Simone at the age of six or seven, wearing a nurse's cap, holding a toy stethoscope to her mom's chest. "This is Simone and her mom, Ms. Baker, about seventeen years ago. Like Ms. Lopez, Simone is from Basking Rock. So is her mom. Simone always wanted to be a nurse, like her mom, who's served us all in local hospitals and nursing homes for twenty-three years."

Terri clicked to the next photo. "Here she is graduating from Basking Rock High School back in 2015. Same year as Veronica. Right after this, Simone went on to nursing school. In her first two years, she was on the dean's list. She was on her way to achieving her childhood dream. But then something happened. When she was just twenty, her health started to fail." While I leafed through some papers on my table, Terri left up the photo of Simone smiling in her graduation outfit. She was holding a bouquet of pink tulips and a balloon, and she looked radiant.

"*Here* we go," I said, standing up straight again with a five-page printout in my hand. "This is the medical report she finally got. The results of her MRI and her lumbar puncture and all the procedures she went through. And it says, 'multiple sclerosis.'"

I held the report up to face the jury, even though they were too far away to read it.

"At twenty years old, folks, that's what she finds out. She's looking at something that's likely to put her in a wheelchair one day and could leave her unable to care for *herself*, much less care for others as a nurse. She's looking at having to give up her childhood dream. That, ladies and gentlemen, is challenging. It's much more than that. It's devastating."

I set the papers down. "Next to that, what's a few nasty words from some high school girls? Yeah, it's true that Veronica had bullied Simone in high school. Matter of fact, that photo right there was taken in Simone's senior year, when the bullying was going on."

I turned and looked at it with them. "Now, does that look like an emotionally devastated young woman? Does that look like somebody who's going to be carrying a years-long, murderous *grudge*?"

I shook my head like that was absurd. Terri started clicking through the half dozen other high school photos we'd chosen. I said, "Does *this* one look like that? Does *this*?" Simone on the debate team. Simone at the prom. Simone laughing with friends.

"No, ladies and gentlemen, the devastation in Simone's life came later, when she was twenty, and it had nothing to do with Veronica. And when that devastation hit, she *overcame* it. Ever since her diagnosis, she has made it her single-minded mission to learn how to keep herself as healthy as she possibly could and to teach other young women with their own health problems how to do the same. And, in the case of Veronica, to help her become an influencer too, so she could get her own positive message out there. She *mentored* Veronica. She thought the world needed Veronica's message."

Then I sighed, looked at the floor, and shook my head. "But then, ladies and gentlemen, a tragedy occurred. The management company they both worked with had them hold a party at Simone's house. A party on film, for all their internet followers and subscribers to see. It was basically a showbiz event, planned and catered by management."

I gave Terri a look, and she brought up the slides: first Simone's cute little house with the rose bushes outside, and then her airy, elegant living room on a normal day.

"This is how Simone's house normally looks. But once management and their staff got done with it—the lighting guys, the caterers, all of that—and the party was underway, it looked like this."

Terri showed the photos that looked like a New York nightclub. Simone's living room was packed. Stage lighting stained gorgeous, dancing people red and green.

"Honestly," I said, "it was more than Simone could keep control of. Her multiple sclerosis means she gets tired real easily, and this whole situation was not anything she was used to. She's been a member of Grace Baptist Church her whole life. She does not touch alcohol, and she had her mom there at the party as her chaperone. But for the other guests, the alcohol was flowing, and maybe other things too. Matter of fact, Veronica's boyfriend got himself so drunk he wasn't able to drive himself and Veronica home."

Terri clicked to a picture of Austin and Veronica. She was in her chair beside Simone's kitchen island, looking tired, and Austin was leaning like he was about to fall off his stool.

"And Simone did not send them away, of course. Even though she was tired, even though the party wasn't intended to last overnight, she wasn't going to let them put themselves in danger, driving when they were impaired. What did she do? She offered them her guest bedroom. And she showed them where the bathroom was, and she brushed her teeth, and she went to bed."

I gestured to Simone and said again, "She went to bed." The jury looked at her, and then their eyes came back to me as I walked toward them.

"What happened after that? I don't know. Simone doesn't know." I started pacing up past the jury box. "How did Veronica end up taking too much Valium and some illegal opiate—heroin, apparently? We don't know." I paced back down. "With a party like that, with at least fifty-eight people there that we know of, including some who weren't invited but managed to sneak past security, a lot of things can happen. A lot of things can go wrong. One of those fifty-eight people knows what happened that night, for sure. But that person is not Simone.

"And I have to tell you," I said, "when I took this case, when I looked through the police files, I was *astonished* to find out that, out of the *fifty-eight* people at that party—many of whom came down from Charleston, and some all the way from Atlanta—out of all those people, the police only interviewed five of them. Only five." I looked at several jurors in turn.

"That's not even one in ten. *Look* at these people." I gestured to the nightclub photos. "Nine out of ten of them, the police never talked to. Not one single question. The only people they investigated at *all* were the two people who stayed. Not the fifty-six people who drove home or flew home and left Veronica to die."

Terri clicked to a picture of Veronica. I looked at it. "I don't think that does her justice," I said. "I don't think that's right."

I turned back to the jury. "You've all heard of reasonable doubt," I said. "It's the foundation of the criminal justice system in the United States of America. You cannot convict Simone Baker in this court-room unless the government eliminates from your mind *all* reasonable doubt as to whether she committed this crime. But how can they do that, when nearly five dozen partying strangers went home without so much as one question? How can they do that, when all that evidence got away?"

Terri clicked to a photo of Simone and Sofia hugging and crying at the funeral. "That's Veronica's cousin Sofia," I said. "All of us here in

Basking Rock were devastated by this young woman's death. But convicting Simone on a scintilla of purely circumstantial evidence, when 90 percent of those city guests who'd been partying with Veronica went home and were never asked one single question would be wrong. And two wrongs don't make nothing right."

I took a moment to look at each juror and then said, "Thank you, and God bless."

31

MONDAY, SEPTEMBER 21, 2020

R uiz walked Detective Davis through his direct, going methodically through each step of the crime scene investigation. Davis was a heavyset guy, about fifty, a twenty-six-year veteran of our local police force. He knew his job, but I got the sense he knew it so well that he just went through the motions. There was not one glimmer of curiosity or liveliness in his face.

The jurors mostly looked bored but dutiful. That was generally how jurors looked when the lead detective testified, except when he had something dramatic or gory to say, which Detective Davis did not.

I was watching him closely, trying to get a sense of where his weak points were. Not the weak points of his investigation; as far as securing the crime scene, examining it thoroughly, and questioning Austin and Simone, it was pretty solid. I already knew the one gaping hole in his investigation was the failure to question everyone who'd been at the party. The cops hadn't even asked each guest and worker what time they'd left. Without an exact time of death, the killer truly could have been anyone.

So what I was looking for now wasn't that. I wanted to know what chips he had on his shoulder. What lines of questioning, in other words, would make him defensive or angry. That kind of reaction mattered more than words. In the posttrial interviews I'd done with jurors over the years, many had told me that was the kind of thing they remembered most.

I wasn't going to get a chance to ask those questions today—he'd only started at two thirty, and the day's proceedings would end no later than five. But I needed to figure him out.

By the time Davis had walked us through his initial questioning of Austin and Simone at the scene, it was almost ten to five. Judge Calhoun said, "Mr. Ruiz, I wonder if this might be a natural place to break," and Ruiz agreed. Calhoun announced that to the jury, gave them the usual instructions about not discussing the case or watching the news, and dismissed them for the day.

Terri and I walked Simone and her mother to their car and saw them off. I looked behind us as we walked, peering all around the court-house parking lot; Terri knew why.

As we got to her car, she said, "I'll be up to the hotel after I give Buster a walk."

I'd rented a room twenty minutes up the coast. I'd gone back to my house to get some things, in broad daylight, but I didn't think I'd be capable of sleeping there until Dupree was under lock and key.

———

Around ten that night, we were in my fourth-floor hotel room going over the day's trial transcript. I'd ordered expedited delivery of the last two and a half hours, to see the detective's testimony. I didn't need the opening statements, but to get same-day delivery, even the limited part I did need had set Simone back more than $300.

"He didn't have any photos of the side door," Terri said, reviewing her list of the exhibits Ruiz had used when Detective Davis was on the stand. "Which is strange, from a police perspective, since that's the closest door to the guest bedroom."

"Yeah. We'll see what he says tomorrow, but it does look like he started from the assumption that somebody who was already in the house overnight must've done it."

Terri's phone rang. The screen said the call was from New York City. She waved a hand to say she wasn't going to let it interrupt our work.

"No, go ahead," I said. I'd long since learned to pick up every time, since you never knew when somebody with knowledge about your case might call.

"Hello?"

I couldn't make out words, but I heard a female voice in a state of excitement or distress.

Terri looked at me, eyes wide. "Don't worry, honey," she said. "I got you. You're going to be okay." She was listening intently. "Uh-huh, yes. Listen, I'm not in the city myself right now, but I'll send a friend over. Hang on. It's all right. Just give me one second."

She put her phone on mute and said, "It's Marushka! Remember—"

"Of course. What does she need?"

Marushka's voice came out of the phone again. She sounded like she was crying.

"Honey, I got you," Terri said. "We'll get you out of there in a minute. We'll get you somewhere safe." She listened for a second. "No. You will *not* be deported. We'll find you a lawyer. We'll get you every-thing you need. Hang on a minute." She hit mute and looked at me.

"She says she's escaped from her house. That was the word she used. And she's, quote, 'hiding from them.'"

"My God." I picked up my phone to dial Cardozo. "That sounds like textbook human trafficking. Where is she?"

———

Cardozo sent two FBI agents to pick Marushka up, and we waited for news. We asked him to send female agents, because, as Terri explained, "She said she called me because I'm a woman."

It was getting toward midnight. I couldn't concentrate on Davis's testimony or even the trial. Terri was sitting at the desk, while I was on the couch, looking at the ceiling, thinking about all the signs I'd missed.

Terri said, "We don't need to hear back from Cardozo to know it's probably Apex that she's scared of. I mean, they own the house she just escaped from."

"Yeah," I said. "And they're who she works for. If she's legal to work in this country at all, they must be who got her the visa. She's completely dependent on them."

"So they're traffickers."

I nodded. "And they used Simone and Veronica as *bait*."

After talking to Cardozo, I'd pulled up one of the transcripts of the OtherWorld chats. Whoever it was who'd played as Simone, they were an expert-level groomer. The girls and young women who'd been invited on private Journeys were given every sign that they were making friends with an influencer they really liked—a woman whose fame and success they admired or even wanted to achieve themselves. It was safe to assume that whoever had played as Veronica had done the same thing.

I wondered where Ilona was. Then I remembered Terri saying her phone had been on two Basking Rock IP addresses after she disappeared.

"Oh God," I said. "The Broke Spoke. You'd get the truck stop Wi-Fi in there."

She looked at me. "Are you talking about Ilona?"

"Yeah. And the— My God. You know how I saw them carrying rolled-up carpets in and out? And dumpsters? I wonder if there were girls in there. People being trafficked right under my nose."

"Don't beat yourself up too much."

I cracked a smile. "I should only beat myself up a little?"

She laughed.

I reached for my phone and pulled up Cardozo's number again. He was going to need to send some agents down here.

Before hitting dial, I leaned my head back on the couch for a second.

"We've only got three or four *days* left in this trial," I said. "And I don't even see any basis for requesting a continuance yet. We know what it all adds up to, but how do I convince Ruiz or the judge that Marushka's problems have anything to do with Veronica getting murdered?"

I had no doubt now that it had been murder. And the killer was probably someone from Apex, though I could not imagine how I might prove that.

I slapped my hands on my eyes, sighed, and said, "I guess now we know why Dupree's so interested in this case."

———

32

TUESDAY, SEPTEMBER 22, 2020

In the morning, Ruiz finished his direct of Detective Davis. It was plodding and boring, but that just helped make his investigation sound thorough. He justified his decision not to track down every party guest and worker by saying that, in his experience, overdose deaths happened very quickly.

"If that poor girl was an addict," he said, "and God knows she was not, then maybe I might think some guest or other gave her the heroin early on and she carried it around all night. But somebody killed that girl. And that somebody must've still been there right before she died."

Ruiz let that sink into the jury's minds, and then he said, "No further questions, Your Honor."

After that direct shot to Simone's defense, I did my cross. Davis explained why he'd paid no attention to the side door by saying, "The defendant there, Ms. Baker, she told me she'd deadbolted it the night before." I said, "Okay, then," trying to move to the next question, but he kept going: "And it was still deadbolted when we arrived."

There were no breakthroughs, none at all. In fact, when I'd questioned why he hadn't bothered to interview anyone else, his nonchalance gave the impression that there was no need. I sensed the window closing on the jury's willingness to doubt anything about the investigation and I didn't dare push it further.

———

I checked my phone at lunch. Still nothing from Cardozo, despite my message reminding him that whatever he learned might be crucial to my trial. Terri and I hadn't told Simone about Marushka's call or what it meant. She was stressed out enough. I didn't want to weigh her down further with the idea that, even though the truth was right up there in Charleston, we might not get what we needed to prove it, and we almost certainly wouldn't get it in time.

———

After lunch, Ruiz put Officer Shepton on the stand. He was the one who'd pulled Simone over and found, or "found," the syringe on the floor of her van. The direct was quick, and simple, and damning. As he walked the jurors through what had supposedly led him to pull Simone over and search her vehicle, I saw several of them—all White —nodding like it made perfect sense. Her left taillight, he claimed, had been broken, and that was against the law. It was a safety issue, and his duty was to protect motorists. And fortunately, that had led to the discovery of the syringe, with the victim's own fingerprints on it.

During a break in testimony, Simone whispered to me. The taillight certainly was broken, she said, when she picked it up at the impound afterward, but she was adamant that it hadn't been before.

But we had no way of proving that, and even if she'd wanted to, it was too late to try to throw this evidence out. The time for that decision had passed when we chose not to file a pretrial motion in limine to exclude it.

When I did my cross, Terri put up photos from the traffic stop, and I drew the jury's attention to how immaculate Simone's van was. The syringe itself was in evidence, in a little plastic bag, and I held it up when I asked Shepton if he didn't think it was a little strange that something like that could roll around the pale gray carpet of a spotless vehicle for over a month without Simone or anyone else seeing it. He said he didn't know. I wasn't really asking for his answer; I just wanted that question to be in the jurors' minds.

I did get him to admit, for what it was worth, that Simone's finger-prints weren't found on the syringe. It was better than nothing, but not by much. Unless the jury believed Shepton had planted it, we still had no explanation for what it was doing in Simone's van.

Next I went through a detailed review of his work experience on the force. I was trying to lull Ruiz into a state of glazed boredom so I could ask a question I wasn't supposed to ask.

"And in your work as a police officer," I said, "would you say you've been honest?"

"Of course."

"All the time?"

"Yes, I have to be."

Ruiz let me ask, I figured, because we both knew police officers' disciplinary records were mostly confidential in South Carolina. Only suspensions and terminations were public, and Shepton's evidence planting hadn't gotten him punished quite that hard. If he'd been disciplined for anything he did in Simone's case, I could've gotten that in discovery, but his records from other cases were out of my reach.

Thanks to Terri, though, I knew the facts: "But, Officer Shepton, isn't it true you were disciplined just last fall for planting an ounce of marijuana in the pocket of a man you stopped on the street? And wasn't your evidence planting caught on the security camera of a nearby store?"

Ruiz was up and shouting "Objection" before I'd finished, and Judge Calhoun banged his gavel hard.

"Your Honor," Ruiz said hotly, "this line of questioning is irrelevant and misleading."

Calhoun looked at me.

"It's impeachment evidence, Your Honor. Officer Shepton claimed he was honest in his work, and that opens the door to letting me show that he's not."

Calhoun considered for a moment. Roy had told me that Calhoun was strongly on the side of the police, but as a matter of evidence law I was right, so it surprised me when he said, "I'm going to sustain, and order that it be struck. Ladies and gentlemen of the jury, you are to treat that last exchange as if it never occurred."

So the jury couldn't discuss it when they went back to deliberate. But at least they'd heard it.

———

Ruiz's last witness of the day was Austin. The kid was dressed like he was going to a funeral, and soon, everyone on the jury understood why. His testimony was heartbreaking, and his love for Veronica was so palpable that it felt like everybody in the courtroom wanted to bring her back to life just so he didn't have to go on without her.

The possibility of throwing him under the bus to save Simone evaporated. If I even hinted at that, they'd turn on her.

I saw the courtroom clock ticking toward five and hoped to God we didn't end the day with him saying something bad about Simone. I didn't want that percolating in the jury's minds overnight. I saw the judge glance at the clock, and to my relief, he asked Ruiz if it might be a good time to pause.

"Uh, Your Honor, if I may, just one more thing."

Calhoun nodded. I made sure my face did not betray my annoyance.

"Austin," Ruiz said, and sighed. "Again, I am so sorry you're having to relive all of this here. But can you tell me, toward the end of that evening, what were the last few things that happened before the two of you went to bed?"

Goddammit, I thought, but I kept my face serene.

"Well, um." He thought for a second. "So, uh, Simone over there, the defendant, she had told us where the restroom was, and the guest bedroom. There wasn't hardly nobody there by that point. And, uh, I believe she went to the restroom, and Veronica and me, we were in the kitchen."

His voice caught, and he looked off to one side to get ahold of himself.

Ruiz said, "Take all the time you need, Austin."

"Yes, sir. Thank you, sir. Um, so we were in the kitchen, talking, and she had sent us these cocktails, in goblets. I mean, Simone had."

A question mark appeared in my head. Sent?

"Uh-huh," Ruiz said. He'd noticed that word, too, I was sure, and didn't know which way to pivot.

"And Veronica," Austin said, looking up toward the ceiling, lost in his memories, "she said, 'Oh my goodness, thank you. I wish I could give *you* one!' To the catering guy, I mean." He made a sound that was half chuckle, half sob. "Because that's just how *nice* she was. She was nice to everyone, whether she knew you or not."

"Uh-huh," Ruiz said, moving on. "And did you drink those cocktails?"

Austin said they had, and within minutes they'd both felt sleepy. So tired, he said, that they'd gone straight to bed.

The day's proceedings concluded, and the jurors were dismissed. As soon as the last one was gone, Terri and I locked eyes.

"I've got their numbers," she said. "All of them." She didn't have to explain she meant the caterers.

"I guess we'll be going to Charleston tonight."

———

33

TUESDAY, SEPTEMBER 22, 2020

After explaining our mission to Simone, we peeled out of the courthouse parking lot, planning to make phone calls from the road.

"It can't have been Shawn he was talking about," Terri said. She was in the passenger seat with her laptop open, looking at her list of the caterers' names, phone numbers, and photographs. "Austin would've recognized him and kicked his ass right out of there."

"And I doubt it was Delacourt," I said. "Austin's been working for him at the Broke Spoke. He wouldn't call him 'the catering guy.'"

After a second, I added, "Damn. What the hell does Austin know? Do you think part of what's going on there really *is* just a renovation? I can't see that kid helping traffic young women, for God's sake."

"Yeah, I don't know. But if there's anything going on that's connected with Marushka, or Ilona…" She shook her head. "I mean, there might be, so we obviously can't call Delacourt."

"Right, and besides that, he's on Ruiz's witness list. Supposedly, he was going to testify that Simone served those drinks. But with what Austin just said, I wouldn't be surprised if Ruiz doesn't put him on."

"Which leaves these four guys. I sure hope one of them can testify."

"And Shawn," I said, getting my phone from the cup holder. "Whatever else happens, I think we need to put him on the stand. I'll see if Laura can draft up a witness summons and take it to the night judge to get it signed."

———

By the time we got to Charleston, it was a quarter to seven and Terri had talked to three of the four caterers. They all claimed not to know what she was talking about. One said he didn't remember the party at all, although we had photos of him there.

As I rolled into downtown, our moods had deflated quite a bit. Three times over the past hour she'd called caterer number four, who she referred to as "the cute one," but it kept going straight to voicemail.

"Can you pull over by that Starbucks there?" she said. "I want their Wi-Fi."

I did. There was parking right out front, for once, since the workday was over.

I looked at the café and said, "Want a latte? I might get one."

"Cappuccino," she said, without looking up from her screen. "Thanks."

———

It took me ten minutes of waiting in the socially distanced line outside before I brought back our drinks. When I opened the door and sat down, Terri was giddy. "I found him," she said, "on Instagram. He's having dinner at a Vietnamese restaurant over in Cannonborough."

That was a trendy neighborhood with the kinds of places that the paper's what-to-do-in-Charleston section referred to as "eateries."

She took her cappuccino and said, with a big smile, "Go! Go! Go!"

"You're just excited 'cause he's cute," I said, smiling back at her.

I put us in gear and pulled out.

———

The restaurant was so trendy we decided not to go in; everyone there looked about twenty-five at the most, and we'd be taken for either parents or cops. After we'd waited a little over an hour on the other side of the street, Mr. Cute Caterer—whose name, Terri had reminded me, was Tyrone—came out with a couple of friends. Terri was halfway across the street before I'd even opened my door. I saw one friend head off, perhaps to get a car, while Tyrone and a young woman stood on the sidewalk looking at their phones.

And he remembered. This young man remembered. Terri used all her powers—her friendliness and her authority and her reading of his body language and the shifting expressions on his face—to get him to stay and talk to her while his friends went on to the next place. She used everything she had to get him to tell us what he knew. Looking at the photos on her laptop, he pointed straight to Shawn and told us that's who'd asked him to serve cocktails to the last two guests.

"He'd already mixed them," he said. "He just handed them to me, like on a tray, and told me to bring them over and say they were from Simone."

"Thank you so much," Terri said. "Now, Tyrone, Simone's freedom is at stake here. Will you help her? Will you appear in court to say what you just told us?"

I could see the answer in his eyes before he spoke: regret mixed with the certainty that he had to look out for himself. "Oh, uh-uh," he said, stepping back, holding his hands up to ward that idea off. He smiled apologetically. "I'm sorry, but I—I'm not comfortable going up in front of no judge. And besides, I didn't get a real good welcome from Basking Rock that one time, myself. So, uh-uh. Just, no."

———

34

WEDNESDAY, SEPTEMBER 23, 2020

We got to court a little after 8 a.m., having made no progress. We had not been able to convince Tyrone to testify voluntarily, and we couldn't get a summons without his address. Terri's earlier research had found that he'd been couch surfing with various friends for a few months, and we didn't know whose place he was currently staying at. Since she couldn't try to find him while we were in court, she'd asked a friend to track him down.

Even if we did locate him, witnesses you had to drag onto the stand didn't tend to be cooperative. I wasn't expecting Shawn to be, either —he'd been served, and a deputy would go get him if he didn't show up himself—but I didn't need him to cooperate. In fact, the madder he was, the better.

Judge Calhoun was punctual. At eight thirty on the dot, he had the bailiff bring in the jury. It was time for me to cross-examine Austin. Without Tyrone, and with no news from Cardozo, I had only one card left to play.

"Morning, Austin," I said. "And thank you for giving your testimony in this case. I know you've been through a lot this year and last, both inside and outside this courtroom."

He nodded, then glanced at the court reporter. The day before, she'd reminded him a few times to give his answers in words. He leaned toward the microphone and said, "Yes I have, sir."

"So, Austin, you said something important yesterday. You said that right before you and Veronica went back to the guest bedroom, a catering guy brought you cocktails. Now, would you be able to recognize him again, do you think?"

"Uh, I don't know, sir."

"Well, let's give it a try, okay? You just look at some pictures and answer as best you can."

I nodded to Terri. She brought up a photo of Delacourt on the big screen.

"Is that him?"

"Oh, no, sir. That's Mr. Delacourt."

"Uh-huh. And what about him?"

Terri went through the first three caterers she'd spoken to the night before, and although he paused on the one other Black guy, he said no to each one. When Tyrone came up, he answered, "Oh, yeah, maybe. I couldn't swear to it, but I think that might be him."

"Uh-huh, thank you. Now, just to be sure, here comes the last caterer who was there that night."

The screen displayed a photo of Shawn, standing in Simone's kitchen in his catering uniform.

"What the—" Austin gawked at it, then looked at me, and then Ruiz.

I said, "You recognize this individual?"

"How did he— Was he *there*?"

"Well, as you can see, yes, he was. Did Mr. Ruiz not *tell* you that?"

Austin looked at Ruiz with an expression of absolute betrayal.

The jurors were shifting in their seats, excited, not understanding what was going on.

"Austin, could you tell the jury who that is?"

"That's Shawn Gifford! He used to *stalk* Veronica for like two years! He was obsessed with her! She had to get a restraining order! How'd he get in? *How*?"

"Well, I hope we'll be finding that out. But can you tell us where he's standing, there?"

"In Simone's kitchen."

"And if you'd known he was there that night," I said, "if you'd spotted him in that crowd, what would you have done?"

"Objection," Ruiz said. "Calls for speculation."

Calhoun said, "He can testify about what he thinks he'd do. Overruled."

"I would've beat— I would've put him the hell out and beat him until — Oh my God." He looked like he was going to cry. "Oh my God," he howled. "Oh, God, Veronica, I wish I'd *known*!"

I had no further questions.

————

35

WEDNESDAY, SEPTEMBER 23, 2020

R uiz put the coroner on last, right after Austin. At first the jury wasn't really paying attention—Austin's anguish was still hanging in the courtroom—but Ruiz managed to get everyone refocused on the fact that the Valium, which the coroner testified could easily have been mixed into the two cocktails, was not what had killed Veronica.

"And what would've happened, in your medical opinion, if, after drinking that cocktail, nothing more had been given to Veronica?"

"Oh, she would've had a good night's sleep."

"So, according to the autopsy you performed, the amount of Valium she ingested could not have killed her?"

"Absolutely not. It was plenty, it was more than you'd take for anxiety or pain, but not even close to lethal. She would've had a nice deep sleep and woke up fine the next morning."

"But she didn't," Ruiz said, shaking his head at the tragedy.

"No, she didn't. Poor kid."

"And, as for the heroin, could *that* have been mixed into her drink?"

"Oh, no. It doesn't dissolve right. It makes it taste all wrong—that's not a substance that perpetrators use to spike drinks. Valium, yes. Muscle relaxants, barbiturates, any of those things, I've seen them many times. But not heroin, no."

I cross-examined him briefly, getting nothing useful, and then Ruiz rested his case. It wasn't the best note to end on, but I knew he had what he needed. And it wasn't the end; before the jury retired to deliberate, he'd give an hour-long closing argument, and it would be at least as good as his opening.

For lunch, we ate sandwiches in our windowless office again. I had a message from Noah, his daily hello to let me know he was okay. Still nothing from Cardozo, and Terri hadn't heard back from her friend or Tyrone. As we were eating, a knock came on the door. The bailiff leaned in and let me know that Shawn Gifford had shown up, and he'd put him in the witness waiting room.

I'd been planning to put Simone on and be done. No magic seemed to be forthcoming from Cardozo, and even if we found Tyrone and dragged him in, I didn't see what he could add that would impact the jury any more than Austin's testimony already had.

No lawyer ever wanted to call a witness without knowing at least the gist of what he was going to say. I'd subpoenaed Shawn as a last-ditch Hail Mary, but in the cold light of day I knew a hundred things could go wrong. He might say Simone had invited him to the party—which would make the jury hate Simone. And that wasn't the only damage he could do. He might claim she offered him heroin, or that he saw her and Veronica shooting up together. That could get her convicted of manslaughter. If he had no conscience and wanted to save himself by sacrificing Simone, he could say she asked him to drug Veronica to make it easier for her to deliver the fatal dose.

I explained all that to her.

I advised against putting him on.

She wavered. She prayed on it and then said, "I still don't know. I kind of feel like we should, but I'm scared."

She asked Terri. After a long, thoughtful pause, Terri said, "I think this jury loves Veronica, and they love Austin. I think they need somebody to hate. And I don't want to let that be you."

———

I decided to put Simone on first. If we all felt good after that, we'd let Shawn crawl back to his parents' basement.

She was sworn in, and she told her story. She was real, and she was dignified. She looked at the jury and talked right to them. She was a communicator by trade, I realized, and she was good at it.

She told the jury she hadn't even wanted to have the party—she didn't drink or do drugs; she liked a quiet life—but her management company insisted. She told them in her own words what had happened there, all the way up until she went to bed, and what happened the next morning when Austin started screaming Veronica's name.

I asked her, "Now, Simone, I think every man and woman on this jury has one question that they'd want to ask you if they could. And that question is, did you kill Veronica?"

"No," she said, and she meant it. "I didn't. I would *never*. I wish I'd sent her home in an Uber. I wish I'd never had that party. I wish so much, for her family and for Austin, and just for *her*—I wish she was still here!"

"And, Simone, have you ever used heroin?"

"Oh my *God*, no. I am a committed Baptist. I was raised up in the church. I don't drink, I don't dance, I don't do any of that. I wouldn't even know how."

"Thank you."

———

When Ruiz did her cross, his tone had changed. He seemed deeply disappointed in her. Such promise, such talent—such a waste. She'd let herself get caught up in her big-city showbiz, and what a price we'd all had to pay.

He showed the jury video of Simone and Veronica's argument on the night of the party. He showed them the angry texts and DMs, blown up to fill the five-foot screen the whole courtroom was staring at. "Isn't it true," he said, "that you accused Veronica of stealing your ideas and costing you tens of thousands of dollars, if not more?"

It was true—she had made that accusation online. She tried to explain that Apex had cooked up the controversy as a publicity stunt, but the questions he peppered her with made her sound like she was complicit in their deceit.

He was painting her as a vindictive liar, not simply to make the jury believe she was capable of murder, but to make them want to punish her for *something* even if they decided the evidence didn't go quite that far. After ripping apart her character, he softened, and I could see he was aiming for a manslaughter conviction. Wasn't it true, he asked, that young people like her sometimes made mistakes? Got in with the wrong crowd, passed drugs around, just to fit in? The syringe, he suggested, she'd taken in a panic when she'd realized Veronica was actually dead. Then she left it in her van, maybe out of guilt. Maybe she almost wanted to get caught.

Her denials were heartfelt, but he'd done his job. Two of the female jurors were shaking their heads, their mouths pressed tight. I could feel the judgment coming from them.

Ruiz didn't make Simone cry, so there was no chance for redemption. Just a burning, goddamn shame.

All I could do on redirect was give her a chance to clarify that she hadn't made the mistakes Ruiz was suggesting. She hadn't passed drugs around just to fit in, or at all. She hadn't seen any syringe, much less taken one from the scene, and she didn't know Veronica was dead until she heard Austin screaming the next morning and ran into the guest room.

But the damage was done.

We could not end on that note. I had to call Shawn. The bailiff brought him in. He was dressed properly, the way he dressed at work. I asked him about his job at the furniture store. I asked him where he lived, so the jury would hear him say his mom's basement.

He was very nervous, understandably. He told Judge Calhoun he hadn't had a chance to get himself a lawyer, and Judge Calhoun told him he was just a witness; he had the right to talk to a lawyer if he wanted, like any American, but since he wasn't on trial here himself, we weren't going to stop things while he did.

I asked him how he'd snuck into the party. We went through that step by step; he'd actually gone and gotten himself hired by the catering company.

"Wouldn't you say that's pretty devious?" I asked. "Pretty calculating?"

"I, uh, I don't work full time at the furniture store," he said. "I'm allowed to have another part-time job."

"That's not what I'm talking about. I'm talking about Veronica. You knew she didn't want you there, didn't you."

"I, uh… Do I have to answer that?" He was looking back and forth between the judge and me. "Or can I—I've seen on TV—can't I take the Fifth?"

"You may," Judge Calhoun said. "If you feel your answer may incriminate you, the Constitution allows you to remain silent."

"Shawn," I said, "you knew Veronica had taken out a restraining order against you, right?"

"I take the Fifth."

"You knew she didn't want you there—that's why you disguised yourself and snuck in?"

"The, uh, I'm taking the Fifth!"

"Did you mix Valium into some cocktails and ask Tyrone Lewis to serve them to her?"

"I—that's— Your Honor, I—"

"Shawn Gifford, did you drug Veronica and Austin that night? Did you knock them out so that you could sneak in and have your way with her?"

"That's— I— You can't— I'm not on trial here!" He was twisting in his seat, looking at me and Ruiz and the judge.

"Your Honor," I said, "can you direct the witness to answer?"

"Mr. Gifford, please answer the question."

"Which one?"

I nodded. Fair point. "First, Shawn, I'll remind you that you swore to tell the truth. Now, did you have drugged cocktails served to Veronica?"

"I—I'll take the Fifth. You can't do this to me, but—"

"Shawn, did you mean to have your way with Veronica?"

We all could see the truth on his face. I was glad I hadn't said "rape." That wasn't how he'd thought of what he was doing, so that word might not have brought the truth to his face.

Calhoun said, "Mr. Gifford, you do have to answer in words."

"I take the Fifth."

I still didn't know who had killed Veronica, or why. I didn't think Shawn had; giving her Valium in a drink and then shooting her up with heroin, or morphine, once she blacked out didn't make much sense.

I did know that if I asked the question I had in mind, his answer could save Simone or destroy her.

But she'd already gambled everything on this. She'd never taken the safer path. And I didn't think she'd want me to take it now.

I summoned a tone of fire and brimstone and said, "Shawn, I know what you did. You snuck into that party, and you drugged Veronica and her boyfriend—so tell me what you did next: Did you run away with the evidence when you saw she was dead? And did you hang on to it until you got a chance to hide it in Simone's van?"

"What? No! I—" He was looking frantically around the courtroom.

I knew he hadn't done that. The syringe from her van was not what had delivered the fatal dose. But the jury thought it was, and I needed a story that they could believe—one in which the killer was not Simone.

Shawn said in desperation, "You can't do this! You can't do this! I'm not a murderer! I'm taking the Fifth!"

I let that sink in. It was my turn to speak, but instead, I waited. I let the courtroom get real quiet.

Then I said, "Thank you. I have no further questions."

————

Ruiz delivered a strong closing argument. He truly believed in his cause, and his devastating cross of Simone had given him all the material he needed.

When it was my turn, I came back to my theme of the police failing to fully investigate. "As you saw here today, Mr. Ruiz and the police did not even know that Veronica's stalker was at the party. But we know that now. We know that he disguised himself, and he snuck in, and he intended her harm. And we know that he tricked her into taking one of the two drugs that killed her. We know all that from ten minutes of his testimony on the stand."

Every juror's eyes were on me. The electricity of Shawn's testimony was still in the air.

"What more might we know about Veronica's death if the police had done their job? If something that crucial was missed, what else do we still not know? There were fifty-eight people at that party, and fifty-three of them were never asked what they saw. Or what they did. Or what their motives might have been.

"You saw this morning what we found out when I put just *one* of them on the stand. You saw one small piece of the evil that descended upon Ms. Baker's house that night, at a party that she didn't plan, or want, or control. And you know that her van was parked outside her house, and around town, for six weeks before that syringe was found—

anybody could've planted it during that time. Can you really look at Simone Baker—this churchgoing Baptist who doesn't even drink—and say, without *any* reasonable doubt, that out of all those people, *she's* the one who injected Veronica Lopez with the drug that killed her?"

The jury deliberated all afternoon. At five o'clock, the judge told them to come back the next day and keep going until they reached a verdict.

I lay awake most of the night wondering if there was anything else I should've said or done.

———

36

SUNDAY, OCTOBER 18, 2020

While we waited on the jury deliberations, I paced Roy's office for the second day in a row. I needed to be within ten minutes of the courthouse in the event the jury had questions, but I was wearing a trail in the carpeting and getting on both Roy and Laura's nerves.

Granted, I was getting on my own nerves too.

So, Roy kicked me out. Suggested I go hang out at the library, the diner, or pretty much anywhere but near him. I agreed. I needed to get out of there but until Dupree was behind bars, I didn't dare go anywhere that wasn't secure.

Noah was still up at the cabin with Squatter and he was going stir-crazy, too. Internet was nonexistent and he had to drive away from the property to get enough bars where he could download his school assignments, and then return to the cabin to work. When I'd spoken with him, he made it sound as though he was living in some ice age. When I'd pointed out that before the internet, research was conducted by hand, he'd scoffed reminding me that the cabin wasn't equipped with a library.

Terri downloaded some more files for him and had driven out to the cabin the day before to drop them off. She claimed that Buster was missing Squatter and it would give both dogs some playtime, but she was worried about Noah too. My son might talk a good game at times, but he was still young and while I didn't share everything that was going on with the case and Dupree, he knew enough to be concerned. Plus, this was the first time he'd ever spent this much time on his own; especially overnight.

Thankfully I'd gotten good news from Cardozo the day before, but he'd cautioned that Noah should stay at the cabin until after the trial verdict. He wouldn't say why and I figured I'd wait to question him.

I had my bag over my shoulder and was just saying my goodbyes to Roy and Laura when my phone rang.

The jury had reached a verdict.

I thanked the clerk and quickly texted Terri and Simone to let them know before I pocketed my phone. It had been two days. I had no idea if the timing of the verdict was good news or bad. Some attorneys thought they knew a verdict from how long the jury took, but I never bought into that—a jury is always unpredictable.

My feet felt like lead as I slowly made my way to the door and Roy stopped me before my hand touched the doorknob.

"Leland. This may well be good news. The prosecution's case was weak with no verifiable evidence. You know that and the jury will have seen it too," he said.

"But Ruiz."

"Ruiz paints a good story. That's his job, but a story is just a story without the evidence."

I nodded my head in response. I wanted to believe him. I did. But a young woman's life was on the line, and not just hers. This case might well be a lynchpin for something much bigger and as much as I needed a finding of not guilty, I worried about what was to come. If even twenty percent of what I suspected was going on around here proved to be true, things in Basking Rock were about to implode and there was no telling how deep this all went.

———

When I got to the courthouse, Terri was already waiting out front and Simone and her mom had just arrived. Everyone had been sticking close eager to get this over with.

We entered the courtroom and I looked around at the mostly empty seats. Ludlow, who had been absent during the trial, now sat behind Ruiz and the glare he gave me had me wondering if he had any part in what was going on around here. A part of me didn't think so, but I disliked the man enough that I sort of wished he did. Shaking my head at the direction of my thoughts, we all rose when the bailiff called for it and the judge entered the courtroom.

Sitting down, Judge Calhoun reviewed the paper that was handed to him before giving it back to the jury foreman.

"Has the jury reached a verdict?"

"We have, your honor."

"What say you?"

I could hear a buzzing of white noise in my ears as I scanned the jurors to see if I could figure out their decision before the foreman spoke. Most of the jurors weren't making eye contact and that was worrisome. I looked to Terri who was holding Simone's hand and she gave me a brief nod.

"We, the jury, in the charge of manslaughter, find Simone Baker. Not guilty."

The buzzing ceased, as though it was never there, and I heard the quiet gasp from Simone who quickly turned to hug Terri, her eyes welling up. The emotions became contagious and I looked to see Terri crying as she held tight to Simone in relief, and the sniffling coming from behind us was Simone's mother.

Swiping at my own tears, I vaguely heard the rest of what was said until Ruiz called out that he'd like the jury polled.

I nodded my head in agreement although I didn't see the point. It wasn't as if there was opportunity for jury tampering, and if there had been, it wouldn't have gone Simone's way. Leland knew that in every cell of his body.

As they listened to each juror announce their not-guilty verdict, I could feel the tension slowly ebbing away. There would still be some wrap up and potentially other problems, but Simone would be able to handle them without the threat of imprisonment hanging over her shoulders.

This young woman would finally have her life back.

Judge Calhoun thanked the jury for their time, their service and as he was dismissing them, I couldn't resist looking over my shoulder at Ludlow. The fury was rolling off him in waves as he got stiffly to his feet. He pulled his phone out and sent a text. While he was putting his phone away, Ludlow caught me looking at him and for just a split second, Leland caught a flash of fear on the man's face.

Walking Simone and her mother out of the courthouse and into the late afternoon sunshine, I smiled at Simone who seemed to be walking on air as she talked animatedly about how happy and thankful she was. They'd all been under so much pressure and to get a not guilty verdict was life changing.

"What will you do now?" Terri asked as everyone stopped in front of Simone's van.

"Is it okay if I tell my followers about what happened?" Simone asked.

Terri turned to look at me and I gave a nod. "Within reason," Terri told her. "I think it's okay to talk about your feelings and the verdict, but maybe leave some of the details out until everything is wrapped up."

Simone gave her a heart-stopping smile. "Deal."

"What about you, Ms. Baker? Any plans?" Terri asked her.

The woman gave them both a true smile. "For the moment, I'm thinking a celebration is in order. Would you two like to join us?"

I wanted to say no but from the hopeful looks on the women's faces, I didn't dare. Smiling at them. "That sounds great. If you're hungry, we could go get some seafood or did you have something else in mind?"

"No. That sounds perfect. But first. Mr. Munroe, I have to thank you for saving my daughter. If it wasn't for you and Ms. Washington, I don't know what would have happened."

I was surprised when she hugged me. The woman wrapped her arms tightly around me and squeezed tight. Turning her head, she kissed my cheek. "Thank you, sir."

I hugged her back, feeling more of that tension ebb from my body. Normally, I would bask in the accolades, but I couldn't seem to do it this time. This case wasn't over yet. Simone might be safe, but there were others out there in danger and until everyone was behind bars, Noah and I still weren't completely safe.

—————

SUNDAY, OCTOBER 18, 2020

Late Sunday morning, I drove Noah and Terri up to Charleston. We were meeting Cardozo at the cemetery, along with Simone and her mother after they got out of church. Simone had been found not guilty on all charges, and she was so grateful that I wanted to show her what she had enabled me to do.

Elise had a headstone now, a beautiful one made of pure white marble, with a grand piano and music notes carved on it below her name. I'd ordered it right after the trial, and it had just now been installed.

As we drove, Noah said, "I wish they'd allowed spectators in court. I wish I could've seen the case firsthand and then all of you when the verdict came back."

"Yeah," Terri said. "It was real emotional."

I said, "I have to admit that I was worried. There were too many what-ifs going on and when the jury had reached their verdict, it felt too fast. Then at dinner, when I got Cardozo's message, the whole day became downright surreal." Cardozo had finally texted to let me know they got Dupree. Two officers had been shot during the arrest, but they were expected to be okay.

Later on he'd told me more, but I couldn't share it with Noah. At least, not until the case against Dupree and Girardeau was over. Simone, Terri, and I were helping with that, telling Cardozo everything we'd learned, so he could pull the net tight around the traffickers.

Because we were involved, he'd spoken a little more freely to me than he usually did. About the morphine, for instance: it was how the traffickers moved the girls. Knocking them out made it easier.

With everything we'd told him, plus the help of the FBI, Cardozo had tracked Ilona down. Federal agents had rescued her and five other girls from a house in North Carolina where they were being held. Ilona was in bad shape, strung out on the drugs they'd hooked her on, but at least she was alive. Simone had gotten her into an excellent rehab center and was footing the bill.

And Delacourt had turned state's evidence, throwing Girardeau under the bus. His catering and restaurant businesses had served as fronts, laundering money for the cartel. He'd even gone along with Girardeau's request to drug Veronica after the party, but he'd heard someone coming, probably Simone's mother, and left the injector pen behind in his rush to get away. He claimed he hadn't meant to kill her; he'd thought he was just helping them move her somewhere. Just getting rich by helping the worst men in Charleston satisfy their appetites. I hoped he knew enough to help us put them all away.

I wasn't sure what Girardeau's intentions had been, or the intentions of whoever he'd been working with at Apex. Were they trafficking Veronica to someone, or were they getting rid of her because she wouldn't shut up about her fans who'd gone missing?

Either way, I figured, Delacourt might have given Austin a job out of sheer guilt.

And whenever the case against Dupree and Girardeau was over, Austin would finally know the truth, and so would we. It might not be any comfort to him, but at least he wouldn't wonder anymore.

———

We pulled up by the cemetery gates. Simone and her mother were already there, in their Sunday best. We got out and walked over. Simone started to say thank you, and then she just grabbed Terri in a hug. Her mom gave me a nod. That was all, but I knew what she meant.

I saw Cardozo crossing the street. He was carrying a bouquet of lilies, for the grave, I figured; he had known Elise well. When he got there, we all walked through the shady, moss-covered old part of the cemetery together.

At Elise's grave, Cardozo said, "That is a nice stone. A real nice stone. She would love that."

Simone said, "It's so beautiful! Was your wife a musician?"

"Yes, she was."

"You should've heard her play," Cardozo said, setting the lilies down. "Just the coolest stuff. Like ragtime, and I think—what was that? New Orleans jazz?"

"Yeah," Noah said, kneeling to set a bunch of blue Stokes' asters down. The asters, Elise's favorite flower, grew wild. He'd spotted them on our drive, by the side of the road outside Basking Rock.

The sunlight had a sad autumn tinge to it, and the air was cool.

I could finally honor Elise the way I wanted to. This stone on her grave would outlast me. Passersby who might not even be born yet would get some sense of who she was.

The wind picked up. It was getting colder, but the day was still beautiful.

I saw Terri shiver. I took off my jacket and gave it to her.

"That's a nice quote," Noah said, reading the stone. "I think Mom would like it."

Carved below Elise's name and dates was the title of one of her favorite tunes—she loved Sinatra's version: "The Song Is Ended (but the Melody Lingers On)."

END OF INFLUENCING JUSTICE
SMALL TOWN LAWYER BOOK 2

Do you enjoy compelling thrillers? Then keep reading for an exclusive extract from *Interpreting Guilt*.

To be notified of Peter's next book release please sign up to his mailing list, at www.relaypub.com/peter-kirkland-email-sign-up.

ABOUT PETER KIRKLAND

Loved this book? Share it with a friend!

To be notified of Peter's next book release please sign up to his mailing list, at www.relaypub.com/peter-kirkland-email-sign-up.

Peter Kirkland grew up in Beaufort, South Carolina. While he had always loved writing, his academic and debating skills made law seem like the obvious career choice. So, leaving his pen and paper behind, Peter worked as a defense attorney for many years. During this time, he saw both obviously guilty clients and a few that he felt were genuinely innocent of the crimes that they were accused of. But no matter what, Peter was always determined to give the best possible defense for his clients and he's proud to say that he won more cases than he lost.

But the more he practiced in criminal law, the more he found himself scribbling away at the end of a hard day to clear his mind and reflect on his current cases. One day, years later, he found himself absent-mindedly reading through his old journals and found he had the beginnings of a story hidden inside his notes. That the tales from the courtroom were deep and rich in characters, twists and turns, and he remembered how much he enjoyed writing before studying law. Peter began reading legal thrillers voraciously and turned the reflections from his journal into a fictional manuscript and decided to try his luck at being published.

New to the industry, Peter would love to hear from readers:

BLURB

A murder from the past hides an even darker secret.

A boating accident has left one Basking Rock teenager dead and three others traumatized. Defense attorney Leland Munroe is determined to prove his client wasn't responsible, but circuit solicitor Pat Ludlow will stop at nothing to keep his own son out of trouble. Even if it means ruining an innocent young man's life.

While Leland prepares his case, a second desperate client approaches him about an injustice from the past. Two decades ago, Maria Guerrero was convicted of murdering Peggy Ludlow, the solicitor's first wife. The evidence was stacked against her, but her son is positive his mother is innocent. If Maria didn't kill Peggy, though… who did?

As Leland navigates the two cases' twists and turns, he and his loved ones are caught in the crossfire. Leland has committed his life to fighting for justice… but this time both his career and his freedom may be on the line

Pre-order your copy of *Interpreting Guilt* (Small Town Lawyer Book Three) from www.relaypub.com/books/interpreting-guilt/

EXCERPT

Chapter One:

March 29, 2021

It was a pretty night, or it would've been, if we hadn't been talking about the death of a teenage boy. Terri and I were standing in the moonlight looking out over St. Helena Sound, trying to get a sense of how well folks on the shore could've seen the accident. The moon was right around full, like it had been on his last night, so the black water was flickering with a million shards of white. A bridge loomed to our left. The boat he'd been riding on, or driving—that detail was in dispute—had crashed into a piling about forty feet out.

Terri took another few photos and tucked her phone back into her pocket. "You want to go get a bite back at that crab shack?" she asked.

"Yeah. I think we got what we need here."

We walked under the cement arch of the bridge and up the empty beach. It was a little bit chilly, but nothing a fried shrimp basket wouldn't fix.

"It'd be easier if we could find some damn way of proving that couple lied," I said.

The couple I was referring to had been down under the bridge, cheating on their spouses, when the crash occurred. They'd both identified my client as the driver.

"Unless they were wearing night-vision goggles," she said, "I don't see how they could be sure from that far away."

"When they heard the kids' names," I said, "down at the police station, I'm sure their memories got real clear all of a sudden."

Three boys and a girl had gone boating that night. Only two of the boys had come back, and only one of them—the one who was not my client—was the son of the district solicitor. The prosecutor, in other words. The man in charge of meting out justice over all six counties and 3,400 square miles of our judicial district.

The Ludlow name went a long way in these parts.

We walked for a few seconds, silent. I could hear the water lapping on the shore.

Terri must've sensed my mood, because in a gentle voice, she asked, "You getting used to it yet? Being on the wrong side of the law all the time?"

We rounded a stand of palmettos, and I saw, a ways off yet, the yellow-lit windows of the crab shack. Ten or twelve people were inside enjoying themselves.

"I'm not on the wrong side of the *law*." To me the law was a higher order, better than all of us.

But I knew what she meant. I'd spent most of my adult life as a prosecutor up in Charleston, until my own failings had cost me that career and the only way to keep my son and myself afloat was to move back to my dirt-cheap hometown and turn to criminal defense.

I said, "I guess what I'm on the wrong side of now is the law*man*."

"Mm. Well, you know, down here, that's the same thing."

A little over an hour later, after we'd eaten and caravaned back to town in our separate cars, I pulled up in front of my house. Noah was sitting on the porch with our Yorkie, Squatter, waiting for the crab legs he knew I was bringing.

He scooped Squatter into his carrier, came over to set him on the back seat, and then climbed in on the passenger side. We were heading for the causeway so he could eat at one of the picnic tables on the thin strip of beach there. He'd been stuck inside most of the day, working on a project for his criminal justice class, and wanted a change of scene as much as he wanted the food.

Before I even put my foot back on the gas, he'd torn through the plastic bag and cracked a crab leg in half.

"I know you're hungry," I said, "but could you hold off on the crab legs until we're out of the car? They're a mess."

"Can I at least have some fries?"

"Yeah, if you're careful."

He ate one and said, "Isn't it about time you got your own car?"

I laughed. I was still driving the Chevy Malibu my boss, Roy, had leased for me back when I was at my lowest point financially. I'd had a beater whose broken rear windshield I'd replaced with plastic sheeting and duct tape, and the sight of that abomination sitting in the parking lot of his law office, next to his shiny BMW, had driven Roy over the edge.

The abomination was Noah's now. Eating crab legs in that thing could only improve it.

"There's still a few months left on the lease," I said. "Besides, when do I have time to shop for a car? I've got three hearings next week alone."

"More drunk and disorderly rich boys?"

"Couple of those. But the other one's interesting. Preliminary hearing for a woman who shot her husband in self-defense."

"That the one where you'll be gone overnight?"

"Mm-hmm." That client was a two-and-a-half-hour drive northwest, in Aiken.

"I guess you're famous now," Noah said, reaching between our seats to hand a fry to Squatter in the back. "Jet-setting all over the state."

"I guess." I laughed. "Although I'm not sure driving a Malibu into the middle of nowhere counts as jet-setting."

At an intersection, passing headlights lit up Noah's hair. It was bright blue these days. I thought it looked ridiculous, but I hadn't said anything and wasn't going to. I knew how lucky I was. Of all the bad decisions a kid could make, that was nothing at all.

At the strip of sand that passed for a beach, he set his meal on the nearest picnic table, pulled a glow-in-the-dark ball out of the pocket of his hoodie, and tossed it for Squatter to chase. The dog had some mobility issues, being well past his prime, but his enthusiasm was undimmed. His ears perked up, and he wobbled away into the darkness.

After polishing off a crab leg, Noah said, "I can't believe I only got one semester left."

"I know." He was set to graduate in December with an associate's degree in criminal justice.

He sighed, looking out at the water, and said, "It sucks that Mom can't see it."

"Yeah."

I'd known a lot of people who would've added something comforting to that—something along the lines of how they were sure the person you'd lost was looking down from heaven.

I wished I was one of those people.

I said what I could: "She'd be so damn proud of you."

He gave a little laugh. "Yeah, no. It's just community college. I mean, maybe if I was graduating from Vanderbilt."

"Naw, you don't need to go to the Harvard of the South to make her proud. She knew what you were going through. She was there."

In high school, Noah had gotten addicted to prescription painkillers. We almost lost him, twice: to our own little family opioid crisis and then to Elise's DUI crash, which had taken her life.

"Addiction's hard as hell," I said. "A lot of folks never make it out."

"Yeah," he said, picking up the ball that Squatter had dropped on the sand and tossing it again. "She sure didn't."

After he'd finished his take-out dinner, Noah reached into his other pocket, pulled out a baseball, and held it up to suggest a game of catch. The ball looked brand-new, so bright white it was almost as vibrant as the one Squatter was gnawing under the picnic table.

We got into position a few yards from the table, and Noah tossed the ball my way. It had been a good two years since he'd so much as watched a baseball game—the injuries he sustained in the car accident had cost him a baseball scholarship to college, and for a long time it seemed he couldn't stand thinking about the sport at all—but his arm was as loose and natural as ever. I stepped farther away so he could enjoy the game more.

A perfectly aimed pitch smacked my hand. "Watch out for Squatter," I called, throwing the ball back.

"Yeah, I can hear him."

Squatter's dog tags jangled as he toddled back and forth between us. The only other sound was the surf, and once in a while a car passing by on the causeway. We played without talking, until my own lack of talent sent the ball too far off to one side and Noah fell over trying to catch it. I winced. His legs still didn't have the strength and agility they'd had before the accident, and I doubted they ever would.

He picked himself up and tossed the ball to me. I caught it and returned it. I'd taught him as a kid to get back in the saddle, not to give up just because you failed or fell. It was good to see he'd taken the lesson to heart. I just worried that he might take it too far.

Knowing your limits could be a good thing, especially if you were planning on going into a dangerous field. Noah was enthused about becoming a private investigator, but he was twenty years old and correspondingly ignorant.

And I could tell from his throws that he was getting cocky. He threw a curveball, which I failed to catch. The next one, a changeup, sent me and Squatter chasing after it nearly into the water. Noah had both arms raised, cheering for himself.

"You know there ain't no girls here. You don't need to show off," I called.

He laughed and said, "You should talk. Saw your face on the front page the other day. What's next, you going to start doing infomercials?"

"God, no." I threw the ball back. "And you know it wasn't my choice to be in the paper."

"Yeah, I figured that out once I read it."

My throw had sent the ball into some spartina grass. Noah was sweeping his hands through the long blades, looking for it.

I looked around to confirm we were still alone on the beach—the bad press coverage of my boat-crash case had made me a little paranoid—and then said, "Seems like old Fourth wants to take me down a notch."

I was referring to our local media magnate, Dabney Barnes IV. His family had run all the newspapers in the nearest half-dozen counties for generations, and in recent decades they'd also started the first local internet provider and the biggest regional websites.

"Just one notch? You sure?"

"Well, I don't know," I said, walking over to help him find the ball. "I didn't read past the first paragraph of that article."

"Huh," he said. "Well, you might want to."

———

Pre-order your copy of *Interpreting Guilt* (Small Town Lawyer Book Three) from www.relaypub.com/books/interpreting-guilt/

Printed in Great Britain
by Amazon

39455142R00185